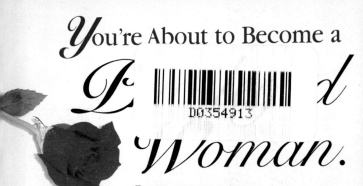

*Y*ou're About to Become a

Woman.

INTRODUCING
PAGES & PRIVILEGES™.

It's our way of thanking you for buying
our books at your favorite retail store.

— *G*ET ALL THIS *F*REE —
WITH JUST ONE PROOF OF PURCHASE:

◆ Hotel Discounts up to 60% at home and abroad

◆ Travel Service - Guaranteed lowest published
  airfares plus 5% cash back on tickets

◆ $25 Travel Voucher

◆ Sensuous Petite Parfumerie collection ($50 value)

◆ Insider Tips Letter with sneak previews of
  upcoming books

◆ Mystery Gift (if you enroll before 6/15/95)

*Y*ou'll get a FREE personal card, too.
*It's your passport to all these benefits– and to
even more great gifts & benefits to come!*

There's no club to join. No purchase commitment. No obligation.

As a *Privileged Woman,* you'll be entitled to all these *Free Benefits.* And *Free Gifts,* too.

To thank you for buying our books, we've designed an exclusive FREE program called *PAGES & PRIVILEGES*™. You can enroll with just one Proof of Purchase, and get the kind of luxuries that, until now, you could only read about.

*B*IG HOTEL DISCOUNTS

A privileged woman stays in the finest hotels. And so can you—at up to 60% off! Imagine standing in a hotel check-in line and watching as the guest in front of you pays $150 for the same room that's only costing you $60. Your *Pages & Privileges* discounts are good at Sheraton, Marriott, Best Western, Hyatt and thousands of other fine hotels all over the U.S., Canada and Europe.

*F*REE DISCOUNT TRAVEL SERVICE

A privileged woman is always jetting to romantic places. When <u>you</u> fly, just make one phone call for the lowest published airfare at time of booking—<u>or double the difference back</u>! PLUS—

you'll get a $25 voucher to use the first time you book a flight AND <u>5% cash back on every ticket you buy thereafter through the travel service</u>!

FREE GIFTS!

A privileged woman is always getting wonderful gifts.
Luxuriate in rich fragrances that will stir your senses (and his). This gift-boxed assortment of fine perfumes includes three popular scents, each in a beautiful designer bottle. <u>Truly Lace</u>...This luxurious fragrance unveils your sensuous side. <u>L'Effleur</u>...discover the romance of the Victorian era with this soft floral. <u>Muguet des bois</u>...a single note floral of singular beauty. This $50 value is yours—FREE when you enroll in *Pages & Privileges*! And it's just the beginning of the gifts and benefits that will be coming your way!

FREE INSIDER TIPS LETTER

A privileged woman is always informed. And you'll be, too, with our free letter full of fascinating information and sneak previews of upcoming books.

MORE GREAT GIFTS & BENEFITS TO COME

A privileged woman always has a lot to look forward to. And so will you. You get all these wonderful FREE gifts and benefits now with only one purchase...and there are no additional purchases required. However, each additional retail purchase of Harlequin and Silhouette books brings you a step closer to even more great FREE benefits like half-price movie tickets...and even more FREE gifts like these beautiful fragrance gift baskets:

L'Effleur...This basketful of romance lets you discover L'Effleur from head to toe, heart to home.

Truly Lace...A basket spun with the sensuous luxuries of Truly Lace, including Dusting Powder in a reusable satin and lace covered box.

ENROLL NOW!
Complete the Enrollment Form on the back of this card and become a Privileged Woman today!

Enroll Today in *PAGES & PRIVILEGES*™, the program that gives you Great Gifts and Benefits with just one purchase!

Enrollment Form

☐ *Yes!* I WANT TO BE A *PRIVILEGED WOMAN*.

Enclosed is one *PAGES & PRIVILEGES*™ Proof of Purchase from any Harlequin or Silhouette book currently for sale in stores (Proofs of Purchase are found on the back pages of books) and the store cash register receipt. Please enroll me in *PAGES & PRIVILEGES*™. Send my Welcome Kit and FREE Gifts -- and activate my FREE benefits -- immediately.

_____

NAME (please print)

_____

ADDRESS   APT. NO

_____

CITY   STATE   ZIP/POSTAL CODE

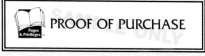

PROOF OF PURCHASE

NO CLUB!
NO COMMITMENT!
Just one purchase brings you great Free Gifts and Benefits!
(See inside for details.)

Please allow 6-8 weeks for delivery. Quantities are limited. We reserve the right to substitute items. Enroll before October 31, 1995 and receive one full year of benefits.

Name of store where this book was purchased_____

Date of purchase_____

Type of store:

☐ Bookstore   ☐ Supermarket   ☐ Drugstore

☐ Dept. or discount store (e.g. K-Mart or Walmart)

☐ Other (specify)_____

Which Harlequin or Silhouette series do you usually read?

_____

Complete and mail with one Proof of Purchase and store receipt to:

U.S.: *PAGES & PRIVILEGES*™, P.O. Box 1960, Danbury, CT 06813-1960

Canada: *PAGES & PRIVILEGES*™, 49-6A The Donway West, P.O. 813, North York, ON M3C 2E8   PRINTED IN U.S.A

▶ DETACH HERE AND MAIL TODAY! ▶

"These are my children, Paige and Aaron," Rachel explained.

Paige closed her book, Aaron turned away from the fish tank. They both moved to stand beside Rachel.

Seth found himself being studied intently by two pair of eyes. He always liked kids—and they always liked him. He gave them an easy grin. "Hi. How's it going?"

Neither child returned the smile.

"This is Mr. Fletcher," Rachel explained. "He's a friend of your uncle." She turned to Seth. "Thank you again for seeing me."

"Of course. I'll call you after I look over the paperwork."

She nodded and ushered her children out of the office.

Seth stood at the window and watched the family climb into a practical compact car. *What a serious trio they are*, he thought. They reminded him of his own family....

Dear Reader,

Welcome to Silhouette **Special Edition**...welcome to romance. This month of May promises to be one of our best yet!

We begin with this month's THAT SPECIAL WOMAN! title, *A Man for Mom,* by Gina Ferris Wilkins. We're delighted that Gina will be writing under her real name, Gina Wilkins, from now on. And what a way to celebrate— with the first book in her new series, THE FAMILY WAY! Don't miss this emotional, poignant story of family connections and discovery of true love. Also coming your way in May is Andrea Edwards's third book of her series, **This Time Forever.** In *A Secret and a Bridal Pledge* two people afraid of taking chances risk it all for everlasting love.

An orphaned young woman discovers herself, and the love of a lifetime, in Tracy Sinclair's latest, *Does Anybody Know Who Allison Is?* For heart-pounding tension, look no further than Phyllis Halldorson's newest story about a husband and wife whose feelings show them they're still *Truly Married.* In *A Stranger in the Family* by Patricia McLinn, unexpected romance awaits a man who discovers that he's a single father. And rounding out the month is the debut title from new author Caroline Peak, *A Perfect Surprise.*

I hope you enjoy all these wonderful stories from Silhouette **Special Edition,** and have a wonderful month!

Sincerely,

Tara Gavin
Senior Editor

Please address questions and book requests to:
Silhouette Reader Service
U.S.: 3010 Walden Ave., P.O. Box 1325, Buffalo, NY 14269
Canadian: P.O. Box 609, Fort Erie, Ont. L2A 5X3

Gina Ferris Wilkins

A MAN FOR MOM

SPECIAL EDITION®

Published by Silhouette Books
America's Publisher of Contemporary Romance

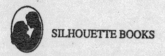 SILHOUETTE BOOKS

ISBN 0-373-09955-X

A MAN FOR MOM

This edition published by arrangement with Harlequin Enterprises B.V.

® and TM are trademarks of Harlequin Enterprises B.V., used under
license. Trademarks indicated with ® are registered in the United States
Patent and Trademark Office, the Canadian Trade Marks Office and in
other countries.

Printed in U.S.A.

GINA FERRIS WILKINS

This award-winning author published her first Silhouette Special Edition in 1988, using the pseudonym Gina Ferris. Since then, she's won many awards, including the Reviewer's Choice Award for Best All Around Series Author from *Romantic Times* magazine. Her books have been translated into twenty languages and are sold in more than one hundred countries. However, now we're pleased to present Gina to readers under her own name—Wilkins.

GINA WILKINS says...

"I've always wanted to write under my own name because I'm very proud of my books, and seeing my name on the covers is the fulfillment of a lifelong dream. But when I first sold to Special Edition, I was still a new author. So, I took the name Gina Ferris, which I chose because I was watching the movie *Ferris Bueller's Day Off* while I was trying to come up with a pseudonym. Still, it's always concerned me that some readers thought I used a pseudonym because I didn't want to be identified with romance novels. They were wrong. When I thought the time was right, that I had enough readers under each name to make the transition, I asked to make the change and I'm delighted that we're doing so. It makes my family happy, too—my husband and children are very proud of my career."

THE CARSON FAMILY

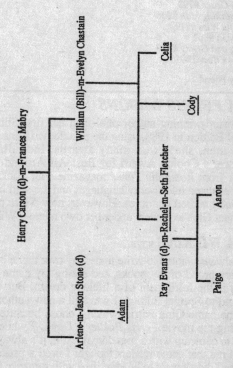

Henry Carson (d)—m—Frances Mabry

Arlene—m—Jason Stone (d)

William (Bill)—m—Evelyn Chastain

Adam

Ray Evans (d)—m—Rachel—m—Seth Fletcher

Cody

Celia

Paige

Aaron

Prologue

"You're a very fortunate woman, Frannie. You have a wonderful family."

Frances Carson looked up from the huge bouquet of mixed flowers that had just been delivered to her front door, and smiled at Lila Twining, her best friend since elementary school. They'd known each other nearly seventy years, their friendship having survived childhood spats, wartime marriages, births of children and grandchildren, and family tragedies, including the deaths of both their husbands. They still lived within a few blocks of each other in a quiet neighborhood in Malvern, the small Arkansas town where they'd been raised. They had coffee together several mornings each week—like this bright Wednesday in early September.

Frances set the floral arrangement, a joint gift from her son's offspring, Rachel, Cody and Celia, next to a bouquet of roses that had been delivered only an hour earlier. Two cards were already displayed on the antique sideboard, one from her daughter, one from her son and his wife. "Yes, I am fortunate. Both my children and all four of my grandchildren remembered that today *would* have been my sixtieth wedding anniversary."

With a faint smile, Frances touched a fingertip to one velvety rose petal. "I wonder which of his cousins called Adam and ordered him to send flowers?" she mused aloud, naming her eldest grandson, the only child of her daughter, Arlene, and the late Dr. Jason Stone. She answered her own question before Lila had a chance to speak. "Rachel, probably. She's the one who is always so serious about her responsibilities, particularly to her family."

"Maybe Adam remembered to send the roses all by himself," Lila commented, though even she didn't seem to take the suggestion very seriously.

Frances laughed. "Now, come on, Lila," she said. "We both know my Adam too well to believe that."

Lila smiled in return. "Rachel probably called him," she conceded.

"It doesn't matter. It was still sweet of him to send the roses. He didn't have to."

"Whatever his shortcomings, Adam adores you and you know it, Frances Carson. And so do Rachel, Cody and Celia. You're a very fortunate woman," Lila repeated.

"Yes," Frances agreed again. "I've had a great deal of love in my life. From my parents, then Henry and our two children, and now from my grandchildren and two darling great-grandchildren. If only..." Her voice trailed off wistfully.

"If only?" Lila prodded curiously.

"If only I could know that my grandchildren will find that same satisfaction for themselves. It isn't right that all of them should be grown and single, Lila. Growing older without the companionship of a lifelong mate—none of them knowing the happiness Henry and I found together as the years passed."

"They're still young, Frannie. They have time to find their mates."

"Not so young anymore," Frances argued. "Adam's thirty-eight, Rachel thirty-one, Cody almost thirty. Celia will be twenty-four soon. I was married and had my first child by then."

"You really shouldn't group Rachel with the others," Lila suggested gently. "She would still be happily married if poor Ray hadn't died so young."

"I know," Frances agreed sadly. "It broke my heart for her, of course. But it's been three years, Lila, and she hasn't even dated anyone since. She's too young to put away all her dreams and live only for her work and her children."

"She *has* changed since Ray's death," Lila agreed, her faded blue eyes sorrowful. "She's so serious all the time now."

"Yes." Frances sighed deeply. After a moment of comfortable silence between the friends, she spoke again. "I have little money and not much in the way of valuable possessions to leave my grandchildren, Lila. But there is one legacy I would leave them if I could. I would give each of them the treasures that I found with my Henry. Love. Fulfillment. Adventure. Compassion. Loyalty. And laughter. Especially laughter."

Lila sighed, too. "I'd like my grandchildren to have those things, too. They're all married, of course, and I can only hope... but there's little we can do about their lives, Frances."

Frances looked thoughtfully at the two floral arrangements sitting on her mother's old buffet table. "I wonder..."

Chapter One

Seth Fletcher held his breath as he placed the card carefully on the top of the structure looming on the desk in front of him. His house of cards was five stories high, with two-story wings branching off to each side. He wondered idly how to give the illusion of turrets once he reached the top. Maybe if he carefully stood a few cards on end . . .

The absolute silence in the one-man law office was broken when a woman suddenly cleared her throat from the doorway. Seth's hand jerked and playing cards cascaded across his desk, a few fluttering to the floor. His impressive structure was now no more than a pile of cardboard. He sighed and looked toward the source of the architectural disaster.

What he saw made him forget the cards. His eyebrows rose in interest.

The woman was tall, slender, dark haired. Her face was a perfect oval, her skin fair and clear, eyes large and dark. Her mouth was soft, lightly painted. She wasn't smiling, but he knew her smile would be beautiful. He looked forward to it.

He didn't like her clothes, though. She wore a plain gray suit—tailored jacket, straight, knee-length skirt, high-necked white blouse. Her gleaming dark hair had been tucked into a prim little roll that emphasized her fine bone structure but made him long to pull out the hairpins and hide them somewhere. He wondered if it was long, if it curled, if it felt as soft as it looked.

"What can I do for you?" he asked, fantasizing about all sorts of interesting answers.

"You're Seth Fletcher?" She seemed to almost hope he'd deny it.

He bit the inside of his lip against a smile. Maybe she didn't think an attorney should be building card houses in the middle of a weekday afternoon. He knew some people who'd agree with her. But Seth no longer made it a practice to try to live up to other people's expectations.

"I'm Seth Fletcher," he assured her. He shoved a lock of sandy brown hair off his forehead and belatedly realized that it was past time for a trim.

"Oh." She glanced from his casual blue sweater and jeans to the cards strewn in front of him on the massive oak desk, looking as though she wasn't sure whether to sit down or take to her heels.

He decided to make it a bit easier for her. He cleaned his desk top by the simple process of sweeping a hand across it, letting the cards tumble to the floor at his feet and out of her sight. And then he gestured toward one of the two small leather chairs positioned in front of his desk. "Have a seat. Tell me what I can do for you, Ms....?"

"Evans," she supplied. "Rachel Evans. My brother recommended you to me."

He couldn't think of anyone named "Evans" at the moment, so he asked, "And who is your brother?"

"Cody Carson. Carson is my maiden name," she added.

Maiden name. Damn, she's married. He masked his reaction as he nodded and said, "Oh, sure, Cody. He's a great guy."

"Yes." She folded her hands in her lap. She sat so straight, so still, that she could have been a statue.

Seth had a bit of trouble picturing this woman as Cody's sister. Cody Carson was notorious for his love of a joke—especially the elaborate practical jokes he arranged—a self-admitted overgrown kid in a man's body. Seth couldn't remember ever seeing him without his lazy grin, and knew Cody wouldn't be caught dead in a severe gray suit. This woman didn't even *look* like Cody. Though her skin was fair, her dark hair and serious dark eyes were in direct contrast to Cody's unruly blond mop and laughing blue eyes.

"So you're Cody's sister," he said, as though repeating it would make it more creditable.

"Yes," she said again. "Mr. Fletcher—"

"Please. Call me Seth. Cody and I have been friends for a long time. Now, what can I do for you?"

She frowned lightly, as though wondering what his relationship with her brother had to do with them, then continued. "I'm afraid I don't have an appointment. Cody just recommended you to me this afternoon, and since I had to pass your office on my way home from his place, I decided to stop by and make an appointment with your secretary."

"But you found an empty desk in the reception area," Seth finished for her. "My secretary is out for the afternoon—a doctor's appointment. She's going to have a baby in a couple of months."

"I see. I'm sorry I, um, interrupted you. I'll call your secretary in the morning to set up an appointment."

Seth raised an eyebrow, fighting a grin that he knew would annoy her. "Now why would you do that when you're already here? As you can see, I'm not exactly swamped with work this afternoon. Why don't we pretend you have an official appointment, and you can tell me what you need right now."

He reached for a pen and drew a pad of paper in front of him, prepared to take notes.

She gave him a suspicious look, as though trying to decide whether he was laughing at her. When he looked back at her without smiling—though it took some effort on his part—she relaxed. "All right. If you're sure this isn't an inconvenient time for you...."

Pen poised, he waited for her to tell him why her brother had recommended legal counsel.

The all-business approach seemed to put her more at ease. The slight frown between her eyebrows eased and she leaned forward in her chair. "The attorney I've always used for my business affairs retired last month and now someone is threatening to sue me. I don't know if he'll actually take it that far, but if he does, I'll need representation."

"Of course. Why is he threatening you?"

"It's ridiculous," she said, her tone annoyed. "I own and operate Evans Industries, a commercial waste trucking company. It's a small company, only three trucks and four full-time employees other than myself. Frank Holder was employed as a driver for two years until I had to fire him six months ago. Now he's claiming that the firing was personal, that I harassed him and deliberately sabotaged his performance sheets for personal reasons. He's even insinuated that I—" She had to stop to take a deep breath, obviously fighting a wave of temper.

"What is he implying?" Seth asked patiently, watching her rein her emotions back under tight control.

She made a face. "He's suggested that he and I were involved in a non-business relationship and when he broke it off, I retaliated by firing him. That's a lie, of course. Anyone I know can testify that there was absolutely nothing of any personal nature between myself and that—that man."

Seth wondered again about her marital status. Was there a husband involved? Commercial-waste disposal seemed an odd business for a woman to own and operate alone. And then he had to wince at his own sexism, knowing instinctively that Rachel Evans wouldn't appreciate his opinion. He knew full well that gender had little, if anything, to do with career choice. His own sister was an engineer, a field once almost exclusively occupied by men. He could almost hear Linda laying into him over his errant thought, had she been privy to it.

"Why did you fire Holder?" he asked simply.

"Inadequate job performance. Frequent absences, excessive mistakes, rudeness to customers, improper care of his truck and other equipment. He was also frequently insolent to me as his employer—he resented working for a woman and made little effort to hide that resentment. I could have dealt with that, if he'd performed his work adequately. But he didn't, so I fired him, after several warnings."

"You have paperwork to back all this up?"

"I certainly do," she replied with a gleam in her dark eyes. "Reams of it. I also have witnesses lined up to support my position, and letters of complaints against him from my customers. I kept dated, detailed records of calls of complaints about him. I even have a warning letter from my insurance company saying that if he had one more accident, they would no longer provide coverage for him."

Seth grinned. "Sounds as though you have everything covered. I'm not sure you even need my services."

She shook her head, without returning his smile. "I want this handled professionally. I'm very serious about my reputation and the reputation of my company. I want it made clear that I will not back away from a confrontation because of Holder's blustering threats."

Seth's grin vanished. "Threats?" he repeated. "Personal threats?"

"Very vague ones," she admitted. "Not enough to prosecute on, I'm sure. But he knew that I understood them."

Seth's fingers tightened around his pen. "You send me copies of everything you have, and I'll take care of this," he promised. "It'll never get to court, I can almost promise you that."

What might have been relief passed through her dark eyes, so swiftly masked that Seth almost missed it. She obviously didn't want him to know quite how worried she'd been—one of those I-can-handle-everything-myself types, apparently. Having grown up in a family of superconfident overachievers, Seth knew the type all too well.

Rachel glanced at her watch. "I'd better be going. Thank you for making time for me. I'll send the copies first thing in the morning. As for your fee—"

Seth broke in with a wave of his hand. "Forget it," he said, oddly embarrassed about talking money with her. "I don't think this will take long to settle—guys like Holder usually back down as soon as they get their bluff called with a nasty letter from an attorney. Just consider my services a favor to a good friend's sister."

Rachel's chin rose regally. "No," she said coolly. "This is *not* a favor for a friend's sister. I came to you only because Cody assured me that you are a very competent attorney, Mr. Fletcher. I fully intend to pay you for your services—at your standard rate, of course. I expect to be billed accordingly."

Some men, Seth reflected, might be annoyed by her less-than-gracious refusal of his generous offer. He, of course, was above that. "Fine," he said, a bit more curtly than he'd intended. "I'll bill you."

"Fine. But—uh—thank you for the offer," she added belatedly.

He only shrugged, his pride still smarting from the rebuff, despite his efforts to remain objective. "I'll see you out," he said, standing when she did.

She started to speak—probably to refuse that offer, as well—then wisely kept quiet.

Seth was startled to find two small children sitting quietly in his waiting room, curled up in the comfortable, oversize chairs arranged against one wall. A dark-haired little girl of about seven was reading a brightly illustrated book while a boy who was probably a couple of years younger was totally absorbed in watching the fish swimming around in a tubular aquarium set up in one corner of the reception area.

"These are my children, Paige and Aaron," Rachel explained. The children looked up in response to their mother's voice. Paige closed her book, Aaron turned away from the fish tank, and they both climbed out of their chairs and moved to stand beside Rachel.

Seth found himself being studied intently by two pairs of eyes—Paige's as large and dark as her mother's, the boy's a lighter hazel. He'd always liked kids, and they always liked him. He gave them an easy grin. "Hi. How's it going?"

Neither child returned the smile. Aaron reached up and took his mother's hand, crowding a bit closer to her side. Paige glanced from Rachel to Seth and back again.

"This is Mr. Fletcher," Rachel explained by way of introduction. "He's a friend of Uncle Cody's."

"It's very nice to meet you, Mr. Fletcher," Paige recited in a clear, oddly mature voice.

Aaron murmured something from behind his mother. It might have been "Nice to meet you," though Seth couldn't be absolutely sure. He couldn't help smiling at the formality of their manners. His own mother had been a real stickler over that sort of thing.

Rachel smiled faintly at Seth, a polite, businesslike smile that could have been as easily directed at his computer. "Thank you again for seeing me," she said.

"Of course. I'll call you after I look over the paperwork," he promised.

She nodded and ushered her children from the office. Seth stood at the window that looked out over the small parking area in front of his office building and watched the family climb into a practical compact car, in which they all fastened their seat belts before Rachel drove away. What a serious trio they were, he thought with a rueful shake of his head. They reminded him of his own family—a daunting resemblance, as far as he was concerned.

Still shaking his head, he let the curtain fall back into place and turned away from the window.

Rachel was headed wearily toward her bed when the telephone rang that evening. She glanced at the clock on her nightstand as she lifted the receiver of the bedroom extension. It was just after ten o'clock. She knew who was calling without even asking. "Hello, Celia."

Her younger sister giggled at the other end of the line. "Someday you're going to be wrong."

"But I wasn't tonight," Rachel said with a slight smile in her voice. "Besides, no one else ever calls me after nine."

"I know," Celia said with a sigh. "Everyone figures you're already tucked cozily into bed, along with the munchkins. Rachel, we have *got* to get you a life."

"I have a life, Celia," Rachel said patiently. "A very busy one. One that tends to start very early in the mornings, remember? Ten o'clock's pretty late when one has to be up before sunrise.''

Celia grumbled something about Rachel's busy schedule—which Rachel ignored since she'd heard it all before—then asked, "Did you call Adam about Frank Holder?''

"No. But I did talk to Cody."

"Cody?" Celia repeated in dismay. "Rachel, I told you to ask Adam for advice. What would Cody know about dealing with a guy like Holder?''

"You know how busy Adam always is," Rachel replied, shaking her head at the thought of trying to catch their big-shot doctor cousin. She was very fond of Adam, but she had never liked asking him for help. He was always so darned perfect, so completely in control. He would help her, of course—in fact, if Adam knew Holder was giving her trouble, he'd probably find the jerk and personally put the fear of God into him—but Rachel couldn't imagine Adam ever asking anyone for help for himself. She'd always envied his cool self-sufficiency, and had tried to emulate Adam during the three long years since Ray's death had left her in charge of the business.

Which was why she hadn't gone to Adam for advice on handling Holder. She hated to admit it, but it was a pride thing. Cody had been easier to approach, because Cody knew all about getting into trouble.

"Sure, Adam's busy," Celia conceded, "but he always makes time for us when we need him. And he is certainly capable of dealing with Holder for you."

"I'm perfectly capable of dealing with Holder by myself," Rachel said defensively. "I hired an attorney this afternoon. He assures me that he'll take care of it, that the case will never even go to court.''

"You found a new attorney?"

"Yes. Cody recommended him."

"*Cody* recommended him?"

"Celia, would you stop repeating me? You sound like a cockatoo."

"Sorry. I guess Cody knows the guy professionally, huh? Probably keeps him on a retainer."

"Oh, come on, Cody doesn't get into trouble that often. Not *legal* trouble, anyway. Actually, this is a friend of his. They went to college together—before Cody dropped out, of course."

"Well, I would hope *this* guy finished, since he's calling himself an attorney. You're sure he knows what he's doing?"

"He seemed competent enough," Rachel replied, trying not to think about the elaborate playing card structure Seth had been concentrating on when she'd arrived at his office. Or about how young he'd looked, with his shaggy, sandy hair tumbled over his forehead and falling into his wide-set green eyes. Or the way he'd been dressed—jeans and a sweater, rather than the suit and tie she'd expected. But Cody had assured her that Seth Fletcher was a very good attorney, and that his rates would be reasonable.

She remembered Seth's offer to handle the case for free, and her pride rebelled again. She might be on a tight budget, but she didn't need anyone's charity. She'd never even accepted Adam's offers of financial assistance after Ray died—and she certainly had no intention of taking advantage of a total stranger in that way!

"What's his name?" Celia asked.

"Seth Fletcher. He has a one-man office on West Poplar."

"He must be pretty young to have his own law practice, if he went to school with Cody."

"He's Cody's age, I guess. Two or three years younger than I am."

Rachel sometimes felt years older than her age, especially when she talked to Cody, who was twenty-nine, or Celia, who was twenty-three. Rachel had married at twenty-one, had two children by the time she was twenty-six, had been widowed at twenty-eight, and now, at thirty-one, was the sole owner and manager of the business her husband and his father had started twelve years ago. Ray had inherited his father's share of the business two years after he and Rachel married; now it was hers alone.

She'd never intended to run a trucking company, but when she'd found herself alone with a mountain of medical bills to pay and two small children to support, taking over the business had seemed the only answer. At least it was already established, and paying its own way, along with a moderate profit.

It hadn't been easy. Between fierce competition from other haulers, increasingly stringent government regulations, and rapidly rising prices of gas, tires, wages, insurance and dumping fees, there'd been times when Rachel had wondered if she could remain afloat. But somehow she'd survived this long, and the company was still paying its way and making that moderate profit for her children, so she kept on. One day at a time. One crisis at a time. One heartache at a time.

"I hope this Seth Fletcher can take care of everything for you," Celia said, breaking into Rachel's solemn thoughts.

Rachel forced a light tone. "All I want him to do is to get Holder off my back. The rest I can take care of by myself."

Celia sighed gustily. "Don't you always. I'd better go. Let me know if there's anything I can do to help you, okay?"

"Of course."

"I mean it, Rachel."

"I know you do."

"But you'll still try to handle everything alone," Celia said in resignation. "Just like always."

"Good night, Celia."

"G'night. I'll talk to you again soon."

Rachel replaced the handset in the receiver and snapped off the bedside lamp before crawling under the handmade quilt that served as a spread on her queen-size bed. She lay still for a moment, listening to the quiet of the night, reassuring herself that the children were sleeping soundly. And then she rolled onto her side and pulled the covers to her chin, one hand stretched in front of her to the side of the bed where her husband had once slept. And she fell asleep alone. Just like always.

Chapter Two

On an impulse he didn't bother to examine too closely, Seth stopped by Cody's club on the way home from his office the next afternoon. It had been a couple of weeks since he'd seen his friend, and he considered that reason enough. Besides, it was an unseasonably warm September afternoon. A cold drink sounded good.

Country Straight was a country-western dance club Cody and a friend had founded on the outskirts of Percy, Arkansas, a couple of years earlier. Despite predictions of financial disaster, the place had become a success, even with a limited menu of barbecue and burgers, and the surprising fact that nothing harder than beer was served from the fancy antique bar. There weren't many places for the younger crowd to hang out in north central Arkansas, but that wasn't the only reason Country Straight was so popular. Primarily, it was because Cody and Jake had worked hard to make it the sort of club where just about anyone could feel comfortable going in for a casual meal or a couple of hours listening to music and dancing or relax-ing.

Cody had once admitted to Seth that the club was the first thing he'd ever cared enough about to make him work that hard.

He sure hadn't cared enough about college grades, Seth thought with a grin, remembering a few escapades the two of them had gotten into at the university—a few times only hours before final exams had started. Had Cody not dropped out after the second year, Seth might never have graduated, himself. And wouldn't his parents have loved *that?* he thought with a wry grimace.

It was still too early in the evening for a crowd to have gathered at the club. Only a half-dozen tables were taken; the music and conversations were low and relaxed. Seth could feel his neck muscles loosening within minutes of stepping inside, which was exactly the atmosphere Cody and Jake had carefully planned. Later, the music would pick up in volume and the dance floor would fill and the party would be in full swing; but for now, it was just a place to unwind and visit with friends.

A loose-limbed blond man in black jeans and a black-and-purple Western shirt sauntered around the end of the huge antique oak bar to one side of the room, his hand-some face creased with a grin. "Hey, Seth. How's it go-ing?"

"Can't complain. How's everything with you, Cody?"

"Oh, fair t'middlin'," Cody drawled. "Want a drink?"

"Yeah. The usual." Seth slung a leg over a bar stool and leaned his elbows on the bar.

Cody placed a foaming mug of light beer in front of Seth, then took the bar stool beside him, a half-empty bottle of mineral water loosely clasped between his hands. Cody had been a heavy drinker in college, one of the rea-sons his grades had been so poor. But ever since Seth had moved to Percy six months ago to set up his own practice, he hadn't seen Cody drink even a beer. Seth and Cody had lost touch for a while after Cody left college, and Seth had discovered more than a few changes in his friend during the past six months. He'd wondered a bit about the differences but hadn't asked. He figured if there was anything Cody wanted him to know, he'd get around to telling him eventually.

"Has my sister called you yet?" Cody asked, pushing a bowl of peanuts invitingly toward Seth.

Seth dug out a handful of the peanuts, popped several into his mouth, then spoke around them. "Yeah, I talked to her." He swallowed before adding, "She came by the office yesterday and outlined her problem. Sent me all her records on the ex-employee this afternoon. I glanced over them. She's got herself well covered. Shouldn't be any problem legally—her paperwork's as precise and conscientious as any court could ask of her."

"That's Rachel. Precise and conscientious." Cody smiled faintly at the description. "So there won't be any problems, huh?"

"Probably not legally," Seth clarified. "Personally, well, it sounds like the guy is a real jerk. I'm hoping to scare him off with a couple of stern, legal-sounding warning letters, but he could cause her trouble."

Cody scowled. "I offered to bust his face for her but Rachel made me promise to stay out of it. She was afraid it would only give him legal ammunition against her. Still, if he doesn't leave her alone..."

He left the rest of the threat unspoken. It wasn't necessary for him to complete it. Seth knew how loyal Cody was to his family, how close they were to one another. It was one of the many things he'd always envied about Cody. His own family wasn't close. Just the opposite, in fact, particularly where he was concerned.

"Give me a chance to do the lawyer thing first," he said easily. "If that doesn't work, I'll help you bust the guy's face."

Cody's quick grin returned. "I'll hold you to that."

Seth took a sip of his beer, then asked casually, "Rachel's your older sister, isn't she?"

"Yeah. She's almost three years older than I am, which makes her almost four years older than you, buddy."

Seth shrugged. "Big deal."

Cody's left eyebrow rose. "So, what did you think of her?"

"She seems very—efficient," Seth answered cautiously. But he was thinking of that quick flash of temper that had sparked in her dark eyes and left him wondering what other passions seethed behind that serene exterior she projected.

"She had her kids with her," he added. "They were certainly well behaved. I never even knew they were in the waiting room until I walked her out."

"Yeah, Paige and Aaron are exceptionally well behaved," Cody agreed in amusement. "They're more like Rachel than their uncle Cody was at their ages."

"That I believe."

"They're nuts about me, of course."

"I'm sure they are. Must be nice for them to have someone their own mental age to play with," Seth remarked, tongue in cheek.

Cody punched his arm. "Watch the attitude, bud. This is my bar, you know. Just because you're a big-shot lawyer doesn't mean you can come in here slinging insults."

Seth smiled. "You going to have me thrown out?" he challenged.

"I just might." Cody glanced around, his attention lingering for a moment on a petite red-haired waitress who was just passing with a tray of drinks. "Hey, Dana," Cody said to her, and motioned grandly toward Seth. "Throw this bum out after you deliver those drinks, will you?"

The waitress smiled lightly. "Sorry, boss. I'm too busy for bouncing at the moment. Guess you'll just have to handle it yourself."

Cody sighed deeply. "Forget it, then. This is a new shirt. I wouldn't want to risk wrinkling it."

Dana moved on. Seth chuckled and finished his beer, along with the remainder of the peanuts. When he thought enough time had passed, he asked nonchalantly, "How come your sister's husband isn't taking care of this Holder guy? Or is she divorced?"

"She's widowed. Ray, her husband, died a few hours after a car wreck three years ago."

Seth didn't quite know how he felt upon hearing that news. For some reason, he had hoped Rachel was single, but he was dismayed to hear that she'd lost her husband, and her children their father, so tragically. "Oh. Sorry. She didn't say."

"She doesn't talk about it much. She and Ray were pretty tight. It was tough for her. If it hadn't been for the kids, she..." He finished the sentence with a grim shake of his head.

"You said it's been three years? Surely she's dated since then."

Again Cody shook his head. "Not even dinner. Celia's practically thrown men at her during the past year, but Rachel's dodged them all. She keeps saying she isn't ready, she's too busy with the business, she wants to spend time with the kids. All excuses. I think she's just afraid to get back into the dating scene after so long. Can't say I blame her, really. It *can* be a jungle out here, can't it?"

Seth didn't answer. He was thinking that a beautiful, intelligent woman like Rachel Carson Evans shouldn't be hidden away like a rare, fragile piece of art. She should go out. Have fun. Take down that tightly bound hair and let those lovely lips curve into a smile. And he was thinking, with a touch of characteristic cockiness, that he knew just the man to help her get over her fear of dating again.

The next morning Rachel answered the telephone in her office to hear Seth Fletcher's voice on the other end of the line. "I've been looking over this paperwork, and I can't see that you have anything to worry about," he said to assure her. "The letter from the insurance company alone justified your decision to terminate the guy's employment, even had it not been for the other complaints against him. You certainly couldn't be expected to employ a man who put you in danger of losing insurance coverage for your business."

"So what's our next step?" Rachel asked. She was relieved to hear the attorney's confidence that Holder hadn't a legal leg to stand on. She'd thought her decisions were well documented, but it was nice to have the confirmation.

"There's really nothing else for you to do at this point. All you have are some vague threats on Holder's part about taking you to court. He hasn't even retained an attorney, as far as I can determine. He'll probably let it drop now, but if he doesn't, then we call his bluff. Be sure and keep records of any interaction you have with him—not that I have to remind you."

"No," Rachel agreed with a faint smile. "My husband taught me very early about the C.Y.A. School of Business."

"The... oh, the Cover Your, er, Assets School, right?"

"Something along those lines," she agreed dryly.

Seth chuckled. "You learned your lessons well. I've rarely seen such detailed record keeping. You've even got Holder's signature on most of the letters of reprimand."

"He didn't want to sign them, but I always made it a condition for him to return to his job after one of our meetings."

"Good practice. He can't say he wasn't warned plenty of times about cleaning up his act."

"He told one of my other employees that his signatures were forged on those letters."

Seth paused. "He doesn't really expect anyone to believe that, does he?"

"Who knows what he expects? He's usually drinking heavily when he does most of his talking."

"If he continues to harass you, you can have a restraining order issued against him. As for him suing you, I'm still of the opinion that it would never get to court. My advice to you now is to wait and let him take the next step, if any."

"All right. I'll do that. Thank you." Rachel pushed a stray strand of hair out of her face and glanced at the pile of bills in front of her, waiting to be sorted and paid. "You'll send me a bill for your services?" she reminded him.

"Rachel, I haven't done anything," he returned in what sounded like amused exasperation. "I've only glanced over the paperwork and advised you to wait. If we have to pursue this, then I'll bill you at my usual rates, okay?"

She frowned, trying to decide if he was laughing at her. She wondered if he was so casual with all his clients, or if he considered theirs a first-name-basis relationship because of his friendship with her brother. It wasn't that she minded him calling her by her first name, exactly, but there was something about Seth that made her defenses go up. Something she couldn't quite define.

Seth gave her another moment of silence, then said, "You still there?"

"Yes, of course."

"Good. I was wondering if we could have dinner together tomorrow night. Someplace casual, where we can talk and get to know each other. How about it?"

"Dinner?" Rachel repeated blankly, blinking in surprise at the invitation.

"Yeah. Why don't I pick you up at seven?" He seemed to take for granted that she would accept.

She shook her head, almost as though he could see her. "I'm sorry, but I—"

"Oh, I guess you have to arrange for a baby-sitter, don't you? Tell you what, I'll call back later this afternoon."

"That won't be—"

"If you can't find anyone, don't worry about it. We'll just take the kids with us. I like kids. It'll be fun."

"But I—"

"Damn, my other line's buzzing. I'd better take it. I'll call you later, okay? Bye, Rachel."

"But, Seth, I—"

She was talking to a dial tone. She stared at the receiver in her hand for a full minute before she quickly shook her head and slammed the handset down on its base. "Of all the—"

She felt as though she'd just been railroaded. Talk about a bulldozer dinner invitation! The man hadn't even given her a chance to answer—yes *or* no! And it would have been no, of course—would still be no when he called her back. She'd get her refusal through to him if she had to shout to get his attention.

Why had Seth Fletcher asked her to dinner? The man was years younger than her, for heaven's sake, she thought in exasperation, though she was aware that she was exaggerating a bit. Still, he was younger by at least three years. And very good-looking, if one preferred the hard-bodied, lifeguard type. Surely there were lots of single young women who'd jump at the chance to go out with him. Why would he be interested in having dinner with a widowed mother of two? He'd even offered to take the kids along with them! How very odd.

She looked again at the piles of paperwork on her desk and sighed. Now she'd have to spend the rest of the day worrying about Seth's call. She really should just call him right back and make it quite clear that she wasn't interested in having dinner with her attorney. A business relationship was all she wanted with him—or with any other man for now.

Maybe there'd come a time when she'd be ready to date again. But not yet, she thought with the faint touch of panic that always accompanied the possibility. No. Not yet.

She reached determinedly for the first stack of bills. She frowned deeply at the figure printed at the bottom of the invoice from the tire company. Something was going to have to be done about this, she thought firmly, picking up the telephone. She was beginning to suspect that she was being charged for new tires she didn't really need. Well, she'd take care of that soon enough!

She punched the buttons fiercely, trying to concentrate all her attention on business. But Seth Fletcher's dinner invitation stayed at the back of her mind, refusing to be completely forgotten as she went about her usual routines.

It was after four when Seth called again. Rachel was just about to lock up and make her daily run to the bank and post office when the call came through. As soon as he identified himself, she took a deep breath and began to speak, "Seth, I wanted to talk to you about your invitation...."

"Couldn't get a baby-sitter, huh? No problem. We'll find a kid-friendly place and we'll all get to know one another. How about Bubba's Barbecue?"

"Please let me complete a sentence."

He chuckled, and he didn't sound offended by her curt tone. "Sorry. What would you like to say?"

She spoke very clearly. "Thank you for the invitation, Mr. Fletcher, but I'm afraid I have to refuse. I'm sorry you didn't give me a chance to say this earlier, to save you the trouble of calling again."

"Oh, but calling you is a pleasure, Rachel. If you're tied up for tomorrow night, how about Saturday evening?"

"No, I—"

"Sunday lunch? Or we can take the kids to the skating rink Sunday afternoon. Do they like roller skating?"

"They've never tried it. But—"

"Never skated? Then we really should take them. I just happen to be an expert at the sport, myself, and I'm a great teacher. Not that I'm bragging, of course, but—"

"Mr. Fletcher," Rachel all but shouted into the telephone.

"It's Seth," he reminded her. "Was there something you wanted to say?"

"Yes. I want to say no. Thank you, but no."

"To which? Dinner? Lunch? Skating?"

"All of the above. This isn't a good time for me."

"So, when is a good time for you?" he asked insistently.

"I, uh—" She didn't quite know how to answer. "I'm just not interested in dating right now," she said finally. "Not even casually."

"I see."

She frowned, wondering if it could possibly be that easy. "I'll let you know if Holder gives me any more trouble," she said carefully. "Thank you again for looking over my paperwork. I wish you would charge me for the time you spent with it."

"We've already discussed that, remember? When I do something worth charging for, I'll send you a bill."

She sighed, but gave in to the inevitable and dropped the argument. At least he seemed to have given up on asking her out.

"By the way, Rachel . . ."

"Yes?" she urged when he paused.

"When we finally go out together . . . something tells me it's not going to be casual."

Her mouth opened, but nothing came out. It was just as well, since he'd already hung up.

For the second time that day, she found herself holding a telephone receiver and listening blankly to a dial tone. A moment later, she muttered an unladylike expletive and slammed the telephone home with enough force to make the instrument jingle a protest.

She was definitely going to have to talk to her brother about this fruitcake he'd recommended as a lawyer!

There was a long line at the bank. Rachel shifted restlessly from one foot to the other, checking her watch every two minutes, fretting about the other errands she had to run before she picked her children up at the day-care center where they stayed each afternoon after school. She was going to be lucky if she made it to the post office before the window closed, she thought, inching forward in the slow-moving line.

She made it to the post office, but with less than five minutes to spare. She was breathless and tense and working on the beginning of a headache. She hated being rushed.

She arrived at the day-care center to find Aaron in tears because he'd broken the zipper on his windbreaker. Paige was perturbed that she'd fallen on the playground at school and gotten the knees of her new pink jeans filthy. Neither child was in a particularly good mood during the drive home, though they perked up a bit when Rachel suggested they pick up something for dinner. She didn't like to buy fast food often, but she hadn't had time to go to the grocery and she was too tired to cope with cooking this evening.

"I want a Chicken McNugget Happy Meal," Aaron immediately spoke up.

"No, tacos," Paige argued. "Can we have tacos and cheese dip, Mama? Please?"

"No, a Happy Meal," Aaron insisted. "They're giving Batman toys in the Happy Meals this week. Please, Mama, I want a Chicken McNugget Happy Meal."

Rachel massaged her throbbing temple with her right hand, keeping the left gripped tightly around the steering wheel. "We'll get a Happy Meal for you, Aaron, and tacos for you, Paige." It meant another fifteen minutes in a take-out line, but she figured it was worth it just this once to avoid the confrontation.

The telephone was ringing even as Rachel unlocked her front door and struggled inside with sacks of food and the stack of paperwork she would work on after dinner. She dumped everything onto the dining table and snatched up the closest receiver. "Hello?"

"You sound breathless," Celia commented.

"I just made it through the door."

"Oh. Sorry."

"I still have to feed the kids. Is anything wrong, Celia?"

"No. I just wanted to ask if I could borrow your silver jacket for tomorrow night. You know, the one with the crystal beads."

"I only have one silver jacket, Celia, and yes, you're welcome to borrow it."

"Thanks. I love the way it looks with my black silk dress."

"Why don't you just keep it," Rachel said with a shrug, digging fast food out of paper bags as she balanced the phone on her shoulder. "I've only worn it a couple of times. I never seem to have the right occasion for it."

"Oh, I couldn't do that. Cody bought it for you for Christmas a couple of years ago, didn't he?"

"Yes, but he won't mind. He'll probably never even know." To change the subject, she asked, "Do you have a date with Cleve tomorrow night?"

"Uh, no. Not with Cleve."

Rachel didn't like her younger sister's tone. Nor did she care for her sudden suspicion. "Damien Alexander wouldn't happen to be in town, would he?"

"Well, yes, he is," Celia admitted defensively. "And I'm going out with him. We're just going into Little Rock for dinner and a symphony performance, Rachel. It's no big deal."

"And after the symphony performance?" Rachel couldn't resist asking.

"After the symphony, he'll be bringing me home," Celia retorted. "Darn it, Rach, if you weren't loaning me your jacket, I'd..."

"I know, it's none of my business, really," Rachel conceded. "You *are* twenty-three years old. It's just that I can't trust this guy, Celia. There's something about him that doesn't ring true."

"You don't trust him because you've never met him. You've read about him in a couple of gossip magazines, so you've decided he's a sleazy playboy. That isn't fair, Rachel. Damien is really a very nice man. He's always been a perfect gentleman with me."

"So far," Rachel muttered.

Celia responded with a gusty sigh.

"All right, I'm sorry," Rachel said, rubbing at her temple again. "I'll butt out. But, Celia—be careful, okay?"

"I'm *always* careful," her sister grumbled. "That's why I'm probably the oldest living virgin in central Arkansas. I appreciate your concern, Rachel, but it's only a date.

Something you should try yourself, occasionally," she added archly.

Rachel winced at the unconscious reminder of Seth Fletcher's dinner invitation. She wouldn't tell Celia about it, of course. Celia would demand to know why she'd refused.

Actually, Celia seemed more Seth's type to Rachel. And Rachel would much rather see her little sister involved with a nice young attorney friend of Cody's than an older, jet-setting, shady hotel magnate like Damien Alexander. Maybe she'd talk to Cody about arranging an introduction for Celia and Seth.

Rachel and her children had just completed their nutritionist's nightmare of a dinner when the phone rang again. Leaving Paige and Aaron engrossed in an old *Partridge Family* rerun on cable TV, Rachel answered, half expecting it to be Celia, asking to borrow something else for her date the next evening. She was delighted to hear her paternal grandmother's voice on the other end of the line.

"Granny Fran!"

"Hello, darling. I'm calling to thank you for the beautiful flowers. I'll call the others after you and I have talked."

"I'm glad you enjoyed the flowers. How are you feeling?"

"Very well, thank you. How are you and the children?"

"We're fine. Paige is making all *A*s so far in second grade. And Aaron's thoroughly enjoying kindergarten."

"That's wonderful. I'd love to see them. They must have grown several inches since I saw them last month."

"Not quite that much," Rachel said with a smile. "But I'm sure they want to see you, too. Maybe we'll get down to Malvern one weekend soon to visit you."

"Actually, dear, I was thinking about coming to visit you, instead. Lila's going to stay with her daughter in Denver for a couple of weeks and it will seem lonely here without her morning visits. I thought, if you don't mind, that I'd—"

"I would *love* to have you stay with me for however long you like!" Rachel interjected sincerely. "You know how often I've asked you to come visit. The guest room is all ready for you. When can you come?"

"Sunday? I know this is short notice, but you did say the invitation was a standing one. If it's a bad time—"

"It's not a bad time. Paige and Aaron will be thrilled."

"You're sure it wouldn't be too much trouble for you? I'll help around the house, of course. It will be so nice to cook for a family again."

Rachel didn't bother to protest; the truth was, she knew that her grandmother thoroughly enjoyed cooking for others and would be delighted to do so for Rachel and the children. "You won't be any trouble," she assured her. "And we'll work out the details when you get here. I'll come pick you up Sunday morning."

"No, thank you, dear, that won't be necessary. I'll ask Adam to bring me."

"Adam?" Rachel repeated skeptically.

"Yes. He has that fancy new car he's been bragging about. This will give him a chance to use it," Frances said with a touch of smug certainty that her eldest grandson wouldn't refuse her. "Besides, I can use the time in the car to have a talk with him. Adam's been getting a bit big for his britches lately, don't you think? Someone needs to remind him that he's still the same little boy who fell out of my apple tree and broke his nose."

Rachel swallowed a laugh at the thought of Adam's discomfort at being lectured for two hours within the close confines of his expensive new sports car. Yet she knew he wouldn't risk hurting his grandmother by giving her one of his famous put-downs. Granny Fran was probably the only person in the world who could get away with lecturing Dr. Adam Jason Stone.

"Let me know if Adam's unavailable," she said. "I'll come pick you up."

"Thank you, dear. I'd better call the others now. I think I'll start with Adam," Frances mused, sounding as though she was greatly anticipating the call.

Rachel was smiling when she hung up, but her smile quickly faded. She really was looking forward to her grandmother's visit, and she knew that Granny Fran wouldn't be any trouble, but there was always some pressure involved in having a houseguest. And additional pressure was one thing she *didn't* need right now!

She took a deep breath and reached into a kitchen cabinet for a bottle of aspirin.

All it would take to top this day off, she thought as she swallowed two chalky tablets with a gulp of lukewarm tap water, would be a call from her mother, who called frequently from Saint Louis to fret about Rachel's health and the well-being of her poor, fatherless children. Rachel's father had been transferred to Saint Louis some six years earlier, and Evelyn Carson still worried about her three fully grown children and two young grandchildren being an entire state away from her guidance.

Rachel had just rinsed her glass and put it away when the telephone pealed again. Somehow she just knew it was her mother. She groaned and buried her face in her hands for a moment before reaching resolutely for the telephone.

What an exhausting day this had been!

Chapter Three

Seth knew he was taking a chance when he pulled into the parking lot of Rachel's office Friday afternoon. There was the possibility that she would tell him to get lost, tell him he was being more trouble than she'd anticipated when she'd asked for his assistance with her ex-employee. But he wanted to see her. Maybe he just needed to find out why she'd stayed in his mind since that one brief meeting with her. Maybe if he saw her again today, he'd realize she wasn't really all that memorable.

He lingered in his car a moment after parking, looking over her place of business. A small, white frame building sat in the center of the lot, with a neatly lettered sign over the door proclaiming it to be the offices of Evans Industries. The parking lot was paved, decorated only with two large security lamps and a couple of Bradford pear trees on either side of the driveway.

Behind the office building, several trash containers of varying sizes were grouped on a large, paved pad, and two huge Mack trucks were parked behind the other side of the office. A heavy chain-link fence ringed the business, the open gates sporting large padlocks that Seth assumed would be secured at closing time.

He couldn't help thinking that it was a very masculine-looking business. He glanced again at the oversize trucks and smiled at the thought of Rachel behind the wheel of one. He'd bet that was one aspect of her business that she left fully to her employees; he wouldn't have attempted to drive one of those complicated monsters, himself. Mechanics and hydraulics had always been mysteries he'd never been interested in exploring.

Three other vehicles were parked in front of the office—the practical compact he'd seen Rachel driving two days earlier, a battered station wagon and a sportier little red number with personalized plates that read "Celia C." He recognized the name of Cody's youngest sister. He was about to meet the remaining Carson sibling.

He hesitated for a moment outside the closed door, wondering whether he should knock. But, since it was a business office, he finally decided to just turn the knob and go on in.

A heavyset woman with flaming red hair and a purple knit pantsuit sat behind a computer in a minimally furnished reception area, her fingers flying across the keyboard as she entered numbers from a stack of paperwork on the desk beside her. She looked up when Seth entered. "May I help you?" she asked curiously, apparently surprised to see him.

Seth would have bet this was the owner of the station wagon outside. "I'm here to see Rachel. Is she in?"

The woman glanced at a closed door to her right. "Yes, she's in. Is she expecting you, or should I ask if she has time to see you?"

Seth bit the inside of his lip against a smile at her obvious reluctance to stop what she was doing in order to announce him. "I'll just knock on the door."

She gave him a cheery smile. "Okay. I have to finish these load reports, anyway." She turned back to her work.

Seth tapped on the closed door, hearing muffled feminine voices through it. The voices stilled, and then Rachel called out, "Come in."

He saw the startled surprise that crossed her face when he opened the door and stepped through. She masked it quickly, replacing it with mild curiosity. "Seth," she greeted him. "Has something happened with Holder?"

At least she'd used his first name, he thought in satisfaction, remembering how she called him Mr. Fletcher whenever she was trying to keep him at a distance. "No, nothing's happened," he assured her. "I just wanted to see my new client's offices."

"New client?" asked the young woman who was sitting in a chair beside Rachel's desk, a beaded silver jacket draped over her lap.

Seth turned to her with a smile. He'd been wondering if the younger sister would resemble his friend Cody any more than Rachel had. He discovered that she actually resembled both her siblings. Celia had Rachel's dark hair and delicate oval face, and Cody's bright blue eyes and dimpled smile. It was a striking combination, particularly when accompanied by a slender figure and long, shapely legs, both nicely displayed by a snug white sweater and a short red skirt. She wore her hair soft and free to her shoulders; red highlights gleamed invitingly in the deep brown depths.

Celia Carson was a beautiful young woman, and yet Seth found his attention turning immediately back to Rachel, who wore her hair in the same tight twist he'd seen before, and had replaced the unexciting gray suit with an equally nondescript navy one. She was watching him, and

Seth got the impression that she was trying to judge his reaction to her sister. "Celia," she said, without looking away from Seth, "this is my attorney, Seth Fletcher— Cody's friend. Seth, this is my sister, Celia Carson."

"Nice to meet you, Celia," Seth said easily, glancing away from Rachel only long enough to smile a greeting at the younger woman. "Cody's told me a lot about you."

"I'm afraid I can't say the same," Celia responded, her voice low and musical. "Cody doesn't talk much about his wild college days."

Some of the "wild" episodes flashed through his mind as Seth nodded and said gravely, "That doesn't surprise me."

"So, tell me, Seth—were you a bad boy, too?" Celia asked with a teasing smile.

"Celia," Rachel murmured in warning.

Seth shrugged and rested a hip against one corner of Rachel's desk, making himself comfortable. "Depends on who you ask," he replied, thinking of his disapproving family. He turned back to Rachel, effectively changing the subject. "I take it you haven't heard anything more from Holder since you came to me?"

"No. But weekends are when he's at his worst," she explained. "He goes out drinking every Friday night, and by Saturday he's mean and vindictive. That's usually when I get the calls from him."

"At your home?" Seth asked with a quick frown.

"Sometimes. Sometimes here at the office."

"You work Saturdays?"

Celia snorted delicately. "Rachel works *all* the time," she muttered.

"Celia," Rachel said again, less subtle this time in her warning.

Seth filed that little tidbit of information away for future reference. "If he calls you again this weekend," he said to Rachel, "I want to know about it. I can help you with this, Rachel, but only if you keep me fully informed." He snatched up a pen and a sheet of memo paper from a holder on her desk and scrawled his home telephone number. "You can reach me here if I'm not at the office. If you get my machine, leave a message and I'll get right back to you. Okay?"

She nodded. "I'll let you know if he calls. I just hope it won't be necessary."

"So do I," he assured her. And then he grinned. "To be honest, I'd rather you'd call me for personal reasons."

He sensed Celia straightening suddenly in her chair. Rachel's smooth cheeks were suddenly tinged with pink. She gave him a look of warning no less stern than the tone she'd directed toward her younger sister. "Very amusing, Mr. Fletcher."

Unabashed, he held her gaze with his own. "It wasn't intended as a joke, Ms. Evans."

Celia cleared her throat and stood. "Guess I'd better be going. I have to get ready for my date tonight."

Rachel broke the visual contact with Seth and turned abruptly to her sister. "Celia, promise me again that you'll be careful tonight."

Celia rolled her eyes in response to Rachel's worried tone. "Rachel, please. Chill out, okay? It's just a date."

"I know, but—" Rachel broke off with a frustrated glance at Seth, who looked blandly back at her, wondering what had her so concerned about her sister's date. And then she sighed. "All right, I won't say any more. Call me tomorrow."

"I will. Bye, Rach. Nice to meet you, Seth. And, uh, good luck with getting those personal calls from my sis. Trust me, you're going to need it."

Her smile told him she'd recognized his interest in her sister, and that she approved, but without much hope for him. Seth hoped very much to prove her wrong.

"I'm leaving, Rachel. You need anything else before I go?" the large, red-haired woman from the reception area called when Celia walked out of Rachel's office.

"No, that's all, Martha. I'll see you next week."

A few minutes later, Seth and Rachel were alone in the small building. She avoided his eyes as she began to clear her desk with quick, efficient movements. "Was there anything in particular you wanted to discuss, or did you stop by only to embarrass me in front of my sister?" She sounded a bit cross.

"Did I embarrass you, Rachel?" he asked with genuine curiosity.

"Yes, as a matter of fact, you did."

"Why?"

"You implied that you and I were ... are ... uh ..."

"Involved in more than an attorney-client relationship?" he said, supplying words for her.

"Something like that. And it's not true."

"No," he admitted. "Not yet."

She finally looked at him, not bothering to mask her exasperation with him. "Haven't I made it clear that I'm not interested in going out with you?"

He gave her his most winning smile. "I'm hoping to change your mind."

She released a quick, annoyed breath. "Why?" she demanded bluntly.

Seth shook his head with a growing exasperation of his own. "I just think it would be fun. Don't you ever do anything just for fun, Rachel?"

Her gaze fell. She busied herself with straightening a pile of papers that hadn't needed straightening. "I have a lot of responsibility. Running this business, taking care of my children and my home."

"It must be very difficult for you at times," he acknowledged. "But you haven't answered my question. Don't you ever do anything just for fun?"

When she looked back up at him, her expression was so stark it wrung his heart. "I'm not sure I remember how," she said in little more than a whisper.

"Then let me help you remember," he urged, reaching out a hand to her.

She looked from his entreating smile to his invitingly outstretched hand. Her momentary weakness was instantly masked. "I don't think that's a very good idea," she said brusquely. "I need an attorney, Seth, not an escort. If you aren't interested in that position..."

His hand fell. Though he'd told himself to be prepared for another rebuff, he still felt a quick flash of annoyance at her attitude. Damned if he knew why he kept setting himself up this way with her, he thought, pushing away from her desk to stand. "I already consider myself your attorney," he informed her curtly. "You let me know if you hear anything from Holder this weekend. I'll handle it from there."

She nodded, avoiding his eyes.

He walked to the door and was on his way out before something made him turn and say, "I never intended to be an 'escort' for you, Rachel. I rather thought we could be friends."

He didn't give her a chance to respond. It seemed like a pretty good exit line to him.

As exit lines went, it had been a very effective one. Rachel felt like a heel for a long time after the outer door closed with a sharp snap behind Seth Fletcher.

Had she been unforgivably rude? Had his offer of dinner been nothing more than a gesture of courtesy to his new client, to the sister of his good friend? He'd only been in town a few months. He was probably still trying to get to know his neighbors and associates. She'd had lunch a few times with her former attorney, on a professional basis. She'd never included her children, or gone out with him during the evening, but maybe Seth was simply more casual about such things than Al had been. Maybe he was just a little lonely.

She could certainly understand loneliness. She'd become all too acquainted with that condition during the past three years.

It was much easier to accept that Seth had asked her out only as a gesture of friendship than to believe he was interested in a more intimate relationship with her.

She looked somberly at the framed photograph sitting on one corner of her desk. Two men stood in the foreground of the photo, one older, one younger, both looking very much alike. Her husband, Ray, and his father, Herman Evans.

The twelve-year-old snapshot showed them standing in front of their first big truck, an older version of the two that were now parked behind her office. Ray had been in his early twenties, and had looked so proud to be in business with his father, whom he'd idolized. Herman had died only a few years later, leaving Ray to build the business into the moderately successful operation it was now—three trucks, three full-time drivers and one part-time driver, a full-time bookkeeper, over two hundred customers in a hundred-mile radius, and Rachel trying to manage it all.

It should be Ray sitting at this desk now. Ray should be trying to figure out how to meet landfill increases and insurance-rate hikes. Ray should be working up bids and ordering Dumpsters and praying the hydraulic pump on the '89 Mack truck didn't burn out before next month's receipts came in. Had it not been for one irresponsible salesman who'd decided to drive home after celebrating a lucrative new contract, and had ended up killing himself and Ray in a fiery crash at a busy intersection, Rachel would be at home with her children now. Planning dinner, sewing a dress for Paige, helping Aaron learn to read, working in her garden, being active in PTA and Brownies

and Little League, and all those other projects she had no
time for now.

She'd learned the hard way that the price of dreaming
was much too high. She'd dreamed of a long, happy life
with Ray and her children, and that dream had literally
ended in flames.

She wouldn't make herself that vulnerable again. Her
dreams now were for her children and their future. She
would work as hard as she had to work to provide for
them—to feed them, clothe them, educate them, even spoil
them a little, if possible. As for herself—she'd had her
youth, her fun. Now she had her responsibilities.

The sound of her own deep sigh brought her out of the
reverie she'd fallen into. With a start, she glanced at her
watch, then muttered beneath her breath and reached
hastily for her purse. She was running behind—again. She
had to go to the bank and the post office and pick up the
children, and she still hadn't been to the grocery store,
which she would have to do on the way home since she had
no intention of buying fast food again.

Seth Fletcher had managed to put her in a rush once
again.

Her new attorney was turning out to be much more difficult than she had anticipated!

Though she had intended to go to her office for a couple of hours Saturday, Rachel impulsively decided to stay
home. The children were pleased. They usually went along
with her on Saturdays—even kept toys and coloring books
there just for weekends—but they enjoyed spending an
occasional lazy morning at home.

Rachel told herself that the decision not to go to the office that day had nothing to do with Celia or Seth. She
simply had housework to do, and there was nothing particularly pressing to be done at the office that morning.
The drivers knew to call her at home if anything came up

during their Saturday routes and they couldn't reach her at the office.

Leaving the children engrossed in cartoons, she worked especially hard cleaning the guest room, preparing it for her grandmother's arrival the next day. She put fresh white eyelet-trimmed sheets on the old four-poster cherrywood bed, tied back the eyelet curtains to let the autumn sun stream through the only window, dusted the huge cherry dresser and matching wardrobe, placed air fresheners in the small, empty closet. And then she spent a moment admiring the results of her preparations.

The antique bedroom furniture had belonged to Ray's mother, who'd died when he was just a teenager, before Rachel had met him. The mahogany table, eight chairs, buffet and china cabinet in her dining room had also belonged to Ray's mother, as had other select pieces scattered throughout the four-bedroom home she and Ray had bought soon after they'd married. They'd planned to have three children, but Aaron had just turned two when Ray died, and they had scheduled the third child to be conceived when Aaron was three.

Ray and Rachel had been serious about their planning and scheduling. They couldn't have foreseen that their plans would change so abruptly, and so tragically.

But she was getting morose again. She shook off the incipient depression and put away her cleaning supplies. There were so many things left to do before her grandmother's visit.

"What time will Granny Fran get here tomorrow?" Paige asked during lunch.

"I'm not sure," Rachel answered. "Aaron, you're dripping your soup. Watch what you're doing."

Aaron brought his attention back to his lunch. Rachel wondered what youthful fantasy had been playing in his imaginative head. Her five-year-old was quite a daydreamer, unlike his older sister, who was firmly grounded in reality.

"How long is Granny Fran going to stay?" Paige asked.

"A couple of weeks."

"Will she make chocolate-chip cookies?" Aaron asked.

Rachel smiled. "Probably. Granny Fran loves making cookies. Especially for you and Paige."

"Is Uncle Adam going to stay here, too?" Paige asked. Paige always wanted to know all the details, was always the one who worried over the little things. The child was so much like her mother, Rachel thought ruefully.

"Uncle Adam isn't going to stay. He's bringing Granny Fran to us and he'll stay for dinner, but after that he has to go back to Little Rock."

"He prob'ly has to go save some lives tomorrow," Aaron commented matter-of-factly. Aaron's favorite television program was *Rescue 911*. He'd decided that his mother's cousin was a dedicated rescuer just like the ones on the program.

Rachel had never tried to explain to Aaron that Adam was a plastic surgeon, more acclaimed for bolstering egos than for saving lives. She was very fond of her older cousin, who'd been one of the first ones to come to her after the news of Ray's death had reached him. Afterward, he'd made repeated offers of financial assistance, which Rachel had always gently refused. His efforts had been awkward, sometimes bordering arrogance, but she knew they had been sincere.

Paige's attention had already moved to another topic. "Are we going back to that lawyer's office soon?" she asked, looking up from the grilled cheese sandwich she'd been pulling into bite-size pieces.

"What lawyer?" Rachel asked, caught off guard by the sudden change of subject.

"You know," Paige said impatiently. "The one with the fish in his office."

"I liked the fish," Aaron murmured, watching tomato soup cascade in a thick red waterfall from the end of his spoon.

"You mean Seth Fletcher? I don't know that we'll be going to his office again anytime soon. Why?" Rachel asked curiously.

Paige shrugged. "He had a nice smile."

Rachel was startled. Paige hadn't seemed particularly taken with Seth when they'd met three days earlier, nor had she mentioned him since. It seemed Rachel wasn't the only one who'd found thoughts of Seth Fletcher lingering in her mind!

"Aaron, don't play in your soup. You're going to make a mess," Rachel said, her attention conveniently distracted by her son's behavior. "Both of you finish your lunch. I need to run to town and pick up a few things so we'll be ready for Granny Fran."

"Can I have a new coloring book?" Aaron asked, immediately intrigued. "My old one's colored up."

"I need a new pencil case for school," Paige reminded her mother. "Bobby Mitchell broke mine. Ms. Walker made him miss recess," she added in satisfaction.

Rachel willingly agreed to both requests. Shopping was a much less disturbing subject than Seth Fletcher.

Her shopping done and purchases stored away, Rachel was in the kitchen chopping vegetables for dinner early that evening when the telephone rang. She glanced automatically through the window over the sink as she reached for the phone. Paige and Aaron were playing in the backyard where she could see them; it was almost time to call them in, since daylight was rapidly fading. "Hello?"

"I hear you got yourself a new lawyer. You're going to need him."

Rachel swallowed a groan. She recognized the low growl immediately, of course. Just as she knew instantly that the caller had been drinking again. "Frank. I've asked you to stop calling me. Please don't make it necessary for me to file charges against you."

"File charges against *me?* That's a good one," Holder snarled. "I'm the one who oughta be filing charges."

"I haven't done anything to you."

"Yeah, right. I bet you're going to try to make me believe you didn't talk to that personnel director for Carter Trucking, either."

Rachel sighed. "Mr. Loudermilk did call me for a reference. I did nothing but honestly answer the questions he asked me about you. You certainly didn't expect me to tell him that I had no problems with you as an employee, did you?"

"You kept me from getting a job with them."

"I'm sorry. I hope you find another position. But don't ask me to lie for you. I won't do it."

"You bitch. You'll do anything you can to ruin my life, won't you? It wasn't enough that you fired me, now you gotta make sure no one else hires me."

"Frank," Rachel said firmly, cutting into the increasingly loud diatribe. "I am not trying to ruin your life. You're doing a pretty good job of that by yourself. I told you several times that you need to get professional help. Your drinking is..."

His interruption was angry and obscene. "You're going to be sorry you messed with me, you hear?"

"Maybe you'd better just talk to my lawyer in the future," Rachel said coolly. "His name is Seth Fletcher and he's listed in the book. If you think you have a suit, fine. Take it up with the courts. But leave me alone."

"Don't think it's going to be that easy, *Ms.* Evans. You'll pay for what you've done to me. You just wait. You'll pay."

A chill slithered down her spine. Rachel stared nervously at her children, playing so innocently outside. "You aren't threatening me, are you, Frank?"

His laugh was ugly. And then he hung up, apparently satisfied that he'd finally worried her.

Rachel muttered a curse and hung up the phone. She spent the next ten minutes trying to reassure herself that Frank's veiled threats were nothing more than drunken ramblings, that he wouldn't really risk harming her. But there'd been something different in his voice this time. The wildness and irrationality that had seemed to escalate in him during the final year of his employment with her had been more audible than usual. She'd heard that his live-in girlfriend had left him since he'd lost his job, and she knew he'd been drinking more heavily than ever. Had he finally gone over the edge? Was she really in danger from him?

She reached for the phone, then stopped herself with a quick shake of her head. She could handle this, she assured herself. Just as she'd handled all the other problems she'd encountered during the past three years.

Besides, who would she call? Cody would only lose his temper and go beat Frank up or something, which wouldn't help anyone. As for Seth ...

The telephone rang again, making Rachel jump. She answered it warily. "Hello?"

There was no response. Only the sound of someone breathing.

She slammed the receiver home again, knowing exactly who was on the other end of the line. And then she ran to get her purse, and rummaged inside it until she found the slip of paper with Seth's number on it. Without giving herself time to think about what she was doing, she picked up the phone again. She was relieved to hear a dial tone.

A few moments later, Seth's voice came through the instrument.

"Seth? It's Rachel."

Something in her voice must have made him aware that it wasn't a social call. "What's wrong?"

"Holder just called. He—he sort of threatened me, Seth. He worried me. I'm not sure what I should do now. I was hoping you could advise me," she said, trying to sound calm.

"Tell me your address, Rachel. I'm on my way over."

Her fingers tightened on the receiver. She should have known this would be Seth's reaction—maybe she *had* known. "I'm sure that's not necessary," she said. "I just—"

"Rachel," he interjected flatly, "give me your address or I'll call Cody and have him come with me. Now."

She sighed, knowing that this was not an empty threat. Seth meant every word.

She gave him directions to her home.

She hung up knowing he was on his way. And wishing she didn't feel quite so relieved about it.

Chapter Four

Rachel had barely opened the door when Seth took her by the shoulders and anxiously searched her face. "Are you all right?"

Less than fifteen minutes had passed since she'd called him. During that time, she'd convinced herself she'd overreacted, that she shouldn't have called Seth. "I'm fine," she assured him, embarrassed that he'd taken the call so seriously. "I'm sorry I bothered you with this."

Seth shook his head impatiently. "When did he call? What, exactly, did he say?"

"Nothing specific. He was drunk again, and rambling about making me sorry for what I supposedly did to him. He claimed I'm trying to ruin his life and said he would make me pay."

Seth's fingers tightened spasmodically on her shoulders. A quick flash of temper heated his green eyes. "Tell me where he lives."

She sighed. "Now you sound just like Cody. Surely you aren't planning to go beat the guy up? I thought attorneys believed in handling everything through the legal system."

Seth had the grace to look a bit sheepish. "We do, usually. I guess it's different when there's a personal involvement."

Rachel stiffened. "I called you on a professional basis, as my attorney," she reminded him. "This isn't personal."

He smiled and dropped his hands from her shoulders. "Whatever you say, Rachel." His sardonic tone mocked her denial, but at least he didn't look so worried and angry now. She decided that she much preferred his easy smile.

"Have you called the police?" he asked.

"No. I didn't know whether I should."

"As your attorney, I would advise you to call the police and file a report. They probably can't do anything to the guy, but at least you'll be on record with a complaint if anything else happens."

That sounded reasonable. Rachel nodded. "All right. I'll call now."

"Who are you going to call, Mama?" Aaron asked from the doorway to the den. He was looking curiously at Seth.

Seth smiled at the boy.

"Hi, Aaron, remember me?"

Aaron nodded gravely. "You've got the fish."

Seth chuckled. "Right. Where's Paige?"

"Playing Sonic Spinball," Aaron replied.

Rachel started to explain that it was a video game for a system connected to their television set, but Seth spoke before she could. "You've got a Sega system?" he asked Aaron, proving that he recognized the game.

Aaron nodded.

"Want to show it to me? Your mom needs to make a telephone call."

"Do you know how to play Sonic Spinball?" Aaron asked, his eyes lighting up.

"You bet I do. I'm the champ," Seth bragged.

Aaron shook his head. "Uncle Cody's the champ."

Seth shot Rachel a lazy grin that made her pulse do strange things. "You make the call," he urged her quietly. "I have to go defend my video game reputation now."

She chewed her lower lip as she watched Seth turn and follow her son into the den. He was certainly making himself at home, she thought in bemusement.

It was becoming more difficult all the time to think of Seth as nothing more than her attorney. And she'd only known him for a few days!

She made the call from the telephone in the kitchen, knowing that Seth would keep the children occupied until she was finished. On an impulse, she asked for the police chief, Leon Jackson. She doubted that he would be in his office on a Saturday evening, but it was worth taking a chance since she hated to discuss this problem with a stranger. She was both surprised and relieved when Chief Jackson answered.

"Leon? It's Rachel Evans."

"Rachel, it's good to hear from you. What can I do for you?"

Leon had played high school football with Ray, and the two had remained close friends until Ray's death. Few people had been more pleased than Ray when Leon had overcome lingering small-town Southern biases to become Percy's first black police chief almost ten years ago. Leon had been one of the groomsmen in Rachel and Ray's wedding, and Ray had been named godfather to Leon's only son. Leon had stood close to Rachel's side during Ray's funeral.

Rachel explained her reason for calling. "It's not that I want Frank arrested or anything," she added when she'd finished. "He certainly has enough problems without that. And I doubt that he's really a threat to me. But my attorney recommended that I file an official report, just to be on the safe side."

"Your attorney was right," Leon said grimly. "You should have told me sooner that this guy's been harassing you."

"It hasn't been a serious problem yet. Only a few phone calls and a lot of loose talk that others have reported to me."

"You never can tell with a drunk," Leon informed her. "Especially if he goes over the edge, which it sounds like this guy might be very close to doing. Losing his job and his girlfriend—well, it might be enough to cause him to do something stupid if we don't step in."

Rachel sighed, feeling strangely guilty about Frank's problems, even though she knew there was nothing she could have done differently. She'd warned him repeatedly about his job performance, given him as many chances as she could afford to take, and still he'd refused to even try to shape up.

"I'll talk to him, myself, Rachel. Pass along a friendly little warning about what's going to happen to him if he continues to give you problems. You hear from him again, you give me a call, okay? At home, if you can't catch me here."

"Thank you, Leon. I really appreciate this."

"Ray Evans was my best friend," Leon said gruffly. "He would have wanted me to look after you and the kids. Just like he'd have been there for Dolores and my boy if it had been me in that car instead of him."

"Speaking of Dolores and DeShawn, shouldn't you be home with them now?" Rachel asked, lightening her tone to hide the rush of emotion that coursed through her in response to Leon's sincere words.

Leon chuckled, following her lead. "Yeah, I should. I got held up here with paperwork, and Dolores is going to have my hide if I don't get home soon. I'll talk to Holder for you, Rachel. You take care of yourself, you hear?"

Following familiar beeping, blooping sounds from the den, Rachel found Seth cross-legged on the carpet in front of the television set, a video game controller in his hands, his attention focused intently on the colorful action on the screen. Paige sat at his left side, Aaron at his right, both children gravely watching him play and occasionally offering advice.

Paige was the first to notice that Rachel had joined them. "Hi, Mama. Did you make your phone call?"

"Yes, I did. And everything's fine," she added for Seth's benefit when he looked at her in silent question. "How's the game going?"

"Seth's almost as good as Uncle Cody," Aaron announced in some awe.

Seth's eyebrows rose. "I'm sure I'm better."

"I don't know," Aaron said skeptically. "Uncle Cody's awful good."

"Mr. Fletcher said we can call him Seth, Mama," Paige explained. "Is that okay with you?"

Rachel met Seth's gaze, saw that he was laughing at her again, and swallowed a sigh. "Yes, Paige, it's okay with me, if that's what he wants."

"Is dinner ready yet, Mama?" Aaron asked. "I'm getting hungry."

Rachel had completely forgotten her dinner preparations when Holder had called. She thought of the vegetables she'd been chopping half an hour earlier and hoped they hadn't shriveled. "It will be ready soon," she promised her son.

Aaron nodded. "Can Seth eat with us? He's prob'ly hungry, too."

The children waited for her answer in innocent inquiry, Seth with a blandly amused expression that made her long to snarl at him. Trapped by deeply ingrained manners, she could only smile weakly and say, "Of course Seth is welcome to eat with us. Unless he has other plans?"

"Not a one," he assured her briskly, dashing her faint hopes. "What can I do to help?"

"I'll take care of the food," she assured him hurriedly. "You finish your game." She didn't want to think about sharing her snug little kitchen with him. He'd probably make her so self-conscious she'd chop her fingers off!

When Rachel returned to the den to announce dinner twenty minutes later, she found Paige and Aaron watching television, and Seth standing beside the fireplace, studying the framed portraits she'd grouped on the mantel. He seemed to be concentrating particularly on the large photo in the center. It was a family portrait, taken when Paige was three and Aaron not quite a year old. Ray had been wearing his best blue suit and only designer silk tie, and Rachel had worn her favorite red dress. She'd spent a long time getting the children ready, dressing Paige in white ruffles, coaxing her fine dark hair to curl beneath a lacy bow. Aaron had worn a navy sailor-collared suit with a red tie.

The photographer had told them that he'd rarely seen a more attractive family. He'd probably said that to all his photo subjects, but Rachel had been very proud.

Seth turned away from the photograph when Rachel entered, his expression unreadable.

"Dinner's ready," she said.

He smiled. "Good. I'm starving." He walked away from the mantel without glancing back.

Dinner was a pleasant affair. Rachel had prepared a quick and easy chicken-and-vegetable stir-fry dish served over steamed rice, a favorite meal for her children. Rachel considered herself fortunate that her children had always enjoyed fresh vegetables, especially when she heard how much trouble other mothers had getting their children to eat nutritious meals. Seth seemed to like the simple fare, as well, judging from his effusive praise and hearty appetite.

He seemed quite content to be dining with Rachel and her children. He swapped video game tips with Aaron, sympathized with Paige about the difficulties of second grade, asked questions about Rachel's business and seemed genuinely interested in her answers.

Though his easy smile and ready laughter reminded Rachel of Cody, Seth's was a gentler, quieter humor than Cody's effusive high spirits. There were times when Seth's green eyes grew pensive, making her think that he was more serious in some ways than he let on. She wouldn't have been surprised to learn that he had known his own share of heartache, though he hid it well.

By the time dinner ended, Rachel had convinced herself again that his interest in her was merely amicable. He simply hadn't met a lot of people in Percy yet, and he was enjoying the opportunity to share a home-cooked meal, simple as it was, with a friendly family. As for his overreaction to Holder's phone call—well, she was his client. His friend's widowed sister. He probably felt that he was being chivalrous or something in helping her with her problems.

That possibility left a dry taste in her mouth that killed her appetite before she'd cleaned her plate.

He didn't linger after dinner. He thanked Rachel for the meal, and she thanked him for coming in response to her call. After that rather stiffly polite exchange, Seth bade good-night to the children and headed for the front door.

Telling herself she was only being hospitable, Rachel left the children in the den and walked Seth to the door.

"You'll call me if Holder bothers you again?" he persisted, one hand on the doorknob.

She nodded. "I'll call. I've got several other minor legal matters to discuss with you soon... a couple of contracts I'd like you to read before I sign them, two customers who may have to be sued for delinquent accounts. I'll call your secretary to arrange an appointment."

It seemed easier to treat Seth as an attorney rather than anything more intimate. She knew how to act with an attorney; she'd almost forgotten how to behave with an attractive man who'd shown signs of a personal interest in her. Though, of course, she'd probably misread those signs completely, she assured herself.

That suspicious amusement was back in his eyes when he gave her a bland smile. "I'll tell my secretary to expect your call."

She swallowed and glanced downward, uncomfortable with the way he was looking at her. Why did she so often imagine that he was laughing at her? She couldn't think of anything she'd done in particular to amuse him.

She jumped a bit when he unexpectedly cupped her chin in his hand and raised her face to his. With his free hand he touched her hair, which she was wearing loose and straight to just below her shoulders. "I like your hair down," he murmured. "I've only seen it pinned up before today."

"I... uh..."

"And I like seeing you in casual clothing," he added, glancing down at her soft pink sweater and gray wool slacks. "Much more approachable than those suits you wear to work."

She frowned. "Seth, I—"

He kissed her before she realized his intention; just a quick, firm brush of lips. He didn't linger long enough to allow her to resist—or to respond. Yet every nerve ending in her body was suddenly quivering in reaction. She told herself it was only surprise, and annoyance. "Do you make it a practice to kiss your clients?" she asked, wishing her voice sounded cooler and less breathless.

"No," he answered, and this time he didn't even try to hide his grin. "But then I've never gotten personally involved with a client before."

"Seth, you aren't—we aren't—"

He placed a finger over her lips, effectively silencing her sputtering. "Oh, but I am. And I certainly hope we are. But I won't rush you, Rachel. Or at least I'll try not to," he amended. "Good night. Sleep well."

He left her convinced that she probably wouldn't sleep a wink. And that he knew it, darn him.

She did sleep, of course. And she dreamed. Strange, disturbing dreams that made her wake in the middle of the night, restless, edgy, her skin damp and oversensitized. She didn't remember details, didn't even try, but she knew her dreams had centered around a man with laughing green eyes and a lazy, sexy smile.

She was glad it was dark in the room. Relieved she couldn't see her own flushed reflection in the mirror across the room. Or the photograph that sat on her nightstand.

When she finally fell back into a fitful sleep, there were tears on her pillow and on her cheeks. And a deep, aching emptiness in her heart.

Celia arrived early the next afternoon, Rachel's beaded jacket over one arm and a covered dish in her other hand. "I've made broccoli-and-rice casserole for dinner," she said with a self-mocking smile. Broccoli-and-rice casserole was the only dish Celia cooked. She provided it for every family potluck meal. Fortunately, Rachel thought fondly, she made it very well.

She took the jacket Celia held out. "You could have kept this," she reminded her sister.

Celia shook her dark head. "I'd rather have you store it, and I'll just borrow it when I need it."

Rachel chuckled. "How thoughtful of you. Take your casserole into the kitchen and help yourself to something to drink, if you like. I'll be there as soon as I hang this up."

Paige and Aaron were in the kitchen with Celia when Rachel joined them. Excited about their beloved great-grandmother's imminent arrival, they were both chattering like magpies, making Celia laugh at their enthusiasm.

"Why don't the two of you go outside and play for a while?" Rachel suggested. "It's a beautiful afternoon and you need to work off some of this energy."

"It sure would be a great day to swing," Aaron hinted broadly. "I bet I could almost touch the sky if we had a swing set."

Rachel rolled her eyes. "Yes, Aaron, I know you want a swing set. You've only hinted about it a few thousand times now. But today you'll have to be content with your other toys. Now, scoot."

"You'll call us when Granny Fran gets here?" Paige demanded on her way out.

"I promise," Rachel assured her.

She closed the door behind the children, then turned to find Celia looking at her with a quizzical expression.

"What?" Rachel asked.

"The kids told me that Seth Fletcher had dinner here last night."

Rachel gave a mental groan at the unnecessary reminder of something she'd been trying unsuccessfully to put out of her mind all morning. That kiss, for example. And the dreams that had followed it.

"It was business," she said a bit too brusquely. "I'd better baste the ham. It smells good, doesn't it?" She opened the oven door, carefully avoiding her sister's eyes.

"Business?" Celia repeated, sounding skeptical. "What kind of business?"

"Celia, the man is my attorney. That's all."

"Hey, come on, Rach. I saw the way he looked at you in your office the other day. It was more than professional interest."

Rachel did groan then. So Celia, too, had found Seth's behavior curious. So much for pretending she'd only imagined it.

"He seemed very nice," Celia offered. "And you have to admit he's great looking. That smile . . ."

"He's too young," Rachel muttered.

"He's a full-grown male, Rachel. A couple of years' difference in your ages doesn't change that."

"He's . . . cocky," Rachel added, blushing at her own inanity.

Celia laughed. "Aren't they all?"

Rachel sighed, closed the oven door and turned to face her sister. "I'm just not ready to start dating again, Celia."

Celia's smile faded. She reached out and took Rachel's hands in her own. "Honey, it's been three years," she said gently. "It's time."

"Even if it is," Rachel murmured through a tight throat, "I wouldn't pick someone like Seth. He's too . . . too . . ."

"Too dangerous?"

Startled by Celia's choice of description, and the confidence with which she'd said it, Rachel shook her head. "I'm not sure I know what you mean."

Celia's smile, this time, held a wealth of understanding. "I mean that Seth is the type of man who could make a woman do something foolish. Make her forget to be cautious and controlled. A woman might even be tempted to fall in love with a man like that."

A ripple of pain coursed through Rachel in response to the word. "I've been in love," she whispered. "It hurts too badly when it ends, however it ends."

Celia's hands tightened around Rachel's fingers. "I'm sorry, Rachel. I didn't mean to upset you like this," she said contritely. "I only thought..."

Seeing the distress in Celia's blue eyes, Rachel made an effort to shake off her moodiness, which she blamed on tension and lack of sleep. "Look at us, standing here wasting time when there's so much to be done. Do me a favor and make a pot of coffee while I cut up a salad, will you? You know how addicted Adam is to his coffee."

"I also know that he thinks I make the worst coffee in history," Celia said, more cheerful now.

"Oh, that's right, he does. Maybe I'd better make it."

Celia laughed and reached for the coffeemaker. "Don't you dare. Making Adam drink my coffee is one of my most cherished pleasures."

"You're a wicked woman, Celia Carson."

Celia sighed gustily. "Yeah, right. Wicked Saint Celia."

Which, of course, reminded Rachel of Celia's date with the dashing Damien Alexander. It worried her a bit that Celia was very evasive in response to questioning during the next ten minutes. Celia finally, firmly, changed the subject by asking about the children's schoolwork. Rachel went along only because she didn't want to tempt Celia to turn the interrogation back to her own complex relationship—or lack of one—with Seth Fletcher.

The doorbell rang less than half an hour later. Celia went to answer it while Rachel hastily wiped her children's hands and faces with a dampened dish towel and straightened the bow in Paige's hair. Deeming them ready for greeting company, she led them into the living room.

The children broke away immediately to descend upon the tiny, gray-haired woman standing in the middle of the room. "Granny Fran! Granny Fran!"

Their great-grandmother gathered them into her arms. "Paige! Aaron! Goodness, how you've both grown."

Rachel couldn't help laughing. "It's only been a month since you last saw them."

Her grandmother smiled over the children's heads. "I know. But they seem to have grown a foot apiece."

Rachel kissed her grandmother's soft cheek, inhaling the familiar scent of jasmine. "Did you have a nice drive?"

"It only took two hours," Frances replied. "Adam's new car is quite comfortable."

"I usually make the drive from Malvern to Percy in an hour and a half," Adam said dryly. "Gran wouldn't let me drive above fifty."

Rachel turned to speak to her cousin, who had been talking to Celia while the others exchanged greetings. She had to rise on tiptoe to kiss Adam's hard, lean cheek. "I'm glad you were able to fit us into your busy schedule," she joked. "Did *you* have a nice drive?"

"She chewed my butt all the way here," Adam murmured ruefully. "Seems she's gotten the idea that I need taking down a peg or two."

Rachel laughed softly.

"And so you do," Frances informed Adam, proving that her hearing was as sharp as it had ever been.

Adam didn't even bother to look abashed. There was a softness in his dark eyes when he smiled at his grandmother that Rachel never saw there at any other time. Dr. Adam Stone was not a soft man in any sense of the word. Brilliant, capable and reliable, he could also be arrogant, demanding and temperamental. At thirty-eight, he was tall and fit, his dark hair just showing a touch of silver at the temples, his skin firm, tanned and unlined except for shallow creases around his eyes and mouth. His nose had a very faint bump that was the result of his childhood fall from Granny Fran's apple tree. Rachel had often wondered why the talented plastic surgeon hadn't bothered to have that minor flaw corrected. He certainly would have encouraged his patients to do so!

Celia—who was one of the two people in the world Adam could never intimidate, Granny Fran being the other—cocked her head and looked at her older cousin with an impish grin. "Well? Did it work?"

"Did what work?" he asked indulgently.

"Did she take you down a peg or two or are you still on a royal high horse?"

Adam frowned. "I think you've mixed a few metaphors."

"Which means you aren't going to answer, right?"

"I never respond to mixed metaphors," he said gravely.

"Well, I'll answer," Frances said with a shake of her head. "The lecture didn't help a bit. The boy's still as cocky as ever."

Celia giggled and glanced at Rachel. "Aren't they all," she murmured, repeating the words she'd used earlier in reference to Seth.

Rachel sent Celia a look of mild warning and turned back to her houseguest. "I've made the guest room ready for you, Granny Fran. I want you to be sure and tell me if you need anything at all while you're here. Adam, you'll carry her bags into the guest room, won't you?"

"It will be my pleasure," he said with a touch of irony. "Celia, you'd better show me the way. I'm not sure I remember which room is which."

"We're having glazed ham and angel biscuits for dinner," Rachel told him, knowing those were two of his favorites.

"And broccoli-rice casserole?" he asked, slanting a smile at Celia.

Celia laughed. "Of course."

"Pecan pie for dessert," Rachel added tantalizingly. "With ice cream, if you like."

He sighed. "For all that, I'd almost paint the guest room."

Celia snorted. "You've never held a paintbrush in your life."

"Okay, so I'd hire someone to paint the guest room," Adam amended, following her out of the room. "Same thing."

Frances had been holding a colorful shopping bag. She offered it to Paige. "There's a gift for you and one for Aaron in here."

The children thanked her promptly and then pounced on the bag. Rachel placed an arm around her grandmother's shoulders and led her out of the room, leaving the children to exclaim over their gifts. "Would you like a cup of tea?" she asked as they entered the kitchen. "Or Celia made coffee."

"*Celia* made coffee?" Frances repeated. At Rachel's nod, Frances cleared her throat and said, "I think I'll have tea."

Rachel laughed. "Good choice." She filled the tea-kettle and set it on a back burner of her electric stove. "Have a seat. It'll just take a minute."

Frances took a chair at the heavy oak kitchen table, but asked, "Are you sure there's nothing I can do to help with dinner?"

"No, everything's almost ready." Rachel pulled out another chair and sat close to her grandmother. "Cody will be joining us for dinner. He had a golf game this afternoon, but he promised he'd come here directly from the country club."

"That boy and his golf. I think he'll be golfing on Judgment Day."

"Most likely," Rachel agreed.

"I'm glad he's coming. It will be nice having all my grandchildren together for dinner. It's been a while."

"Yes, it has, hasn't it? I wish Mom and Dad were here."

"I talked to them yesterday. Bill still seems to be content with his work in Saint Louis. And I think your mother finally feels at home there, after almost six years."

"It was a hard adjustment for her," Rachel agreed. "After living in central Arkansas all her life, it wasn't easy to pick up and move when she was almost fifty. But it has been a good move for Dad. He seems to really enjoy working with the mental health center there."

Bill Carson was a psychologist. He'd worked for the Arkansas health system for years before accepting the position in Saint Louis. Now, at fifty-six—with several years remaining until retirement age—he still enjoyed the challenges of his work. His wife, Evelyn, a year younger than her husband, hadn't been as excited about the career move, since it had meant leaving her children and grandchildren.

At the time of the move, Celia had just entered her senior year of high school. She had been so upset at the thought of leaving her friends only months before graduation that she'd moved in with Rachel and Ray during that final year of school. Rachel had enjoyed having her younger sister in the household. Celia and Ray had gotten along well, and Celia had been a lot of help with Paige, who'd been just a baby at the time. That experience had left Rachel feeling even more responsible for her younger sister than ever, which explained her intense concern about Celia's involvement with Damien Alexander.

"Speaking of the rest of the family," Rachel said, "how's Aunt Arlene?"

A slight frown creased Frances's brow. "The same as always," she said with a sigh. "Always suffering some imaginary illness, always complaining about one thing or another, always calling on poor Adam to drop everything and rush to take care of her, and then throwing a hissy fit when he can't make time for her.''

'' 'Poor Adam' is quite capable of standing up for himself, even from his mother,'' Rachel said.

''I suppose,'' Frances agreed wistfully. ''I swear, that daughter of mine is enough to try the patience of a saint.''

Rachel hoped her grandmother wasn't comparing Adam to a saint! That *would* be stretching things. She prudently bit her tongue.

Two years older than her brother, Rachel's father, Arlene Carson Stone had never gotten over her resentment at being widowed young. Though her husband had left her financially secure, with enough money to raise her son in pampered luxury and a firmly established place in Little Rock society, she had spent the thirty years since his death bemoaning her fate in being left to raise her ''poor, fatherless child'' alone.

She had called Rachel nearly every day for months after Ray's death to compare their situations and cry buckets of tears over their shared misfortune. Rachel had made herself a firm promise during that time that she would never give in to public self-pity, and that she would never allow herself to become as emotionally dependent on others as Arlene had been since her own husband's death.

''So, tell me, Rachel,'' Frances said, suddenly changing the subject. ''What's been going on in *your* life? I hope you're taking more time for yourself lately.''

Rachel stood and busied herself preparing her grandmother's tea. ''I've been rather busy with the business lately. But I take time off with the children occasionally. We drove into Little Rock just last week to visit the children's museum.''

Frances didn't look particularly impressed. ''But what about yourself? Have you done anything just for fun? Are you seeing anyone new?''

What was it with everyone lately, urging her to have fun and to start dating again? Rachel wondered in silent exasperation. They acted as though she were still Celia's age, rather than a mature woman of thirty-one. "No, Granny Fran, I'm not seeing anyone," she said, sternly ignoring an unbidden mental image of a green-eyed, sexy-smiled attorney.

The front doorbell provided another welcome distraction. "That must be Cody," Rachel said, leaping gratefully on the change of subject. "I'll go let him in. And I'll send everyone else to join you in the dining room now."

As she'd expected, Rachel saw her brother's face through the tiny, diamond-shaped window in her front door. "You're just in time to eat," she said. "I've just sent everyone in to sit—"

She stopped abruptly at the sudden realization that Cody hadn't arrived alone. Seth Fletcher stood behind him, smiling blandly.

"I hope you don't mind," Cody said in a mischievous murmur. "I brought a friend."

[faint text from show-through, illegible]

Chapter Five

Seth spoke before Rachel had a chance to say anything. "Actually, our golf game took longer than we'd expected. I'm just dropping him off here. He assured me someone would take him home later."

He wanted to make it clear that he wasn't inviting himself to her home when she was entertaining her family. He was planning a pursuit of her, but he would try not to cross the boundaries of common courtesy while doing so.

"Come in and meet my grandmother before you go, Seth," Cody urged his friend. "You'll like her. She's cool."

Seth shook his head and took a step backward. "No, I don't want to intrude on your family. I'll meet her another time."

"Don't be silly, Seth. You aren't intruding. There's plenty of food and an extra place at the table. Please join us for dinner," Rachel urged, sounding invitingly sincere.

He hesitated, searching her face for any sign that she would rather he leave. Was it only good manners urging her to ask him in, or did she really want him to stay? As much as he wanted it to be the latter, he was afraid to get his hopes up too much.

She reached out and took his arm, pulling him inside. "Come in," she repeated with a smile.

She dropped his hand immediately after he stepped through the door, but now he was smiling, too, encouraged by her actions. Okay, so maybe she was only being polite; he'd settle for that.

She was wearing her hair down, again. The thick, dark mane gleamed in the light and rippled around her shoulders when she moved. He itched to bury his hands in it; it had been all he could manage not to do so last night. He'd resisted only because he hadn't wanted to take advantage of her when she'd called on him to help her. She was wearing casual clothing again today, a navy-and-white striped tunic sweater with navy stirrup pants and navy flats. The outfit emphasized her slender build and long legs; he liked it. But then, he'd have liked anything that didn't resemble those keep-your-distance suits she usually wore.

He was wearing jeans again, and a white sweatshirt with a screen print of a golfer on the front. She probably thought he didn't own a suit. He did, of course. Two of them. He just didn't wear them unless it was absolutely necessary.

She'd turned back to him and was looking at him with a polite, impersonal, gracious-hostess-to-welcome-guest smile that annoyed him a little. "Everyone's waiting in the dining room," she said. "I hope you like glazed ham."

Cody laughed, his blue eyes glinting with amusement. "Take my word for it, Rach, there is nothing this guy won't eat. He's got an appetite like Godzilla."

Rachel lifted an eyebrow and glanced at Seth's slim waistline. "I find that hard to believe," she said.

"He's got the metabolism of a race car, apparently," Cody teased. "He burns off calories faster than he consumes them."

Rachel sighed enviously. "It must be nice."

Embarrassed by the attention, Seth cleared his throat and motioned toward the dining room. "After you, ma'am."

He noticed that Cody seemed to be watching him rather intently as they followed Rachel to the dining room. Seth had been very careful not to say much about Rachel during the golf game. Now he suspected that he hadn't been as successful as he'd hoped at masking his growing interest in Cody's sister.

He wondered how Cody felt about that. He still wasn't exactly sure how he felt about it, himself.

Celia was standing in the dining room talking to a tiny, silver-haired woman and a tall, dark, rather stern-looking man. Paige and Aaron were already seated at the large table, leaving six empty chairs, Seth noted in relief. Rachel had been honest when she'd said there was an extra place for him at the table.

Cody swooped down on the older woman and snatched her into an enthusiastic bear hug that proved she must not be as fragile as she first appeared. She emerged breathless and laughing.

"Granny Fran, you get more gorgeous every time I see you," Cody assured her. "How do you get younger with passing time instead of older like everyone else?"

"You save your blarney for the young ladies," his grandmother told him with mock severity. "Maybe it'll help you find yourself a wife—and not a bit too soon, either."

Cody gulped audibly and turned to Seth. "Granny Fran, I want to introduce a friend of mine, Seth Fletcher. We were at the university together. He even managed to get a degree or two. Now he's an attorney here in town. Seth, my grandmother, Frances Carson."

Seth smiled and took the woman's tiny hand in his own much larger one. "It's very nice to meet you, Mrs. Carson. Cody talks about you often."

"You might as well call me Granny Fran. Everyone else does," the woman said, looking Seth over with apparent approval. "So you're an attorney. Are you married?"

"No, ma'am," Seth replied, ignoring Cody's snort of laughter.

Her eyes lit up. "Have you met my granddaughter, Celia?"

Now it was Celia who laughed. "Seth and I have met, Gran. But he knows Rachel even better," she added slyly.

A sideways glance let Cody know that Rachel's cheeks had darkened. He was glad he wasn't the one at the receiving end of the look she shot her younger sister. Quickly masking her discomfort, she introduced their cousin to Seth. "Dr. Adam Stone," she said. "He's a plastic surgeon in Little Rock."

Seth and Adam shook hands. Adam glanced from Seth to Rachel and back again but didn't comment on Celia's teasing remark.

"Are you going to eat with us again, Seth?" Aaron piped up from the table.

The other adults visibly reacted to the word *again,* all looking with interest at Seth and Rachel. Seth bit the inside of his lip and nodded. "Yes, Aaron. Your mother and uncle have generously invited me to join you for dinner."

"Come sit by me," Aaron said.

"No, sit by me, Seth," Paige insisted, not to be outdone. "You sat by Aaron last night."

"I'll sit between you," Seth promised, knowing Rachel was probably ready to strangle the three of them.

Though he tried to be discreet about it, Seth studied Rachel during dinner. As the meal progressed and the attention was diverted away from her and Seth, she began to relax, even laughing at Cody's foolishness. Watching her, Seth could imagine what she might have been like as a girl. Still rather serious, of course—she'd probably always been that—but more eager and hopeful.

She was obviously very close to her family—even her cousin, Adam, whom Seth found rather reserved and hard to read. Adam was tolerant of Cody, indulgent with Celia, patient with the children, and respectful toward his grandmother. But Seth noticed a subtle difference in Adam's attitude toward Rachel, a touch of warmth just slightly more pronounced than his obvious affection for the others. Seth wondered if anyone else even noticed. And then he decided that the others displayed the same interesting condition.

What was it that made Rachel so special to them? Pity, because she'd been widowed so young, so tragically? He rejected that possibility almost immediately. Rachel wasn't the type of woman to induce pity. Sympathy, yes, but not pity. She was too competent, too strong for that. He could only imagine how she'd hate the very idea.

But why was he trying to analyze the others' reactions to Rachel when he was still struggling to understand his own? There were plenty of other women he could go out with, women who'd made it clear in various degrees that they wouldn't make it necessary for him to pursue them too strenuously. So why would he even consider a serious involvement with one who would be so much trouble? A woman who was obviously terrified at the thought of an involvement with him—or with anyone, for that matter. A woman with two young children and memories of a dead husband for Seth to compete with. A woman who seemed every bit as rigid and routine-bound as his parents.

He must be a glutton for punishment.

* * *

Adam didn't linger long after dinner, claiming that he had several things to do that evening. Rachel suspected from the way he said it that he had a late date. Not that she believed the woman, whoever she was, was particularly special to Adam. Like the rest of the family, Rachel had begun to suspect that Adam would never marry. He was entirely too set in his ways, too resistant to compromise in any form. Some would have said he was too selfish to marry—in fact, plenty of people *had* said it.

Rachel didn't know if it was selfishness, or more a fear of the sort of clinging possessiveness he'd always received from his smotheringly overprotective mother. He'd once hinted to Rachel that he was afraid a wife would interfere with the little privacy he was able to snatch from his demanding career.

"Dinner was really good," he said to her as he prepared to take his leave.

"I'm glad you enjoyed it. We don't get to see you often enough," Rachel replied affectionately.

He touched a hand to her shoulder, searching her face with too-intent dark eyes. "Everything is okay with you? No business or financial problems? Because if you need anything..."

"Everything is fine," she assured him firmly, pushing all thoughts of Frank Holder's blustering threats to the back of her mind. She'd made her brother and sister promise not to mention Holder to either Adam or their grandmother, and fortunately Seth hadn't referred to the trouble, either. Adam would only insist on trying to take care of her, and there was really nothing he could do that she hadn't already done. "Thank you for caring, Adam."

He smiled a little and squeezed her shoulder before dropping his hand, which was as much affection as she would ever expect him to express. "Call if you need me," he said.

"I will. Drive carefully."

His smile deepened a bit at her motherly tone, and then he was gone. Rachel turned away from the door to find Seth standing behind her in the small foyer. She wondered how much he'd overheard of her parting from Adam. "Is there something you need?" she asked.

He cleared his throat. "Not at the moment," he replied with a cryptic expression. "Cody sent me after you. He said they're about to play Uno and they want you to play with them."

Rachel had to smile. Her grandmother was a fanatic for that card game, never hesitating to rope her family and friends into playing with her. Rachel had expected to be playing quite a bit during her grandmother's visit, but hadn't thought Granny Fran would pull out the deck quite so soon. And then she remembered that Seth had said "they" were about to play. Not "we."

"You'll play with us, won't you?" she asked, telling herself that she was only being polite. It certainly couldn't be that she was particularly reluctant for him to leave. Could it?

Seth hesitated before answering and she suspected that he was worried again about intruding on her family's evening. She thought of him going home to an empty apartment, leaving the rest of them there to laugh over the game, maybe have coffee and more dessert later. "Please stay," she said.

And then she chided herself for being foolish. How could she know he'd be going home alone to an empty apartment? For all she knew, he could have half a dozen people—women, probably—waiting for him to call. She was sure an attractive, personable young man like him would have plenty of options for entertainment on a Sunday evening, all of them more interesting than sitting around her house, playing card games.

If he'd made other plans, or had anything else he'd rather do, it wasn't apparent in his smile. "Thank you," he said. "I'd like that."

She looked at him more closely to try to decide whether he was genuinely pleased with the invitation, or just trying not to hurt her feelings. Their gazes locked—and held. Rachel felt her breath catch in her throat as they stared at each other. She had the oddest feeling that she was seeing him, really seeing him, for the first time. And what she saw was fascinating.

"Mama? Mama," a little voice repeated impatiently.

Rachel snapped to attention, her cheeks warming as she turned too quickly in response to the summons. "What is it, Aaron?"

"Uncle Cody said Granny Fran's getting ready to deal and if you want to play, you and Seth had better get in there."

"We're coming," Rachel replied, pleased to hear that her voice sounded at least reasonably normal. "Seth, go on in and tell them I'll be right there. I'll put on a fresh pot of coffee."

She snatched at the excuse for a few precious minutes to herself. She needed to regain her composure, to remind herself that she was no longer a silly girl, breathlessly susceptible to a sexy smile. Even if she *had* been acting like one for the past few minutes!

It was after nine o'clock when everyone left. The children were yawning, an hour past their usual bedtime, and even Granny Fran had finally tired of beating everyone else at Uno.

"I don't know about the rest of you, but *I* have to work tomorrow," Celia announced, reaching for her purse. "And I just can't tell you how excited I am about it."

After graduating from the University of Arkansas at Little Rock with a degree in business—the only one of the

Carson siblings to actually earn a college degree—Celia had moved back to Percy and taken a job as assistant loan officer of the local bank. She could have found a position in Little Rock or Memphis or Dallas, or joined her parents in Saint Louis, but she'd claimed she hadn't wanted to move away from her brother and sister. Since that decision had been made only a few months after Ray's death, Rachel had always suspected that Celia had been motivated by a desire to offer moral support to her widowed sister.

Lately she'd seen the restlessness growing in Celia, the longing to see new places, sample new experiences. Rachel thought that not-so-secret craving for adventure was one reason Celia had been drawn to Damien Alexander, who was so different from the young men in Percy.

Taking Celia's hint, Cody, too, stood and prepared to leave. "You ready to go, Seth, or do you want Celia to drop me off at my place?" he said, and Rachel remembered that the two men had arrived in Seth's car.

Seth shook his head and stood with lazy grace. "I'd better be going, too. I'm sure Rachel has to get these little monsters into bed," he added, ruffling Aaron's hair.

Aaron laughed. "I'm not a monster," he protested. "I'm just a kid."

Seth grinned. "Same difference."

Aaron squealed and made a ferocious face at Seth, who appeared properly cowed. Paige, not to be outdone, threw her arms around Seth's legs and lifted her face for a good-night kiss, which Seth promptly administered to her cheek with a noisy smack. Rachel marveled that her children, who were usually rather reserved with new acquaintances, had taken so quickly to Seth, treating him much the same as they did their uncle, whom they adored. She had to bite the inside of her lip against a smile when Cody, looking a bit jealous of the attention Seth was getting from his niece and nephew, grabbed them both and made them giggle with good-night nibbles and kisses.

Celia departed with hugs all around for her family and a smile for Seth. Cody hugged his grandmother and Rachel and headed for the door in Celia's wake. Seth bade good-night to Frances, assuring her that it had been very nice to meet her.

And then he turned to Rachel. "It's been a nice evening. Thank you."

"You're welcome." She almost offered him her hand, then told herself not to be stupid.

He hesitated just long enough to make her wonder in near panic if he intended to kiss her good-night again, right in front of her children and grandmother. But he only smiled, gave her a look that promised more to come and followed Cody out.

Rachel let out a breath she hadn't realized she was holding. "Paige, Aaron, it's time to get ready for bed. Go put on your pajamas—and do it quickly," she added, knowing both would try to stall for extra time if they weren't warned.

"That young man seems quite taken with you," Frances said the minute she and Rachel were alone.

Rachel hated herself for blushing like a schoolgirl. She busied herself clearing the oak game table that sat in one corner of the big, comfortable den. "Seth?" she said, trying to sound casual. "He's just a friend—and my attorney, of course."

"I got the impression he'd like to be more," Frances murmured with a smile.

Rachel cleared her throat. "Even if he is... interested, it wouldn't matter. I've given him no encouragement."

"And why not? He's a very nice man."

"He's too young," Rachel said automatically. How many times had she had to remind others, and herself, of that fact?

Frances laughed. "Sweetie, when you get to be my age, you'll see how little difference three or four years makes. Or ten or twenty, for that matter. Age is only a number."

Rachel really didn't want to have this conversation again. She'd already been through it with Celia, and absolutely nothing had been accomplished. She'd never been deliberately rude to her grandmother in her life, and didn't intend to start now, but she was bringing this subject to a close before it went any further. "I'd better go check on the children," she said with a pleasant smile. "They have school in the morning."

Frances had never been slow. Accepting Rachel's change of topic with good grace, she lovingly returned the smile. "All right, dear. I think I'll get ready for bed, myself. It's been a long day and I am rather tired."

"Let me know if you need anything."

"I'm sure I'll be just fine. Good night, Rachel. Sleep well."

Rachel kissed her grandmother's soft cheek. "You, too," she murmured.

She left the room with her fingers crossed, hoping there would be no more disturbing dreams that night.

Seth was in his office the next afternoon, wading through stacks of paperwork on a particularly nasty divorce he was handling, when his secretary called through the open doorway, "Phone for you, Seth."

Comfortable with the informality he'd established with her from the beginning, Seth reached for the telephone. "Okay, Maddie, I've got it. Fletcher here," he said into the receiver.

"Seth, it's Rachel."

His pulse kicked into a higher rate in response to the musical voice. He shook his head at his own folly. One would think he was a randy adolescent in the throes of his first infatuation! "What can I do for you, Rachel?"

"I just talked to Leon Jackson—he's the chief of police," she added.

"Yes, I've met Chief Jackson. Nice guy."

"Yes, he is. He and my husband were close friends."

An odd, hollow feeling coursed through Seth when she referred to her husband. He wondered if she'd mentioned him for some particular reason, or just as a casual comment. "Did Chief Jackson call you about Holder?"

"Yes. He wanted to let me know that he'd talked to Holder personally and warned him about harassing me. He told Holder to pursue any legitimate complaints he thinks he has through the court system, and to keep his distance from me or take the consequences."

"Does he think his warning got through?"

"He seemed to think it did. He said Holder seemed properly intimidated. I hope he's right."

"So do I," Seth agreed. He'd already decided that if the police couldn't stop Holder from bothering Rachel, he was going to take matters into his own hands. She wouldn't appreciate it, of course, but Seth couldn't stand the thought of that jerk causing her any more distress.

"Do you think Holder will go through with his threats to sue me?"

"I don't know, Rachel. I can only repeat that your documentation is flawless. I can't see that you have anything to worry about should this go to court."

A faint sigh of relief came through the line. "All right. I just wanted to let you know about Leon's call. As my attorney, of course," she added hastily.

He knew she was being very careful to make it clear that this wasn't a personal call. He wasn't entirely sure he believed her, or was that only his hormones talking?

"Thanks. Why don't we celebrate Holder's official reprimand over dinner tonight?"

"I'm afraid not," she said coolly. "I have a houseguest to entertain."

"Bring Granny and the kids along," he suggested. "My treat. It'll be fun."

"I'm sorry, Seth, but we have other plans for the evening."

He'd expected this... but he didn't have to like it. "All right," he conceded. "We'll do it another time. Soon." The words were as much a vow as a promise.

"Seth—"

But he didn't want to hear again that she had no interest in him personally. A guy's ego could only take so much rejection in one telephone call. "Oops. Sorry, Rachel, I've got to go. I'll talk to you again soon. Bye."

He heard her sputtering faintly as he hung up the phone. His grin was rueful. He'd probably pay for that, too.

He'd hung up on her *again!*

Rachel slammed her own receiver home and cursed herself for calling him in the first place. It had been an impulse, one she regretted now. The man was impossible. He simply wouldn't take no for an answer. And, though his persistence was just a teeny bit flattering—oh, hell, it was *darned* flattering—she had no intention of letting him railroad her into a date. Not even a date that included her entire family.

She suddenly realized that her fingers were crossed. Annoyed, she uncrossed them and turned her attention to business. But for the remainder of the afternoon, she found it very difficult to concentrate on her reports and responsibilities.

Chapter Six

During the next few days, it became embarrassingly apparent to Rachel that everyone in her family had decided to champion Seth's cause. Celia and Cody were blatant about it. Both asked her point-blank why she wouldn't "just go out with the guy." Neither accepted any of the standard excuses she gave them in reply. Her grandmother was only a bit more subtle, casually bringing Seth's name into conversations, asking if Rachel had talked to him, repeatedly mentioning what a "nice young man" he was.

Even Adam, who rarely interfered in such things, brought Seth's name up when he called Rachel at her office on Thursday to ask how she and Granny Fran were getting along. "He seemed like a decent guy," he said. "Not quite as much the joker as Cody."

Rachel murmured something noncommittal.

"Has he asked you out?" he asked with entirely characteristic lack of tact.

"Yes," Rachel answered with a sigh, knowing just what to expect. "He has. I turned him down."

"Why?"

"I just don't want to get involved with anyone right now."

"You should think about it," Adam advised. "You're still an attractive young woman. You don't want to spend the rest of your life alone. Besides, you need someone to help you with the kids."

"I'm perfectly capable of raising my children alone," Rachel responded coolly, annoyed with his rather arrogant certainty that he knew what was best for her.

"I know you are. Don't be so prickly. It was just a suggestion."

"Hmm." She turned the offensive right back to him. "What about you, Adam? Didn't you turn thirty-eight on your last birthday? Isn't it time you start thinking about settling down and making little Stones?"

"Point taken," he said hastily. "Your social life is your own business."

"Exactly."

"But, you know, I never did ask—why *have* you retained Fletcher as your attorney? Are you in some sort of legal trouble?"

"Just a minor problem with an employee I had to fire," Rachel answered lightly, deliberately downplaying the trouble. "It seems to be all taken care of now, and I probably won't even need Seth's services for that particular problem. Anything else I might need him for will just be the legal formalities required of any small business owner these days."

"You'd tell me if it was more serious than that, wouldn't you?" Adam asked suspiciously.

"Of course I would," Rachel lied sweetly, and then disconnected the call as quickly as possible.

She'd barely gotten in the door that evening before Seth's name came up again. "When are we going to see Seth again?" Aaron asked as he stood in Rachel's bedroom, watching her lace her sneakers after she'd changed out of her work clothes and into jeans and a comfortable sweater.

"I don't know, Aaron. I'm sure you'll be seeing him again sometime," Rachel answered, deliberately vague. "He's Uncle Cody's good friend."

"He's our good friend, too," Aaron said.

"Yes, of course." Rachel reached for her hairbrush.

"I like Seth."

"Yes, dear, so do I. Um—how was school today?"

"Fine. Wesley Kirkpatrick's father came to show us some animals in cages. It was cool. He had a raccoon and a possum and a bat."

Since Rachel happened to know that Wesley Kirkpatrick's father worked for the state parks service, she reacted without surprise. "Sounds interesting."

"I like Wesley's father. He's nice."

"Yes, Martin Kirkpatrick is a nice guy. He and I went to school together." Having lived in Percy all her life, Rachel knew just about everyone who'd lived there more than a year or two. Many of Paige and Aaron's friends were children of Rachel's own childhood acquaintances.

"It must be nice to have a father," Aaron said with a sigh, leaning back against Rachel's bed. "I wish my daddy didn't die."

"So do I, sweetie," Rachel said evenly, though her throat burned with the effort. It broke her heart that Aaron couldn't even remember his father, would never know how much Ray had loved him, how proud he'd been of his children. What a wonderful, patient, nurturing father he'd been to them.

"Timmy Engel's father died when Timmy was a little kid. Now he's got a new daddy."

Rachel bit her lip. Patricia Engel, whose husband had died of cancer a couple of years ago, had only recently remarried. Town gossip had it that Patricia was already expecting a new baby, and was blissfully happy with her new husband.

Since Rachel didn't know quite what to say in response to Aaron's musing, she changed the subject again. "We'd better go find Granny Fran and Paige, Aaron. I'm sure Granny's almost ready for us to eat that pot roast she cooked for our dinner."

"Do you think we could ever get a new daddy, Mama?" Aaron asked with the single-minded tenacity so typical of childhood.

"I don't know, Aaron," Rachel said helplessly. "But we're getting along pretty well as we are, don't you think?"

"Yeah, but it would be cool to have a dad," Aaron said with another little sigh. "Someone like Seth."

Rachel somehow managed not to choke. "Let's go find the others," she said quickly.

She all but bolted from the bedroom, pausing only long enough to turn off the light. Aaron tagged at her heels, already babbling about something else that had happened at school, much to Rachel's relief. It was bad enough that the rest of the family was playing matchmaker. She'd be darned if she'd let a five-year-old start organizing her love life!

She lay in bed that evening replaying the conversation she'd had with her son, wondering if she should have said something different, taken more time to talk to him. She shouldn't have let herself get flustered.

She wouldn't remarry just to give her children a new father, of course. That was certainly no basis for a successful marriage. And even if she *were* to remarry for the sake of the children, it wouldn't be someone like Seth, but someone older, more settled. Someone like...she searched her mind for a viable candidate. Someone like Dan McNeil, she finally decided, picturing her insurance agent, a divorced forty-year-old who'd asked her out a time or two. He'd taken her gentle refusals graciously enough, but had made it clear his interest was still there. All she'd have to do would be to give him a little encouragement.

Maybe it was time to start thinking about going out again, she thought, looking somberly at the photograph on her nightstand. Ray wouldn't have wanted her life to end when his did. He wouldn't have wanted her to be alone. Maybe it had taken Seth's attentions to make her aware that it was time she considered what she wanted for herself besides her children and her work, if anything.

The problem was that she couldn't really work up any enthusiasm about going out with Dan or with any other man. Except, perhaps, Seth Fletcher, the most likely candidate for heartache she could imagine at the moment. Damn it.

Aaron turned six that Saturday, the last weekend in September. Rachel had carefully budgeted during the preceding weeks to allow her to buy the gift Aaron most wanted—a swing set. She bought the nicest set she could afford, with two swings, a plastic glider shaped like a colorfully painted horse, a lookout tower on one end and a bright yellow plastic-clad slide on the other. Of course, the boxes were all marked "Assembly Required."

"How long do you think it will take you to put it together?" she asked Cody on the telephone Friday afternoon.

Cody had volunteered to put the set together while she and the children were away for Aaron's party.

"Keep the kids at the pizza parlor for a couple of hours. Everything will be ready when you get back home," Cody promised confidently.

Rachel mentally added an hour to his estimation. Surely Cody and the friends he'd claimed to have recruited for the project could have the set assembled in three hours. Aaron's birthday party was scheduled at Pizza Palace for twelve o'clock, and she pictured his excitement when she brought him home at three to find the swing set in his backyard, ready for play. She'd bought an inexpensive toy to give him at his pizza party, so he'd have something to unwrap from her, and to serve as a red herring.

The birthday party arranged by the long-suffering staff of the Pizza Palace was everything a six-year-old could have desired. Thirteen noisy guests, all the pepperoni pizza they could eat, followed by chocolate cake and ice cream, pitchers of sugar-and-caffeine-laced soda to turn them into hyper little motion machines, birthday hats, balloons and noisemakers, organized games that didn't stay organized for very long, party favors for everyone and a mountain of brightly colored gifts for the birthday boy to open.

Rachel and Granny Fran were exhausted when the last child departed with her parents at two-fifteen. The pizza parlor staff looked a bit frazzled but were already setting up for the party scheduled for three o'clock. Aaron and Paige were still full of energy.

"Can we go home now so I can play with my new toys?" Aaron demanded, greedily eyeing his stacks of gifts.

Rachel glanced at her watch. "We have to stop by the grocery store first," she said, stalling for extra time. "I need to pick up a few things for this evening. Aunt Celia and Uncle Cody are coming over to bring you their gifts."

"Are we going to have another birthday cake?" Aaron asked, his hazel eyes lighting up in anticipation.

"Of course we are," his great-grandmother replied. "I'm making it myself."

Rachel smiled at her son's delight. Giving her children pleasure was all the joy she could ask for herself, she thought contentedly. She'd felt the same way after Paige's birthday party last June, which Paige had declared to be the very best slumber party anyone had ever had.

She tried not to even think of the inevitable time when her children would leave home. Each birthday celebrated was a step closer to their independence. There were times when she wished she could snatch them into her arms and keep them small and innocent forever.

She deliberately took her time at the grocery store. Her coconspirator, Granny Fran, helped by pausing occasionally to read labels on cans and exclaim over rising grocery prices. The children quickly grew restless, though they were too well trained to make a scene in a public place, and too fond of their great-grandmother to risk hurting her feelings by rushing her through her shopping.

It was five minutes after three when Rachel guided her car into her driveway. She was already frowning at the sight of the black sports car parked at the curb, the only vehicle in sight.

"Isn't that Seth's car?" Paige asked innocently from the back seat of Rachel's car.

"It certainly looks like it," Rachel murmured. She'd specifically asked Cody who he was bringing to help him with the swing set. He'd named two longtime friends, neither of them Seth, to her unspoken relief. She should have known better.

Arms loaded with groceries, Rachel led the way into the house, followed by her grandmother and the children, all of whom were carrying Aaron's birthday presents. The house was empty. "Where's Seth?" Paige asked, puzzled.

"I don't know," Rachel said. "Why don't you and Aaron take his gifts to his room and I'll go see if he's here."

"Maybe they aren't finished putting the swing set together yet," Rachel said to her grandmother when the children followed her instructions. "See if you can keep the kids inside until I call them, okay?"

Frances smiled and nodded. "I'll get them started playing that new board game one of the little boys gave Aaron. It looked like it would take a while."

"Good idea. Thanks." Rachel headed for the backyard to check the progress of the swing set.

Instead of the three or four men she expected to find, there was only one—and it wasn't her brother. Wearing faded jeans and a red-and-white Arkansas Razorbacks sweatshirt that had seen better days, Seth was standing at the top of a stepladder, an instruction manual in one hand, a wrench in the other, and a deep frown creasing his forehead. The swing set was only half-finished, and that half was leaning precariously.

"What in the world—?"

At the sound of Rachel's voice, Seth jerked, dropped the manual and the wrench and nearly managed to fall off the ladder. He caught himself with one hand against the top railing of the swing set, then looked down at her with a half guilty, half sheepish expression. "I'm sorry," he said. "It's not quite finished."

"Seth, why are you here alone? Where are Cody and the others who were going to help him with this?"

"Cody was here," Seth explained. "The other two guys who were going to help him canceled out at the last minute, so he called me. He and I had just gotten started putting the set together when he was called away. Some sort of problem came up at the club, apparently, and Jake couldn't handle it alone. Cody said he'd be back as soon as he could, but I guess the problem was worse than he'd anticipated."

"So he left you to take care of this alone," Rachel concluded.

"I told him I didn't mind," Seth assured her. "The only problem is, I've never put a swing set together. To be honest, I've never put anything together that was larger than a model airplane. I'm sorry, I know you wanted this finished by the time you got home.''

Rachel shook her head, touched despite herself that he was apologizing when he'd certainly had no obligation to give up his Saturday afternoon to put together her son's swing set. "You really don't have to do this. You must be tired and thirsty. Why don't you come on into the kitchen for a cold drink and I'll have someone finish this later."

Seth immediately looked offended. "I can finish it," he insisted. "I've been studying the manual and I know now what I was doing wrong before."

"I'm sure you can finish it," Rachel hastened to assure him, realizing she'd accidentally stepped on his male ego. "I just thought you might be ready for a break."

"No. I want to finish this first. It shouldn't take much longer."

"Then I'll help," Rachel said, pushing up the sleeves of the apple green hand-knit sweater she wore with neatly pressed jeans and comfortable flats. She'd dressed for comfort for the birthday party, and now she was glad she'd chosen such casual clothing. "What can I do?"

Seth smiled down at her. "Why don't you read the instructions aloud as I get to them? It's hard for me to hold the manual and put this together at the same time."

Hoping Aaron would be engrossed in his new toys long enough to give them time to finish, Rachel retrieved the instruction manual from the ground where Seth had dropped it and turned to the page he named.

During the next hour, Rachel saw exactly how determined Seth could be when he put his mind to it. She wondered if he looked this serious and stubborn in court. He attacked the swing set as though it were the opponent and he was determined to win at all costs, and he looked far different from the man she'd caught building card houses on a lazy weekday afternoon in his office. She couldn't help wondering a bit nervously if he went after every challenge with the same single-minded pursuit of victory.

They worked well together. After the first few minutes, she found herself able to almost anticipate his requests, handing him tools before he asked, stepping forward to help him steady a particularly heavy piece of equipment, knowing just when to repeat an obscure bit of instruction from the confusing manual.

"I think these directions were written by someone to whom English was a second language," Seth muttered at one point.

Rachel chuckled. "This from a lawyer? I thought you guys specialized in making the English language especially difficult to understand."

He growled and waved a wrench at her in a mock-threatening motion that didn't intimidate her in the least. To her surprise, she was actually having fun, a realization that only made her nervous again.

A sudden, shrill squeal came from behind them. Aaron stood in the kitchen door, studying the almost-finished swing set with blissful excitement. "A swing set! Thank you, Mama!"

Paige appeared at Aaron's heels, followed by Frances, who looked apologetic at being unable to stall them any longer. "Hey, cool!" Paige exclaimed. "Can we play on it?"

"It's not quite ready," Seth explained. "Give us just a few more minutes."

"Yeah, Paige," Aaron muttered, sounding quite superior now that he'd reached the mature age of six. "Can't you see the swings aren't even on it yet?"

Paige glared at him. "I can see that," she retorted. "I was just asking if it was almost ready to play on."

The children insisted on "helping" with the final steps in the assembly of the set, which added a good half hour to the process. It was almost five-thirty when Seth announced that he was finished. He refused to let the children play on the set until he and Rachel had tested every part of it for sturdiness and safety, checking to make sure there were no exposed metal parts and no loose connections, climbing into the tower to determine its steadiness, even sliding down the slide and swinging on the swings to verify that they'd hold his weight, as the promotional materials had assured him they would.

The horse glider was rated only to hold a hundred pounds. "You try it, Rachel," Seth urged.

Rachel gave him a reproachful look. "Don't I wish."

He looked surprised. "You weigh more than a hundred pounds?"

"Of course I do! I'm five-seven. If I weighed a hundred pounds, I'd be nothing more than skin and bones."

"I certainly didn't mean to imply that there was anything lacking in your figure," he murmured, giving her a quick, appreciative head-to-toe glance. "Just the opposite, in fact."

She blushed and cleared her throat. "You can test it, Aaron," she said quickly. "Seth can stand close by to make sure it looks safe."

They finally proclaimed the swing set ready for action. After giving a few last-minute safety instructions, Rachel and Seth stood back and let the children have at it. Seth looped a casual arm around Rachel's shoulders as they watched the kids play. "I think they like it," he said.

"I think you're right," she replied. She knew she should step away, was determined not to send him any mixed signals, but his arm felt so nice around her, his body so warm and strong against her side. Just for a moment, she allowed herself to relax and enjoy.

A man cleared his throat behind them. "Looks like I'm a little late to help with the swing set," Cody said.

Rachel stepped quickly away from Seth, feeling absurdly guilty at being caught with his arm around her. She turned to her brother with a frown. "Yes, you are. What on earth happened?"

"Plumbing problems," Cody answered morosely. "The bathrooms flooded, and it was spreading fast when I got there. Jake and I have been working our butts off trying to get everything cleaned up in time for opening tonight. I promised him I'd be back by seven, so I can't stay long, but I wanted to give Aaron his present. I'm sorry, Rachel."

Rachel could hardly reprimand Cody for being called away by problems with his business. That was one responsibility she understood all too well. "Don't be silly. Did you get everything cleaned up?" she asked in concern. "Is there anything I can do to help?"

He shook his head and smiled. "Thanks, but everything's under control." He turned to Seth. "And thank you, buddy. This couldn't have been easy to put together alone."

"I didn't do it alone," Seth returned. "Rachel and I worked together on it."

"I see." Cody looked at them in a way that had Rachel's cheeks warming again.

"Have you had anything to eat, Cody?" she asked quickly. "I was just about to offer Seth a sandwich." She glanced a bit shyly at Seth. "You must have missed lunch. I'm sure you're starving."

"As a matter of fact, I am," he confessed. "A sandwich sounds great."

"Humph. Offering a sandwich to a man who's been working so hard all afternoon," Frances grumbled, appearing suddenly in the doorway to the kitchen. "I'll have you know I've got a garden salad, a pot of vegetable soup and a pan of corn bread ready."

"I think I'm in love," Seth announced, slipping his arm around Frances's comfortably padded waist. "Granny Fran, will you marry me?"

Frances laughed and shook her head admonishingly at him. "Stop your foolishness and go wash up," she told him. "Save your proposals for the one who should be hearing them."

Embarrassed to her toes by the blatant matchmaking, Rachel glared at her grandmother, who only smiled blandly back at her. Cody gave a bark of laughter that earned him a killing look from his sister. Seth prudently withdrew to the closest bathroom to wash his hands.

Celia arrived just as the others were sitting down to their early dinner of soup, salad and corn bread. She was easily persuaded to join them. She greeted Seth as easily as she did the others, apparently not at all surprised to find him there. Rachel reflected in concern that Seth was becoming just a bit too much a part of the family lately. What would happen when he met someone who interested him more than she did at the moment? How big a hole would his absence leave after they'd all gotten used to having him here?

She told herself not to borrow trouble, but she'd always been a worrier, always been one to look ahead at consequences and repercussions. And she still couldn't imagine that Seth's flattering interest in her would be more than a passing fancy. Could he *really* have enjoyed spending an entire day building a swing set for her son? Weren't there many more things an attractive single man would rather have done on a warm, beautiful autumn afternoon?

Cody and Celia presented their gifts to Aaron after dinner. Celia gave him two new cartridges for his video game system, and Cody rolled in a bicycle—pre-assembled. Aaron was delighted with both gifts. Rachel whispered a reproach to Cody for being overly extravagant, as he always was with her children. He cheerfully told her that it was his money, and he could spend it as he liked, to which she had no legitimate argument.

Even Seth had provided a gift, which he brought in from his car. "Hey, cool!" Aaron said, tearing the wrappings off a genuine leather football. "Will you play with me sometime, Seth?"

"You bet," Seth agreed. "We'll get up a game of touch, okay? You and Granny Fran and me against Paige and Cody and your mom."

"And what about me?" Celia demanded, while Frances laughed at the idea of playing touch football at her age.

"You can be the water person," Cody replied with a grin.

"You can be the referee, Aunt Celia," Paige said, getting into the spirit of the teasing.

Aaron shook his head. "Aunt Celia can be on our team and Mama can be the referee."

"How come, tiger?" Seth inquired.

"'Cause Mama's the one who's always making everybody follow the rules," Aaron answered logically. "Aunt Celia and Uncle Cody don't care about stuff like that."

The adults laughed—all but Rachel, of course. But even she couldn't help smiling a little at her son's reasoning.

Exhausted by the events of the day, the children were both yawning hugely by eight o'clock. Rachel sent them off for baths, firmly overriding their protests that they wanted to stay up "just for a little longer."

Cody and Celia left at the same time. Frances made an excuse to retreat to the kitchen, leaving Rachel and Seth alone in the den.

"I guess I'd better be going," Seth said, glancing reluctantly toward the door.

Rachel didn't argue with him. "Thank you again for putting the swing set together. I really appreciate it."

"Will you have dinner with me one night this week?" he asked promptly.

She sighed and shook her head. "Don't you ever take no for an answer?"

"Not when it's important," he admitted.

"I'm afraid you're going to have to this time."

He took a step closer to her, and cupped the side of her face in one large, warm hand. "Why, Rachel? Why are you so afraid to go out with me?"

"I'm not afraid of you," she denied immediately, a bit too quickly.

"Then what *are* you afraid of?"

Of the way you make me feel, she almost told him. *Of the strange, breathless excitement I feel when you smile at me. Of the way it feels when you touch me. Of falling for you because I'm vulnerable and lonely and susceptible. Of being left alone again just when I've gotten used to not being alone anymore.*

"I'm not afraid of anything," she said, instead. "I'm just not ready."

His eyes called her a liar. But he didn't try to argue with her. Instead, he leaned over to cover her mouth with his.

He didn't pull away quickly this time. He lingered, his lips moving slowly, seductively over hers, his arms going around her waist to pull her against him. She pressed her hands to his chest, maybe even with the intention of pushing him away, but she got lost somewhere in that kiss and somehow forgot all the cautious, sensible reasons why they shouldn't be doing this.

It had been three years since a man had really kissed her. Three years since she'd known the pleasure of being held in a pair of strong arms, having her breasts crushed against a broad, warm chest.

Seth made her feel as though she were experiencing those sensations for the very first time.

She would never know how long the kiss would have gone on, what might have passed between them had they not been interrupted by two angry voices coming from the hallway.

"Mama! Paige won't let me have the toothpaste. Tell her to give it to me."

"I'm still using it, Mama. Tell Aaron to wait his turn!"

"Mama!"

"Mama!"

Rachel pulled slowly out of Seth's arms, the real world crashing abruptly back down upon her. "Good night, Seth," she said, relieved that the words were coherent.

He started to say something, then stopped. A moment later, after searching her face with eyes that were all too perceptive, he nodded and stepped back. "Good night, Rachel. See you around."

She only nodded and turned to go to her children, leaving Seth to find his own way out.

Rachel was in her office when her insurance agent called Monday afternoon. She rubbed her temples as she greeted him, fighting a headache that was the result of two long, restless nights and too many disturbing thoughts.

"The policy on your trucks is up for renewal, Rachel, and I'm afraid there's been another increase. Want me to look into some other policies for you to try to keep the costs down?"

"Yes, Dan, I would appreciate that," Rachel said wearily.

"You okay? You sound a bit down."

"I'm fine. Just a headache."

"Sorry. I guess this call didn't make it much better."

"Don't be silly. I always enjoy talking to you. And I know you're doing your best for me."

"I'll get a couple of proposals together and fax them to you, okay? You can look them over and let me know which policy you want to take. Of course, if you have any questions about anything, you know you can call me at any time."

"Yes, I know. Thanks."

Dan hesitated, then asked casually. "Or, you know, we could look the policies over together. During dinner? I could explain the various benefits and drawbacks of each one, make a few suggestions, maybe."

Rachel started to politely decline, as she had for the past two years—and then stopped. "All right, Dan," she said abruptly, impulsively. "Let's discuss them over dinner. When will you have the proposals ready?"

"Tomorrow night?" he said, sounding surprised but eager.

"Yes, fine. I'll meet you."

"Yeah, sure. How about Kelley's Steakhouse?"

"Fine. Seven o'clock?"

"You're on. See you then."

"All right. Until tomorrow, then."

Rachel hung up with a snap, feeling quite brave and defiant.

And then she buried her face in her hands and asked herself what the *hell* she thought she was doing.

Chapter Seven

Rachel first mentioned her date that evening, when she asked her grandmother to baby-sit. "I know you didn't come to stay with me to be used as a baby-sitter," she began, "but..."

"Nonsense. I'll enjoy spending the evening with the children, you know that. So Seth finally charmed you into going out to dinner with him, did he?" Frances added with a pleased smile.

Rachel lightly cleared her throat. "I'm not going out with Seth. I'm having dinner with my insurance agent, Dan McNeil. We're going to discuss some new policies for the trucks."

Frances seemed disappointed. "Then this isn't a date?"

"Well...yes, in a way," Rachel admitted. "Dan is single, and he's asked me out a few times. We're combining business and pleasure tomorrow evening." Though at the moment, she couldn't work up a great deal of pleasure about the whole thing, she could have added, but didn't, of course.

"Oh?" Looking torn now between approval that Rachel was going out and slight disappointment in her choice of escorts, Frances studied Rachel's face and then nodded. "All right, you've got a baby-sitter. Now, what are you going to wear?"

Rachel hadn't even thought of that. "Um, I suppose I'll just meet him in whatever suit I wear to work tomorrow."

Frances was shaking her head before Rachel even completed the sentence. "You'll do no such thing. You come home in time to change for dinner. Common courtesy, if nothing else, dictates that you make a special effort to look nice."

"I hardly go to work in rags," Rachel protested, rather offended by the reprimand.

But Frances was so adamant in her opinion that Rachel should freshen up and change before her date that Rachel finally conceded. She told herself she was doing so only because her grandmother was being nice enough to baby-sit for her, and not because she necessarily agreed with Granny Fran's advice.

"Dan McNeil?" Celia said over the telephone that evening. "You're going out with Dan McNeil?"

Rachel sighed in exasperation at Celia's lack of enthusiasm. "I thought you would be pleased that I'm finally going out on a date."

"Well . . . yes, I suppose so . . . but Dan McNeil?"

"Would you quit saying his name? Dan is a very nice man. What could you possibly have against him?"

"Nothing personal. It's just that he's so . . . well, dull."

"Celia—"

"And you know how bitter his divorce was. Men who've been burned the way Dan was always carry scars."

Rachel shrugged, though she knew her sister couldn't see the gesture. "I have a few scars of my own," she murmured. "And Dan isn't dull. He's just quiet."

"Safe, you mean. Predictable."

Rachel reflected that those were the very qualities that had made her accept Dan's invitation. Her reactions to him were safe and predictable, not volatile and alarming. "He's a nice man," she repeated stubbornly.

Celia's sigh was as gusty as Rachel's had been. "All right. It's certainly none of my business who you go out with, but—"

There always seemed to be a "but" after facts that should have been indisputable, Rachel mused.

"I just hope you know what you're doing," Celia completed, unaware of her sister's mutinous thoughts. "Don't jump into anything with Dan just to avoid an involvement with, er, with anyone else."

Despite Celia's awkward effort to be subtle, Rachel knew exactly who she meant. She started to tell her sister in no uncertain terms that she hadn't accepted a date with Dan just to avoid going out with Seth. She kept quiet only because she wasn't entirely sure she could convince either Celia or herself that it was true. Instead, she reminded Celia that this was no more her business than Celia's relationship with Damien Alexander was Rachel's, as Celia had pointed out frequently of late.

There was really nothing Celia could say after that.

"Why are you having dinner with Mr. McNeil, Mama?" Aaron asked the next evening, hanging over the back of Rachel's dressing chair as she freshened her makeup. Paige clumped around the bedroom behind them, balanced precariously in a pair of Rachel's heels. "How come you aren't going to eat with us?" Aaron persisted. "Granny Fran is making spaghetti."

"Mama's going out on a dinner date, Aaron," Paige said, sounding smugly self-important for knowing the difference between dinner out with a gentleman and dinner at home with the family.

"A date?" Aaron repeated, tiny lip curled. "You're not going to kiss him, are you, Mama?"

Rachel's hand slipped, and mascara streaked her cheek. She bit back a curse and reached for a tissue. "We're only having dinner, Aaron."

"Good," her son pronounced firmly. "'Cause if you're going to kiss anyone, I'd rather it would be Seth."

Rachel dropped her blusher brush, scattering rose-colored powder over the top of her vanity table. She snatched another tissue out of the dispenser. "Whatever makes you say that, Aaron?" she asked weakly.

"Aaron said he saw Seth kiss you the first night he had dinner with us," Paige explained.

"I like Seth," Aaron said. "He's cool. He can play video games and build swing sets and tell jokes. And he has fish. Couldn't you go out on a date with Seth, Mama? And could we go, too?"

"Kids don't go on dates," Paige said scornfully, before Rachel had a chance to form an answer. "Only grown-ups do."

"I bet Seth would let us go," Aaron insisted stubbornly. "Wouldn't he, Mama?"

Rescue came in the form of Granny Fran, who appeared in the doorway to shoo the children downstairs. "Your mama has to finish getting ready," she told them. "It's almost time for her to leave."

"I still think she should be going with Seth," Aaron muttered, determined to have the last word as he trudged out of the room.

Paige stepped out of Rachel's heels and followed in her brother's path. She paused in the doorway. "I hope you have a good time tonight, Mama."

Rachel smiled. "Thank you, honey."

"But I think you'd have more fun with Seth," Paige added thoughtfully.

"Downstairs, young'un," Frances urged, her eyes alight with amusement at Rachel's expression.

"Yes, ma'am," Paige said, and obediently disappeared.

"Not a word out of you," Rachel warned her grandmother, pointing her lipstick in a threatening manner.

Frances laughed and held up her hands in a gesture of surrender. "Not a word," she promised. "I'll see you downstairs."

And then she followed the children out, leaving Rachel to bury her face in her hands—and then to hastily repair the fresh damage she'd done to her makeup.

She didn't have a wonderful time.

It wasn't anything in particular that Dan did or said, though Rachel thought he talked a bit too much about his ex-wife and how badly she'd treated him. Nor was there any particular awkwardness between them. They'd known each other for years, so conversation was easy enough, with few stilted silences to fill. Mostly they talked business, his and hers.

Dan was attractive enough in a bland sort of way, and as charming as a salesman learns to be after a few years in his job. But there was little laughter between them. And Rachel couldn't imagine reacting with any enthusiasm should he kiss her, which she intended to avoid.

They saw several mutual acquaintances in the popular restaurant, and Rachel noted the speculation at seeing them out together. Rachel found herself fighting an urge to announce that this wasn't really what it appeared. She and Dan weren't exactly dating. They were, well, "doing dinner."

But the worst part of the entire evening, as far as Rachel was concerned, was that she couldn't seem to put Seth out of her mind. Irrationally, she grew more angry with him as the evening progressed, as though it were his fault that he was haunting her mind, which, she decided, it was.

Rachel and Dan parted amicably in the parking lot beside their cars. He didn't try to kiss her, and Rachel sensed that he probably wouldn't ask her out again. The sparks simply weren't there. And though she'd thought that was exactly what she wanted, she found herself curiously dissatisfied.

She turned the car radio on as she drove home, hoping to lift her spirits with a peppy song. The oldies channel she'd left the radio tuned to was broadcasting a song that had been one of Ray's favorites. Rachel quickly turned it back off, deciding silence was better for now.

She was so engrossed in her own despondent thoughts that she didn't notice the black sports car parked at her curb. But she definitely noticed the man who appeared silently at her side the moment she stepped out of her car.

Looking up at Seth's glowering face, Rachel realized that if she'd been angry with him earlier, it was nothing compared to the way he was feeling at the moment.

Seth was furious.

Except for the overhead security lamps, it was dark outside Rachel's house, and quiet in her comfortably middle-class neighborhood. The air was cool but not yet cold, the sky cloudless and star-studded. Rachel clutched her purse in front of her and cleared her throat, the sound seeming unnaturally loud in the silence. "Seth? What are you doing here?"

"I hear you had a date tonight. Did you have fun?"

"No," she said irritably. "Not particularly."

"Good," he snapped.

She exhaled impatiently through her nose and moved to step around him. "If that's all you wanted to say, I—"

"That is *not* all I wanted to say. And I'm sure you know it," he added, catching her arm. "Damn it, Rachel, what kind of game are you playing with me? What were you trying to prove tonight? That you could hurt me? Well, congratulations. You did."

She was startled. Of course she hadn't been trying to hurt Seth! She hadn't even realized she could.

"I'm not playing any games with you, Seth," she protested weakly. "I simply went out to dinner."

"Fine. If you're ready to date again, you can damn well have dinner with me."

"Maybe I'm not interested in going out with you. Hasn't that even occurred to you, or are you too—"

He jerked her against him and smothered the remainder of the words beneath his mouth.

He kissed her until she was clinging to him, weak-kneed, breathless, and fully aware that there was no way she could continue to deny her interest in him.

"Now tell me why you won't go out with me," he murmured against her cheek, his arms still locked securely around her.

She fell back on the same excuses she'd given everyone else who'd asked. "You're too young," she whispered.

"I'm almost twenty-eight."

"And I'll soon be thirty-two."

"Big deal."

There was no doubt in her mind that her age meant nothing to him.

"We're too different," she said, instead.

"How?"

"You're . . . impulsive and impetuous and unpredictable. I have routines and responsibilities and long-term plans."

"Maybe you need to be a bit more impulsive and impetuous," Seth suggested, his lips moving now against her ear. "And maybe I should give more thought to long-term planning. We could teach each other."

"But I—"

He kissed her again, less forcefully this time, more enticingly. The tip of his tongue teased her lips, inviting her to play. It was an invitation she was helpless to resist at the moment. She parted her lips and helped him deepen the kiss.

"Rachel," Seth groaned when he pulled back a long time later. He was gasping for breath, she was dazed and disoriented. Both of them were trembling. "Ah, Rachel, you're driving me crazy. I'm not trying to pressure you into bed, or push you into a commitment neither of us is ready to make. I only want to be with you. I only want a chance with you. Say you'll go out with me. Just dinner. Nothing more. I swear."

Maybe it was because her mind was still spinning from his kisses. Maybe lack of oxygen had caused temporary brain damage. Whatever the cause, Rachel heard herself suddenly saying, "All right. Yes."

Seth went still. He lifted his head, peering at her through the shadows. "Was that a yes?"

"Yes," she repeated a bit more steadily. "But just dinner."

"When?"

"I, er, Friday?"

"That long?"

"I hate to leave my grandmother again any sooner than that," she explained.

"All right. Friday. I'll pick you up."

"I'll meet you," she said hastily, trying vainly to keep this dinner date on the same basis as the last one. Knowing it was impossible even as she made the effort.

"I'll pick you up," he repeated flatly.

She didn't attempt further argument. Suddenly she needed to be inside, out of Seth's arms, out of his sight. She couldn't think when he was this close to her, when he was looking at her this way. She couldn't make herself behave the way she knew she should.

She pushed against him, and he made no attempt to restrain her. She knew it was because he'd already accomplished what he wanted.

She ran into the house without looking back. She thought she heard him laughing softly at her haste, but she didn't care. She just needed to be inside.

Seth had never prepared more carefully for a date in his life. He cleaned his car, inside and out, he pressed his pale blue shirt and navy slacks, he even took a damp washcloth to his shoes in lieu of the polish he didn't own. He'd had his hair trimmed, though it still displayed that lifelong tendency to tumble onto his forehead. No amount of spit, spray or grease had ever conquered it. He'd given up trying sometime during his teens.

He thought about taking her flowers, then decided that was too clichéd. He considered chocolates, but that didn't seem right, either. Maybe he shouldn't take anything, he mused. He didn't want to appear too eager. Though heaven knew he was.

He finally decided on flowers, then spent half an hour in a florist shop making his selection. The half-dozen peach roses he chose reminded him of Rachel—cool, classy and beautiful. On impulse, he bought a velvety purple African violet for Granny Fran and a cheery little basket of mixed flowers for Paige. Flowers didn't seem quite right for Aaron, so he chose a brightly colored Mylar Garfield balloon with long, curly streamers cascading from the bottom.

He was standing on the doorstep of Rachel's house, hands laden with gifts, when he decided he'd probably overdone it. He shouldn't have brought anything, he thought ruefully. She'd probably suspect him of trying to manipulate her again, which, of course, he probably was.

Lord, he was as nervous as a kid on his first date. His palms were sweating, for crying out loud!

Rachel opened the door just as he was half-seriously considering bolting. Paige peeked out from behind her on the right, Aaron on the left. Seth suspected that Granny Fran wasn't far away.

"You look very nice," he said, all too aware of the children's avid attention.

She looked wonderful. She wore a sleek tunic-and-slacks set in a cool melon color just a shade darker than the roses he'd brought her. The tunic was knit out of something soft and fuzzy, angora, maybe, or cashmere. He didn't really know fabrics, but he knew that it would be all he could do to keep his hands off her. Unless, of course, she gave him a sign that she wanted them on her. In which case, he'd be happy to oblige. He had resolved that he would be on his best behavior this evening, that Rachel would have no cause to regret accepting his rather coercive invitation.

"Thank you," Rachel murmured, as self-conscious as he in front of their giggling audience. "Um—?" She glanced curiously at the flowers and balloon he held.

"Oh." He realized in some amazement that he was damned close to blushing. What on earth—?

"These are for you," he said, shoving the roses into her hands a bit too abruptly. "And Paige, this little basket is for you, and this balloon is yours, Aaron. The other flowers are for Granny Fran."

"Flowers," Paige said, studying her fragrant little basket with wide, shining eyes. "Mama, look! Seth gave me flowers. No one's ever given me flowers before," she added, slanting Seth a shy smile. "Thank you."

"Cool balloon," Aaron approved, lightly batting the bouncing bag of helium. "I like Garfield. Thanks, Seth."

"The roses are lovely, Seth," Rachel said more quietly. "Thank you."

He cleared his throat. "You're welcome," he murmured. "All of you," he added, dragging his gaze away from Rachel's with an effort.

"Granny Fran! Seth brought you flowers! Come get 'em!" Aaron called out, dashing toward the den with streamers floating behind him. "Look what I got."

"Granny Fran's in the den," Rachel said. "I'll go put these in water and join you there in a moment."

Still clutching the African violet, Seth nodded and watched Rachel walk away with the graceful dignity that was so much a part of her. He didn't move until Paige took him by the free hand and tugged him toward the den, impatient to show her great-grandmother her very first basket of flowers.

Dinner with Seth wasn't nearly as comfortable as it had been with Dan, Rachel realized ruefully an hour or so later. There were several awkward pauses this time, and nervous glances and forced smiles. Maybe because this date was so momentous, despite her efforts to convince herself that it was no different than the last one.

She toyed with her food and glanced through her lashes at Seth, who sat directly across the tiny, candlelit table tucked into a secluded corner of the Italian restaurant he'd selected. She found her gaze caught and held by his.

"Well," he said after another one of those awkward little pauses. "This is fun."

His dry tone made her giggle.

Seth's eyes lit up. "Was that a laugh?"

"That was a laugh," Rachel admitted. "A little one."

"Hey, that beats what I've gotten so far," he declared cheerfully. "I was getting worried."

"About what?"

He made a face. "I was afraid your boring date with the insurance agent was starting to seem like a wild time in comparison to this one."

"I never said my date with Dan was boring," Rachel corrected him.

"You didn't have to. I could see it on your face when you got home."

She shook her head in reproof at him, but refused to be led into a discussion of her outing with another man.

Instead, she decided it was time for her to start holding up her end of the evening's conversation. "That was really nice of you to bring flowers and balloons for Granny Fran and the children. Paige was thrilled. Of course, you know she has a serious crush on you now."

"No kidding." He lifted an eyebrow. "Now *that* would be an age difference."

But age was another topic Rachel would just as soon not discuss. She changed the subject again. "Were you and Cody in classes together at the university?"

"A few. He was a sophomore when I entered as a freshman, or at least, he should have been a sophomore. I'm not sure he had enough credit hours to actually qualify."

Rachel shook her head and sighed. "College wasn't Cody's milieu, I'm afraid. He just couldn't seem to get serious about grades and classwork."

Seth looked down at his dinner and Rachel wondered if he was thinking back to some of the adventures he and Cody had shared. She suspected that she would be more comfortable not hearing about many of them.

"Cody's changed quite a bit since I knew him back then," Seth said, glancing up at her.

Rachel nodded. "I'm sure he has. He's told you about the accident, I suppose."

"What accident?" Seth asked, looking confused.

Rachel was surprised that he didn't know, since Seth and Cody seemed to be such good friends. "It happened several months after Cody left college. The night of his twenty-first birthday."

"Cody and I lost touch after he left school," Seth explained. "We didn't see each other again until just over a year ago, when we met by accident in a restaurant in Little Rock. I mentioned that I wasn't happy working in my father's law firm, and he suggested that Percy would be a good place to set up my own office. I decided to check it out. I liked what I saw when I visited, so six months ago, I quit the family business and started my own. I haven't caught up yet on everything that has happened to Cody during the past ten years."

Rachel was intrigued by the twist of his mouth when he mentioned his father's law firm. Why had he been unhappy there? How had his father felt about Seth striking out on his own? Why didn't he talk about his family more? But she filed those questions away for later—if ever.

"Cody was involved in a car accident the night of his twenty-first birthday," she explained, still saddened by the grim memories of Cody's accident and the painfully similar one that had taken her husband's life. "He'd been drinking, I'm afraid."

Seth nodded. "He was quite a drinker when I knew him."

"He hasn't touched alcohol since his twenty-first birthday. Not since he fell asleep at the wheel of his car and plowed into the side of a family's minivan, flipping it into a ditch."

"Oh, God. Was anyone hurt?"

"Yes. Everyone involved was injured—Cody, and a family of four, the children both under ten. Fortunately, they all recovered, though not without a great deal of treatment and therapy. Cody was charged with driving while intoxicated and heavily fined. There was even a possibility that he would spend time in jail. Since it was his first offense, he was given probation. The probation ended some time ago, of course, but as you noticed, he has never been quite the same.''

Seth looked thoughtful, obviously shaken by her tale. ''He still seems to enjoy a good laugh.''

''In some ways, he's even more the clown than he was before,'' Rachel agreed. ''But something is ... different.''

''He and Jake are doing well with the club, aren't they?''

''Very well,'' Rachel agreed, smiling a little. ''We've all been pleasantly surprised that he has stayed with it this long and made such a success of it. It's the first job he's held on to for more than a year since ... well, ever.''

Seth winced. ''I can identify with that one.''

Rachel swallowed. ''Oh.'' Was he warning her that he wasn't one to stay around long, himself? That he was as likely to tire of his one-man office in Percy as he apparently had of his father's law firm? Or was he only making conversation, as she was trying to do?

Seth finished his meal and pushed his empty plate away. He picked up his freshly refilled coffee cup and took a sip, watching her over the rim of it. When he spoke, he had changed the subject again. And this one was even more unsettling. ''Tell me about Ray.''

Though she had finished only half her own meal, Rachel, too, pushed her plate away. ''What do you want to know about him?''

''What was he like?''

''Steady,'' she said quietly. ''Dependable. Patient. Loving.''

''A real paragon,'' Seth murmured, looking grim.

''He wasn't perfect,'' Rachel admitted. ''Celia always accused him of lacking a certain excitement. And he was even more fond of schedules and routines and detailed, long-range planning than I am, if you can believe that. But I loved him.''

''I know you did. I've seen it in your face.''

She bit her lip. ''You seem to be pretty good at that.''

''I'm learning.'' He took another sip of the coffee. ''He'd have been proud of you, Rachel. The way you're running his business and raising his kids. He couldn't have asked any more of you than what you've done.''

She was touched by the sincerity in the simple words. ''I hope he would have been proud. I've tried to do what I thought he would have wanted. We had so many plans, so many dreams ... and they all seemed to be coming true. And then—''

She couldn't finish the sentence. She knew it wasn't necessary. She didn't know how to explain that all those plans, all those dreams had died with Ray. And she didn't for the life of her know how to get them back.

Seth gave her a moment, then said quietly, ''You're a very special woman, Rachel Carson Evans.''

She managed a shrug. ''Not so special. I just do what I have to do.''

He shook his head and smiled faintly. ''It's more than that. A great deal more.''

To her relief, he changed the subject again, this time to something more innocuous, less personal. She couldn't have said later exactly what they talked about for the next few minutes, though it seemed to center around movies and music and books—that sort of getting-to-know-you conversation.

Seth didn't bring up any more sensitive topics, and she was grateful. She thought she'd revealed enough for one evening.

As he'd promised, Seth took her straight home after dinner. He didn't ask to be invited inside. Nor did he press for anything more than a brief good-night kiss, which Rachel made no effort to resist.

"It's not enough, but it's a beginning," Seth said when he lifted his head, touching her cheek with one fingertip. And then he smiled. "A very nice beginning."

Or a very dangerous one, Rachel added mentally.

Chapter Eight

A cold front arrived with the beginning of October, and the trees blazed with autumn colors. The faintest scent of wood smoke seemed to lace the crisp air. Granny Fran mentioned that it was time for her to return home, but Rachel and the children persuaded her to stay for another week. Frances stayed, but only after making Rachel promise to take advantage of the available baby-sitting for the next week.

"I want you to stay because I enjoy being with you," Rachel protested. "Not because I want to use you as a cook or a baby-sitter."

Frances smiled and kissed her granddaughter's cheek. "I know, darling. But I happen to love cooking and baby-sitting for you and your children. You wouldn't deprive me of those two pleasures while I'm here, would you?"

It was impossible to come up with a response to that.

As it turned out, Rachel didn't require much baby-sitting during that week. Seth seemed perfectly content to hang around her house, playing video games with the children, Uno with Granny Fran, talking to Rachel over endless cups of coffee and slices of her grandmother's pies and cakes. Rachel worried about the children's growing fascination with him—not that she was surprised by it. If she couldn't resist Seth, how could she expect two impressionable children to do so?

She was still concerned that his interest in her would soon fade, that she was a novelty of sorts to him. He was so bright and vital and enthusiastic that she sometimes felt dull and boring next to him. But he never seemed to find her dull or boring. He always appeared interested in what she had to say, about her work, her plans, her thoughts, her tastes.

He made it no secret that he was physically attracted to her. He touched her often, though always discreetly, and his eyes sent messages she couldn't help but understand. Twice that week, he lingered after Frances and the children turned in for the night. He and Rachel sat on the sofa in the den, facing the glowing fireplace, talking in low voices. And when he began to kiss her, she didn't resist.

The first night, he pulled back after only a few long, thorough kisses, though he made it clear that he was doing so with great reluctance. After he left, Rachel prepared for bed in a pleasant daze, thinking that the man was certainly a boost to her woman's ego.

The kisses went a bit further the next time. Rachel kept telling herself that she would call an end to it soon, but it felt so nice to cuddle in front of the fire with a warm, sexy man who definitely knew how to kiss. And just what to do with those big, strong hands of his.

Her body ached with long-denied needs, and her palms itched to feel sleek, pulsing skin beneath them. It had been so long. So very long...

"Mama?"

The sleepy voice from the doorway brought Rachel out of Seth's arms as effectively as a gunshot. "What is it, Aaron?" she asked breathlessly, feeling her face flaming with embarrassment as she rapidly straightened her clothing.

Knuckling his eyes, Aaron yawned, obviously only half-awake. "I'm thirsty."

"I'll get you a glass of water," she promised, nervously smoothing her hair.

"I'd better be going," Seth said, his voice rough. He, too, had stood, and was combing his tousled hair with his fingers. He looked at Rachel in mute apology, and she knew he was sharing responsibility for letting the caresses almost get out of hand.

Her hand on Aaron's thin little shoulder, Rachel nodded, biting her lip. Seth touched her cheek as he passed, saying good-night to her and to her son.

Rachel gave Aaron his drink, then tucked him snugly back to bed. "Good night, sweetheart," she whispered, pressing a kiss to his soft cheek.

"'Night, Mama." Aaron turned his face into his Mickey Mouse pillowcase and was asleep before she turned off the light.

Rachel didn't bother turning on the light in her bedroom. She walked slowly across the room and sat on the side of the empty bed, fully clothed, staring at nothing. Did Seth understand the implications of becoming involved with the mother of two small children? Could a single man possibly understand the heavy responsibilities those children represented? Could he accept that their needs would always be of primary consideration to her?

They were so small, so vulnerable. So totally dependent on her, and her alone. Had she been selfish this past week, putting them at risk for heartache and disappointment because of her own foolish infatuation with Seth Fletcher?

She groaned and buried her face in her hands. Her life had been so much easier before she'd met Seth. Busy, of course. Stressful, at times. Sometimes lonely. But safe. And now she found herself dreading the possibility of returning to that safety, if it meant no longer having Seth in her life.

If Seth had had second thoughts after Aaron's untimely interruption, he certainly hid it well when he showed up at his usual time the next evening—just in time to eat. Rachel greeted him a bit awkwardly, but her reserve didn't last through dinner. Throughout the meal, Seth teased with Paige and Aaron, flirted outrageously with both Rachel and Granny Fran, and kept the conversation brisk and light. If he was deliberately trying to put her at ease, he succeeded very well.

The children excused themselves after dinner and went off to play, leaving the adults to linger over coffee. Frances entertained them with an amusing story about her son, Bill—Rachel's father—and the big blue lizard he'd stashed in his pocket on laundry day.

Seth laughed. "Now I know who Cody resembles in the family."

Frances smiled and nodded. "He's very much like his father was as a young man. Bill was never predictable. I suppose that's why he works so well with troubled young people at the health clinic in Saint Louis."

"How long has he worked there?"

"Almost six years now, isn't it, Rachel?"

Rachel nodded. "Celia was just entering her senior year of high school, remember? She lived with Ray and me during that year so she could finish with her friends."

"That must have been difficult," Seth commented. "A teenage girl living with her newlywed sister."

"I wasn't quite a newlywed," Rachel corrected. "We already had Paige by then. It was a bit stressful, suddenly becoming responsible for a teenager. But Celia was always well behaved and easy to get along with. In fact, she was a lot of help with Paige and the housework."

"You rarely talk about your own family, Seth," Frances commented innocently. "Are your parents still living?"

The transformation was immediate and rather startling. Seth's smile faded and his lively green eyes dulled. It was as though a cloud had passed over the sun. "Yes, they're still living," he said cordially enough, but without inflection. "They have a home in west Little Rock. My father's an attorney, and my mother is principal of a public elementary school."

"How interesting. And do you have any brothers and sisters?" Frances asked, studying Seth's face in a way that let Rachel know she wasn't the only one who'd noticed his sudden distance.

"An older sister. Linda. She's an engineer in Dallas."

"A family of achievers, I take it," Frances commented with a smile.

Seth didn't smile in return. He nodded and picked up his coffee cup. "That's my family," he said. "Real achievers."

"They must be proud of you," Rachel said tentatively. "For starting your own law office at such a young age," she added when he looked at her in question.

He made a face. "My family and I aren't what you'd call close, Rachel. As for my office—they've made no secret of their disappointment that I didn't stay with the firm my great-grandfather founded in the early 1900s. I'm the first Fletcher in four generations to break away from the family business."

"Did you become an attorney just to please them, Seth?" Frances asked gently.

"Yes," he admitted. And then he shrugged. "But I like it well enough, especially now that I'm out on my own. I have no regrets."

Rachel wasn't entirely sure she believed him. There were definitely regrets in his eyes. Whether they centered around his career choice or his estrangement from his family, she couldn't have said.

He changed the subject in a way that made it clear he didn't want to talk about his family. He stayed for a while after dinner to watch some television with Rachel and the children, but he left early. Rachel wasn't sure why. Because of what had happened the night before? Because he didn't want to risk getting carried away again? Or because the personal conversation at dinner had made him uncomfortable? Was he pulling back? Or, she thought ruefully, was he only tired and she being unreasonably paranoid?

This was all getting very complicated. And it wasn't as if she didn't already have enough to worry about!

It seemed that everything that could go wrong did on that Friday. The hydraulic pump she'd been worried about gave out, putting one truck out of commission for several days while it was replaced. The backup truck her driver was forced to use wasn't in the best of shape, itself. Rachel could only hope it would hold up until the other truck was repaired. The routes had to be run regardless of her equipment problems, or customers would become dissatisfied and trash would pile up in violation of local sanitary codes.

She was wading through a stack of bills in her office that afternoon when the telephone rang. "Rachel, it's Carl," a gruff voice said when she answered.

She knew from his tone that the driver had bad news. And this wasn't even the man driving the backup truck. "What's wrong, Carl?"

"I've had a little—uh—accident. Hit some overhead wires with the forks and I've made a hell of a mess. Dropped the container, snapped the wires, dented the

Exxon station's awning. I'm real sorry, Rachel. I don't know what happened. You know I've never done anything like this before.''

"It's all right, Carl. Accidents happen," she said, rubbing her temple. "I'll call the insurance company. I assume you've got an accident report?''

"Yeah, I'm taking care of it. Mr. Handy is being pretty nice about it." Handy was the owner of the service station, a longtime customer who was never late with his monthly payments, never had a complaint even when the drivers were delayed. Rachel regretted the inconvenience her driver had caused him, but was secretly relieved it hadn't happened to one of the more difficult or demanding customers. There were several who would not have been so understanding.

Her next call was to Dan McNeil. She quickly explained the problem to him. He promised to file the proper claims as soon as he received all the information. "Everything else going okay for you?" he asked, when they'd gotten that business out of the way.

"Well enough," she replied.

"That's good. Okay, you get this paperwork to me and I'll take care of everything."

"Thank you," she said, relieved that their longtime business relationship didn't seem to be affected by their one mistaken attempt to turn it into more.

Busy filing reports and calling repair shops and ordering parts and finally paying bills, Rachel couldn't leave the office until late. She called her grandmother and explained that she was running late. She was grateful that Frances had been watching the children in the afternoons after school. Usually when something like this came up, Rachel had to go to the day-care center at the usual time, pick up the children and bring them back to the office with her, often with take-out dinners to keep them busy while Rachel worked. Paige and Aaron weren't particularly fond of those overtime days, but they'd long since learned to entertain themselves at the office.

It was almost seven by the time Rachel called it quits. She stacked papers on the reception desk for Martha, her bookkeeper, to take care of the next morning, did the best she could about cleaning her desk and locked the office door as she left. She hadn't had a chance to get to the bank or post office, but she would take care of those errands first thing Monday morning.

Another day, another dozen crises, she thought wearily, throwing her purse into her car. She was locking the heavy security gates when she suddenly had the eerie feeling that someone was watching her.

Acting on instinct, she slid immediately into her car, then closed and locked the doors before glancing around. Her offices were located in an old section of town, with few businesses nearby and no residences in sight. The street was nearly deserted at this hour, and the sun was rapidly setting, leaving deep shadows between the circles of light from the widely spaced streetlamps. The only vehicle in sight was a rusty pickup parked at the curb a hundred or so yards away from her offices. Someone was sitting in the truck, which didn't seem to be turned on.

Rachel shivered at the knowledge that the man in the truck probably had been watching her. She told herself that he must not mean her any harm, or he would have approached her while she was out of the car and vulnerable. Still, she kept her hands tight on the wheel, foot heavy on the accelerator as she passed him, her face averted. She didn't want to look at him, didn't want him to think she was giving him any notice or encouragement, though she'd memorized a description of the vehicle and as much as she'd been able to see of the license tag.

She let out a gusty breath of relief when the truck made no move to follow her as she drove away.

He'd probably been waiting for someone, she told herself as her rapid pulse began to slow. Maybe taking a cigarette break or having an illegal beer. She really was getting paranoid lately to think that he'd been there because of her.

But maybe she wouldn't stay so late at the office alone for a while.

Seth was waiting with her family when she finally arrived home. She was tired and frazzled and her head ached dully, but she managed a smile of greeting and hugs for the children. "I'm sorry I'm so late," she told them as a group. "It's been a rough day."

"We told Seth you do this all the time," Paige announced with a wave of her hand. "I'm sure glad Granny Fran's here so we didn't have to eat takeout at the office tonight."

Rachel almost winced. Paige's breezy explanation made their usual schedule sound worse than it was. "I don't work late *that* often, Paige," she protested.

"It seems like you do," Aaron piped in, to Rachel's exasperation. "That's why we keep toys at Mama's office," he added for Seth, who wasn't smiling. "So we'll have something to do there while she works."

"Why don't you two wash up for dinner," Frances suggested hastily, glancing from Seth to Rachel. "I'll put the final touches on dinner." She turned to hurry out of the room behind the children.

Rachel had the oddest urge to apologize to Seth for being so late. She bit the words back. Why should she apologize? He hadn't even been formally invited to join them for dinner tonight. It had simply become accepted somehow that he would be there. As for her work—it was a demanding, time-consuming job at times, and she couldn't promise she wouldn't work late again. Nor should she have to.

"Problems at work?" Seth asked when Rachel didn't immediately speak.

"A few. Most of it is taken care of already." She had no intention of telling him about her momentary fright outside the gates of her building. He'd probably overreact. She tucked her purse under her arm. "If you'll excuse me, I'd like to change before dinner. I'll be right back."

He caught her arm as she passed him. "Rachel?"

"Yes, Seth?"

He started to say something, stopped, then sighed and shook his head. "You work too hard."

"I have responsibilities," she reminded him, refusing to be softened by the concern in his eyes.

A faint frown creased his brow. He muttered something as she left the room. She thought it was, "I'm beginning to hate that word."

She didn't linger to find out exactly what he'd said.

Frances insisted that Rachel and Seth go out one last night while she was in town, leaving her to watch the children. Seth picked Rachel up early Saturday evening and they made the fifty-mile drive into Little Rock. Seth had made reservations at the local dinner theater. The food was rather bland, served buffet-style—not nearly as good as Granny Fran's cooking, they agreed. But the service staff was friendly and the play was excellent—funny and fast paced, well acted and produced. Rachel enjoyed it thoroughly.

It was late when the play let out, but they were in no hurry. They'd warned Frances that they probably wouldn't get in until the wee hours. Still, Rachel was rather surprised when Seth didn't immediately take the freeway back toward Percy. Instead, he drove into a section of town she didn't immediately recognize. The road curved and climbed, leading them into high, wooded hills lined with nice homes and apartment buildings. "Is this where you grew up?'' she asked, thinking that was the reason Seth had brought her into this part of town.

"Not exactly, though I did spend a lot of time in this area as a teenager.''

They drove up a hill so steep, the car engine whined in protest. Seth downshifted with the casual ease of familiarity. When they reached the top, he turned right onto a paved road that led to a fenced lookout point. One other vehicle was already there, a battered Honda Civic parked at the far end of the lot. Seth pulled into a parking space at the opposite end and turned off the headlights. "This is what I wanted you to see," he said.

Rachel smiled and looked over the edge of the mountain. The Arkansas River was directly beneath them, gleaming like black satin, looking deceptively calm and tranquil for a river with such a dangerous reputation for swiftness and deadly undercurrents. On the other side of the river were more hills, dotted with hundreds of lights— white, red, flickering neon. Above everything, the sky spread clear and dark, the stars barely visible through the glow of the city. "It's beautiful," she said.

Seth reached out and turned on the radio, tuning in a soft-rock station, leaving the volume low. "I used to bring my dates here when I was a kid.''

Rachel fought a smile. "I'm sure you did."

He yawned elaborately and slipped an arm around her shoulders.

Her smile deepened. "Very smooth."

He grinned. "I'm glad you think so."

She settled into the curve of his arm—at least, as much as possible with the console between them. "What did you do after you got your arm around them?''

"Anything they'd let me get away with," he admitted. "Which," he added ruefully, "usually wasn't much."

She wasn't sure she believed that one. She was more inclined to suspect that Seth had always had a way of charming anyone into just about anything he wanted.

He twisted in his seat until he was facing her. "Did anyone ever tell you your eyes are limpid pools?" he murmured in an exaggeratedly oily voice.

She giggled. "No," she admitted. "No one ever told me that."

"Or that your laughter is the sound of fairy bells tinkling?" His green eyes glittered in the darkness, reflecting amusement, and something more.

Rachel tried to cling to the teasing.

"No, I don't think I've heard that one, either."

Seth leaned closer, brushing his lips lightly across her cheek before he breathed, "That your skin is as flawless as fine porcelain, as soft as velvet?"

Her eyelids grew heavy as he tasted the sensitive skin at her temple. "Seth?" Her voice was little more than a breathless whisper.

He kissed the hollow beneath her ear. "Mmm?"

"If these are the lines you used on your dates, it's no wonder you didn't get very far."

"Is that right?" He kissed the corner of her eye, the side of her mouth. His hand slid slowly up her thigh to her waist. "You mean they aren't working on you, either?"

She was melting into his arms like warm caramel, but she was able to say with total honesty, "No. They aren't."

It wasn't what he was saying that was weakening her willpower as rapidly as her knees; it was what he was doing with his all-too-practiced-and-talented mouth and hands. She swallowed a moan when he lowered his head to nuzzle at her throat. She arched her back instinctively to give him better access.

He nibbled his way up her throat to her chin, then nipped lightly at her lower lip. "I'm really sorry to hear that."

She had no idea what he was talking about. She'd lost all track of their teasing conversation the moment his left hand settled warmly over her right breast.

He didn't seem to mind her sudden speechlessness. He took immediate advantage of the situation, covering her mouth with his own. He kissed her with an intensity that momentarily startled her. She realized for the first time that he'd been holding something back in the kisses that had come before. And she knew she was lost, her resistance defeated.

She wrapped her arms around his neck and kissed him back. And for the very first time, she held nothing back, either.

Seth sensed the difference as quickly as she had. He groaned his approval and deepened the embrace, dragging her as tightly against him as the console between them would allow.

Time and purpose faded from her mind, lost in a blur of kisses—long, sensual kisses, short, hot kisses, hard, hungry kisses. The fingers of his right hand moved at the back of her neck, and suddenly cool air caressed her shoulders, her chest, as he slowly lowered the front of her silk dress.

She felt the need to protest. "Seth," she whispered when he moved his head to kiss the upper swell of her breasts above her lace-and-satin bra. Her fingers threaded into his hair, tightening to hold him against her even as she said, "We shouldn't be doing this here."

He nudged lace aside and tasted the soft skin he'd revealed. "Why?"

Why? Surely there was a reason. "The, uh—" She gasped when he ran the tip of his tongue over her rapidly hardening nipple. "The other car," she blurted, seizing on the first excuse that came to her. "They'll see us."

Seth's breathing was ragged, his muscles tense with need. "Trust me, Rachel, they have other things to do than to watch us," he assured her, his voice gruff.

He pulled her nipple into his mouth, and she arched back with a choked cry of reaction. The sensations were so strong, so powerful that she trembled with a need that was rapidly growing to match his. She ached, she throbbed, she gasped with desires that she wouldn't allow herself to examine too closely. For just a moment, she wanted to savor. For just a moment, she wanted to be free to revel in these feelings, in this man.

Seth brought his mouth back to hers, his tongue plunging between her lips to mate with hers. He moved closer, rising slightly above her—and then stopped with an exclamation of frustration when the console brought him up short.

The sensual spell shattered with an almost audible snap. Rachel stiffened, then pulled back, pressing against the door behind her.

Seth resisted her withdrawal only for a moment, then dropped his hands. He tried to smile. "Come to think of it, this is about as far as I ever got here," he said in an obvious effort to lighten her sudden tension.

She managed a shaky smile of her own, though she was sure it was a pitiful attempt. She pushed nervously at her hair, which she'd left down that evening just because she knew he liked it that way. "It's getting very late, and we still have an hour's drive ahead of us," she reminded him. "We'd better be going before Granny Fran starts to worry."

Seth looked at her for a long moment, sighed almost inaudibly, then nodded. "All right. Don't forget to refasten your seat belt," he added as he turned and did the same before starting the engine.

Rachel had to refasten her dress first. Her cheeks were flaming as she snapped the seat belt buckle securely into position. She couldn't believe she'd lost control like that!

She was painfully aware that she had never done so before. Not like that. Not with anyone.

She turned her head and stared out the window beside her as Seth guided the car down the hill toward home.

The drive home was a quiet one, their conversation, what little there was, centered around dinner and the play, Granny Fran's departure the next day—anything but what had passed between them. Rachel kept her hands in her lap, her fingers twisted so tightly together that she could see her knuckles gleaming in the darkness inside the car.

Seth walked her to her door. The house was quiet, the bedroom windows dark, letting them know that her family was in bed. Rachel didn't ask Seth in. "Good night," she whispered, one hand on the doorknob.

He cupped her face in one hand, his eyes searching her expression. "You're okay?"

She managed a better smile this time, though she wasn't sure how she did it. "Of course," she assured him briskly. "Just a bit tired."

He nodded. "Get some rest then. I'll call you."

"All right. Good night, Seth."

"Good night, sweetheart." He brushed a soft, tender kiss across her rather bruised-feeling lips. "Sweet dreams," he added with a smile.

She let herself inside without saying anything else. She locked the door behind her. She was still standing beside it when she heard Seth's car drive away.

She didn't want sweet dreams that night, she thought bleakly. She didn't want to dream at all.

Dreaming could be so very painful.

Chapter Nine

Rachel helped her grandmother pack the next day after lunch. Cody had volunteered to drive her home, claiming with a grin that he supposed it was his turn to hear the get-a-wife-and-kiddies lecture.

"You're sure you have everything?" Rachel asked for the third time.

Frances glanced around the neatly cleaned guest room. "Yes, I have everything."

Rachel sighed. "I hate to see you leave. We've enjoyed having you here." It was true, she had enjoyed sharing a home with her grandmother. And it wasn't just because Frances delighted in cooking and cleaning and baby-sitting; Rachel loved her grandmother and enjoyed being with her. "Do you really have to go so soon?"

"Rachel, dear, I've been here for three weeks. And I've enjoyed every day of my visit. But it's time for me to go home."

"You're really happy living alone in Malvern, now that all your family has moved away?" Rachel couldn't help asking.

Frances smiled gently. "It's been my home for longer than I can remember. My friends are there, and my church and my seniors' group. There may come a time when I can't live on my own, but for now I'm getting along just fine."

"If that time ever comes, you'll always have a home with me," Rachel told her, and meant every word.

Frances kissed her cheek. "Thank you, Rachel. You're a very special young woman, a very dear granddaughter."

"And you're a wonderful grandmother."

"Then maybe you won't mind another little bit of advice from me?"

Rachel tried not to tense. She suspected she knew exactly what her grandmother's advice would be related to. "Of course I don't mind your advice," she said brightly. "I welcome it."

Frances laughed softly. "You don't have to take it quite that far. I know how you young people feel about advice. I once felt the same way. But I offer it only because I love you."

"I love you, too, Granny Fran."

"I know you do. You have a great capacity for love within you, Rachel. Don't let it go to waste."

Rachel crossed her arms at her waist and gripped her forearms as though warding off a chill. "I—er—"

Frances shook her head. "You worry too much. You should allow yourself to have more fun. You need that—and so do your children."

Rachel's eyes widened. "I try to make sure the children have fun," she protested. "I spend as much time as I can with them and—"

Frances held up both hands, palms outward. "Rachel, you're a wonderful mother," she interrupted firmly.

"Your children are happy and healthy and bright and well behaved. I'm very proud of them, as I know you are. And I'm sure they want you to be as happy and content as they are."

"I am happy," Rachel assured her. "I really am."

"And are you having fun?"

Rachel started to say yes but had to hesitate. She couldn't exactly say her life was fun, though she enjoyed her children and her family and friends, sometimes even enjoyed her work. As for fun—it seemed fun had been something she hadn't experienced much in the past few years. Until...

She thought of Seth, and the way he could make her laugh with only a wry look or dry comment.

"I'm very content with my life right now," she protested, though she wasn't sure if she was trying to convince herself, her grandmother, or that persistent image in her mind.

"Contentment is nice," Frances said, patting Rachel's hand. "But you deserve so much more."

The doorbell chimed faintly through the house. Rachel welcomed the interruption almost as much as she resented it. "That's probably Cody."

"Probably," Frances agreed, then smiled. "I'll bet you thought I was going to give you advice about Seth, didn't you?"

Rachel was startled into a laugh. "Well, yes," she admitted.

"I think Seth is quite capable of pleading his own cases," her grandmother said, looking pleased with the pun on his career. She started for the door, then paused to look over her shoulder. "But, in case you're interested, I think Seth Fletcher would be the place to start if a certain young woman was looking to have some fun."

"Mama, Uncle Cody's here," Paige called out from down the hall.

"I'll keep your advice in mind," Rachel promised hastily.

"You do that, dear."

Rachel followed her grandmother out of the bedroom, wondering darkly if Seth had personally requested that little endorsement from Granny Fran.

Seth didn't go to Rachel's house on Sunday. He thought of calling, but kept stopping with one hand on the telephone, unable to make himself follow through. At ten o'clock that evening, he walked away from the silent telephone for the dozenth time that day and cursed himself for being a coward.

He'd been fighting a major panic attack all day. It had started during the middle of the near-sleepless night after he'd left Rachel at her door. In fact, it had probably started at the same time it had occurred to him that he was falling in love for the first time in his life.

He'd always thought this would happen to him someday. He'd vaguely envisioned a wife and children in his future. His distant future. After he'd gotten his law practice firmly established, and somehow resolved the emotional problems his estrangement from his family had caused him. He hadn't expected it to happen now, when he was still adjusting to life in a small town. Still a long way from financial security with his practice. Still trying to decide exactly who he was and what he wanted from life, rather than trying to conform to his parents' expectations of what he should be and want.

He wasn't ready. But it seemed to have happened, anyway.

He was falling hard for a woman still grieving the loss of her husband. A woman with full responsibility for two young children. A woman who spent too much time and energy running her late husband's business. A woman who considered him too young for her, and apparently had doubts about his stability and responsibility. A woman who'd almost forgotten how to laugh.

But even as he mentally listed the drawbacks, he was aware of the qualities he most admired in Rachel. Her loyalty to her children, her extended family, her employees—hell, even to her late husband. Her competence. Her self-sufficiency. Her courage.

He enjoyed watching her with her children, whom she so obviously adored. And they were good kids. She'd done a great job raising them alone for the past three years. He was already very fond of Paige and Aaron, though he was realistic enough to know he'd seen them primarily on their best company-manners behavior. Children, even kids as well behaved as Paige and Aaron Evans, were going to cause problems at times. Major problems as they grew older and were suddenly exposed to the parents'-nightmares aspects of life—drugs, sex, fast cars, the lures of gangs and dares and defiance of authority. Seth shuddered just to think of it. Was he really ready to face those responsibilities, especially as a stepparent?

Even should he decide he was ready for parenthood, would Rachel accept anyone else's intrusion into her relationship with the children? During several of the divorce cases he'd handled, he'd heard distasteful stories of family power struggles, "real" parents played against "steps" by cleverly manipulative children, bitter disagreements on discipline, household rules, monetary responsibility. He'd never quite understood the aversion so many of his single male friends had to dating women with children, but now he could at least acknowledge that there was a basis for their concerns.

He shook his head as he realized just how far ahead his thoughts had taken him. He and Rachel had hardly progressed beyond the getting-acquainted stage and he was already worrying about raising her children. They were a long way from permanent commitments and those long-range plans she was so fond of making. And yet he was aware that the children had to be considered from the beginning. They were as much a part of Rachel as that funny little frown that so often creased her forehead, which invariably made him want to tease her and kiss her and make her smile.

He really should call her, he thought again, glancing at the telephone. He checked his watch. Ten-twenty. The children would have been in bed for a couple of hours, probably. Was Rachel in bed? Was she wondering why he hadn't called her that day? Had she even noticed that he hadn't?

He groaned. Now he was moping around like a lovesick schoolboy, unable to concentrate on anything but the girl who'd caught his interest.

He had some very serious thinking to do before this thing went any further, he decided gravely. And it was time he started thinking with his head instead of his hormones where Rachel Carson Evans was concerned.

Rachel sat in her office Tuesday afternoon, staring blindly at a stack of invoices in front of her and trying to remember what it was she was supposed to do with them. Her concentration had been shot all to hell this week. Though she longed to deny it, she knew it was because she couldn't stop thinking about Seth. Couldn't stop herself from replaying those fervent, heated caresses in his car Saturday evening. Couldn't stop wondering why he hadn't called her since.

Had he lost interest already? Was this his way of letting her know that it wasn't working out? That he was backing off before they went any further? That he'd decided that she wasn't worth the trouble she caused him?

Or was she only being paranoid again?

As though from a great distance, she heard the computer keyboard clattering in the other room. Martha was hard at work, as Rachel should be. Martha had even commented earlier on Rachel's unusual distraction, asking in concern if she was feeling all right, if everything was okay at home with the children. Rachel had made vague excuses about a sinus headache. She couldn't tell the truth, of course. Couldn't admit to anyone but herself that she was brooding about Seth and vacillating about whether she should be the one to make the next move.

Maybe that was all Seth was waiting for.

The telephone at her elbow startled her with its flat buzz. Rachel all but fell upon it, snatching the receiver to her ear. "Evans Industries," she said, trying to sound professional, just in case it wasn't Seth.

"Is this the trash people?" a rather nasal female voice inquired.

The disappointment was immediate, and dismayingly deep. She struggled to push it aside so she could focus on her job. "We are a commercial waste hauling company," she explained in response to the unfortunately familiar question. "May I help you?"

The caller explained that she wanted to rent a Dumpster on a temporary basis. "My husband and me are tearing down an old house," she added. "We'll have some lumber and shingles and concrete blocks and stuff like that to be hauled away."

Rachel swallowed a faint sigh. This, too, was a familiar problem. People assumed anything would go into a regular-size trash container. Building materials, however, were much too heavy for the average Dumpster, which had to be hydraulically lifted high into the air for emptying into the back of the front-loader trucks she used. The larger containers, which were actually loaded onto trucks and carried to the landfill, then returned to the site, were quite expensive in comparison to the smaller boxes.

The customer was shocked by the price Rachel gave her. "Oh, I can't afford that," she exclaimed. "I didn't know it would cost so much."

Rachel gave the woman the telephone number of an acquaintance who owned a small dump truck that he often rented out for just such purposes. "I'm sure you can work something out with him," she offered helpfully.

The woman hung up without even thanking Rachel for taking the time to advise her.

Ten minutes later the phone rang again. Rachel didn't allow herself to anticipate that time, which was just as well, since it still wasn't Seth, but an emotional woman who had just discovered that her husband had loaded two plastic garbage bags full of laundry into the two-yard Dumpster they rented for their small business.

"I was going to stop by the Laundromat on the way home this afternoon," the woman explained. "I put the bags in the back room and he thought they were trash. I've had a few words with him, let me tell you. I've gotten behind on laundry and over half of the clothes we own are in those bags. Please tell me there's some chance of getting them back."

Rachel checked the route sheet, then winced. This woman's container had been emptied early that morning. The truck had been dumped at least twice since then. "I hate to tell you this, but the chances are very slim that you'll get your things back," Rachel said regretfully. "Those bags are probably buried under tons of garbage and cover dirt by now. The landfill we use is the only one for miles around and it receives trash from towns in three counties."

The woman groaned in dismay. "There's no way we could, you know, sort of dig around a little?"

"You could call the landfill and ask," Rachel said, "but I'm afraid I can't offer much encouragement. You should probably call your insurance agent and ask whether you're covered under your homeowner's policy.''

This, too, was a familiar problem. People were always throwing things away by accident, and then dismayed when they couldn't easily recover their property. They seemed to think the garbage was taken somewhere and neatly filed away for future retrieval, Rachel thought wryly after concluding the call. Trash disposal was something every household needed, yet few people ever wondered what happened to the bags of garbage once they were set on a curb or tossed into a container.

Every municipality in the country was struggling to find something to do with garbage amid growing problems with overburdened landfills, increasingly stringent ecological regulations, rapidly rising prices. Recycling programs were underway, even in Percy, but processing costs were high and consumer demand for recycled products much too low. The industry still struggled for recognition from the public and suffered from shortsighted policies of the past and a reputation—rightfully earned, at times—for being haphazardly regulated, viciously competitive, and tarnished by association with organized crime.

There were many times when Rachel wished Ray and his father had chosen to open a grocery store or a construction company rather than a waste-hauling business. Though she knew those professions came with their own sets of problems, there were times when her business seemed destined to self-destruct.

She shook her head when she realized that her thoughts were wandering again from the tasks at hand. At least she hadn't been thinking about Seth that time, she thought with a sigh.

''Rachel?'' Martha appeared in the doorway, solid and dependable looking in her blue polyester blouse and navy slacks, her oversize handbag tucked under one arm, a pencil still stuck, obviously forgotten, into her teased-and-lacquered red-dyed hair. "I'm leaving now. You should be going home yourself, soon."

Rachel glanced at her watch and winced. She'd accomplished much too little that day. And, worse, she knew she'd get little more done should she stay. "I'll leave as soon as I clean off my desk," she promised. "Good night, Martha. I'll see you Thursday."

Martha nodded and turned to leave, then paused. "By the way, Rachel. Do you know anyone who drives a rusty old green pickup truck?"

Rachel's fingers tightened convulsively around the pen in her hand. "Why do you ask that?"

"There's one been driving past quite a bit this afternoon. Seems like he slows down when he gets to our gate, but then he goes on. One time he stopped on the street for a few minutes. I could see him from the window behind my desk. I didn't think anything about it at first, but about the third time I saw him I started to wonder."

Rachel bit her lower lip, remembering the night she'd thought someone in a rusty truck had been watching her. "No. I don't know anyone with a truck like that," she said.

Martha frowned. "Strange."

"Um, Martha? What sort of vehicle does Frank Holder drive?"

Martha's faded eyes widened. "Last I knew, he had a beat-up old van. But he was always trading one worthless piece of junk for another. You don't think it was him in that truck, do you?"

Rachel shook her head. "I have no reason to believe it was Frank," she explained carefully. "And I haven't heard from him since Leon warned him off. I just thought I should ask."

"Why don't you call Leon now?"

"And tell him what? That a pickup drove past the office a few times?"

"You could at least have him find out what Frank's driving these days," Martha suggested.

"Even if it *was* Frank, there's no law stopping him from driving on public streets," Rachel argued. "Unless he calls again, or something like that, I have no basis for a complaint."

"If it is him, then you do have a basis," Martha returned firmly. "Stalking's illegal in this state."

The word sent a cold chill slithering down Rachel's back. "I don't think Frank Holder is stalking me," she protested, mostly because she didn't want to even consider the possibility.

"Nevertheless, I want you to be careful," Martha said. "That Frank was always a wild one when he was drinking. And I heard he had a nasty habit of slapping around that silly little girlfriend of his. I guess that's why she finally got fed up and left him. He's a bad one, Rachel. I think you should ask Leon about that truck."

"I'll think about it," Rachel promised.

Martha didn't look satisfied. "I'll wait with you here until you get your desk cleaned off. I don't want you leaving alone."

"Thank you, Martha, but I'm sure I'll be fine. I'll be careful."

Martha shook her head, her double chin firmly set. "I'm not leaving until you do."

Rachel knew better than to argue when her bookkeeper got that particular look on her face. She surrendered. Ten minutes later, her desk was clean, her purse in her hand, and the two women walked side by side outside to the small parking lot that held only Rachel's car and Martha's old station wagon. Both looked automatically out at the street. Several cars were passing at this time of day, workers on their way home for dinner, but the rusty green truck was not among them.

"I'm sure we overreacted," Rachel said.

"Maybe so. But I still think you should mention this to Leon."

Rachel promised again to consider Martha's advice. Martha didn't drive away until Rachel had secured the gate locks and closed herself back into her own car. They drove down the street together, turning different directions at the next traffic light. Martha waved goodbye.

Rachel headed toward the day-care center to pick up her children. She rather wished Martha hadn't even mentioned the pickup. It was probably just someone driving around, killing time on a lazy afternoon, she reassured herself.

She had enough to worry about right now. She didn't need to add the possibility that she was being stalked by an embittered ex-employee!

Paige had a special request for dinner that evening. "Could we have hot dogs and macaroni and cheese tonight, Mama? Real macaroni and cheese out of a box, not that kind that Granny Fran makes."

Aaron quickly seconded the request.

Rachel grimaced in response to Paige's artless comment. Trust her children to prefer the powdery dry mixed macaroni and cheese to Granny Fran's home-baked casserole! But she agreed to the menu the kids had asked for, since she hadn't planned anything else in particular.

"Is Seth going to eat with us?" Aaron asked hopefully.

Rachel shook her head. "Tonight it's just the three of us."

"We haven't seen him in forever," Paige said with a sigh.

"It's only been three days," Rachel remarked. "I'm sure Seth has other things to do."

What *was* he doing? Why hadn't he called?

Was he, perhaps, sharing dinner with another woman tonight?

She tried not to dwell on that possibility, finding it just too depressing.

It didn't take her long to make the dinner her children wanted. She cooked peas as a side dish; hot dogs didn't seem such a guilty pleasure if they were served with something green, she rationalized. The children seemed to thoroughly enjoy the meal. Rachel could hardly touch a bite.

After dinner she busied herself with housecleaning—doing laundry, mopping floors, scrubbing sinks—anything to keep her mind occupied so she wouldn't dwell on her problems. Any of her problems.

She was on her knees scrubbing a faint soap ring off the children's bathtub when the doorbell rang. She looked in dismay at her damp T-shirt and grubby jeans. Her arms were soapy, her hair pulled back into a loose ponytail. She wasn't wearing shoes. If that was Seth, showing up without warning after not calling for three days...

"I'll get it," Paige yelled.

"Find out who it is first," Rachel admonished, though she knew Paige always asked before opening the door.

Celia appeared in the bathroom doorway a few minutes later. "Doesn't this look like fun," she commented, glancing at the cleaning supplies in the plastic carry tray at Rachel's side.

"I live to attack soap scum," Rachel assured her gravely. "What's up, Celia?"

"Oh, nothing. I just felt like dropping by. Anything I can do to help?"

Rachel looked at her sister's immaculate cream-colored slacks and matching sweater. "I don't think you're dressed for it. But, as it happens, I'm finished here. Let's go into the kitchen for some coffee."

Celia agreed without argument.

Rachel soon noticed that her usually exuberant younger sister was unnaturally subdued that evening. They talked about Paige and Aaron, agreed that they would both miss having their grandmother in town, compared stories of their workdays, though Rachel deliberately avoided any mention of a rusty green truck. Only then did Rachel finally ask, "Is there anything in particular you want to talk to me about?"

Celia looked into her coffee cup, as though she'd found something of great interest in the half inch of lukewarm beverage that remained. "Nothing specific," she evaded. "I just wanted to spend some time with you tonight."

"I'm glad you did. You know I always love talking to you. But I wish you would tell me what's bothering you. I can tell there's something."

Celia shrugged. "Oh, you know. Just the usual stuff."

Which meant exactly nothing. Rachel hazarded a guess. "You're okay financially?"

Celia rolled her eyes. "I'm fine financially."

"Problems at work?"

"Nothing of any significance. It's kind of boring sometimes, but it's okay."

Rachel thought she'd just found a clue to Celia's mood. She still believed her sister was restless, bored with the routines she'd fallen into during the past couple of years. Rachel had warned Celia when she'd moved back to Percy that small-town life had its own charms, but adventure and excitement were rarely part of them. Celia had claimed then that she didn't want adventure and excitement. She just wanted a good job, a secure future, the opportunity to see her family often, she'd said. Rachel had worried then that there would come a time when Celia would want a great deal more than Percy had to offer.

Rachel wanted very badly to ask if Celia was still staying in touch with Damien Alexander. The man was one of Rachel's biggest worries as far as her sister was concerned. The well-known hotelier was a familiar face in the society publications, often photographed at exclusive celebrity parties, usually with a beautiful woman or two at his side. He was rich, handsome, powerful and sophisticated. Celia had met him by accident several months earlier when he'd come into the bank where she worked for a meeting with some local landowners in connection with a resort he was considering building on nearby Greers Ferry Lake.

Rachel wasn't surprised that Alexander had noticed Celia. He was reputed to have a keen eye for beautiful young women. Nor was she surprised that Celia found him fascinating—after all, he was so different from the men Celia was usually surrounded by. But Rachel couldn't help worrying, as usual.

Celia was, at heart, a sheltered, small-town girl. Could she really hold her own with a man of Damien Alexander's reputation? Would she emerge unscathed from an involvement with him, from a sudden exposure to the fast lane? Or would she fall victim to the dangerous temptations just waiting out there to prey on naive young women?

She wanted very badly to ask if Celia had been in contact with Alexander lately, if he had anything to do with her distraction tonight. But she was afraid that Celia would only turn the questioning back to Rachel's own complicated social life, and ask questions about Seth that Rachel wouldn't know how to answer. Maybe the reason Celia hadn't mentioned Seth thus far was because she was concerned about the same thing.

Celia didn't stay much longer. She kissed the children, then turned to hug Rachel. The hug was a bit more fervent than usual. "Celia?" Rachel asked, drawing back in concern. "Are you *sure* there isn't anything you want to talk to me about?"

Celia shook her head and flashed a bright smile that looked completely artificial. "Don't start your famous worrying, Rachel. I'm fine. Really."

"If you need to talk..."

"I know where to come," Celia said. "Good night, Rachel."

Rachel closed the door after her sister with a frown. Obviously something was bothering Celia, despite her denials. She just wished she knew what it was.

This was all she'd needed today, she thought with a sigh. One more thing to worry about.

She thought inconsequentially of Granny Fran, and her advice for Rachel to have more fun. "I'm waiting for that fun to start now, Granny," she murmured. "Anytime would be nice."

There was no answer, of course. Rachel shook her head in self-directed derision and went to finish cleaning the bathrooms.

Seth called that night, after the children were in bed. "I guess you were wondering what happened to me," he said with a note of apology in his voice.

Rachel considered coolly assuring him that he hadn't even crossed her mind. She didn't—both because it would be rude, and because she knew he wouldn't believe her. "Well, yes," she admitted. "I guess you've been busy?"

"Not particularly."

"Oh." He could at least have taken advantage of the excuse she'd offered him. She wondered what he wanted her to say next.

"Why don't we take the kids out for pizza Friday night?" Seth suggested. "We can go to that place that has all the games for the kids to play after they eat."

Rachel found herself chewing her lower lip again. That was one nervous habit she was going to have to stop, or she was going to end up lipless, she thought in exasperation.

"Rachel? What's wrong, don't you like pizza?"

"I like pizza."

"So, what? You don't like me?" Though he still spoke lightly, she knew he wasn't entirely joking.

She couldn't tell him what really worried her. That she wasn't sure they should include the children in their plans during this early, tentative stage of dating. Paige and Aaron were already so attached to Seth—Aaron, in particular. Should she encourage them to spend more time with him? Could they continue to be friends even if nothing further developed between Seth and Rachel, or would Seth disappear from their lives altogether? Would the children be bitterly disappointed if that happened? She already knew she would be.

"Rachel?" Seth said again, and this time he sounded very serious. "What's wrong?"

I'm scared, Seth. I want to know where you've been for the past three days, why you haven't called me, but I don't feel I have the right to ask. I don't want you to hurt my children, and I don't want you to hurt me. But mostly I'm afraid because I've missed you so very badly the past three days.

"Nothing's wrong," she lied. "Pizza sounds fine. The children will look forward to it."

"Great," he said, sounding relieved. "See you then, okay?"

"Sure. See you then."

She carefully hung up the phone, then spent a few wasted moments lightly pounding her forehead with her fists and wondering just how long it would take for the men with the white coats and the straitjackets to show up at her doorstep. She was feeling very much out of control of her life these days.

Chapter Ten

It didn't take Rachel long Friday evening to realize that something was different about Seth. She couldn't quite put her finger on what it was. He teased with the children, and with her, as easily as he had before. He smiled and laughed and talked during their pizza dinner, then enthusiastically helped the children win prize tickets in the game room. But something was different.

Maybe it had something to do with the times she glanced his way and found him looking at her with an odd expression in his eyes. An expression that seemed to be made up of several emotions she couldn't quite identify. She only knew that every time he looked at her that way, she temporarily forgot how to breathe.

He didn't linger long after he drove them home that evening. He kissed Paige's cheek, ruffled Aaron's hair, then sent the children off to change for bed before giving Rachel a kiss that weakened her knees. His voice was rather husky when he stepped back and said, "Good night, Rachel. I'll call you tomorrow."

She blinked. "You're leaving now?"

"Yes. I think it's better," he explained. "If I stay, I'm afraid I'll start pushing for more than you're ready to give," he admitted ruefully. He brushed her cheek with his fingertips, the gesture a sweetly tender one. "I want you, Rachel. I think you know that by now. But I won't rush you."

She didn't quite know what to say. As strange as it felt to admit it to herself, she knew that she wanted him, too. But, as he'd so perceptively pointed out, she wasn't quite ready to do anything about it.

He smiled. "You don't have to say anything now," he murmured, letting her off the hook. "Just think about it, okay?"

As though she'd been able to think about anything else during the past week! "Good night, Seth," she said, settling for something safe and noncommittal.

Moments later, he was gone.

Long after the children were in bed, Rachel paced through her silent house, restless in ways she didn't want to examine too closely. She didn't allow herself to dwell on the things Seth had said just before he'd left. She wasn't ready to consider his admission that he wanted her, nor was she quite prepared to deal with her own feelings, whatever they might be.

She decided to take a warm bath before going to bed. It had been ages since she'd had time for more than a quick shower before work. She pinned up her hair and filled the tub, impulsively adding a packet of the expensive, scented bath powder Celia had given her for her birthday. The floral aroma hung heavily in the steamy air, inviting her to relax and enjoy. She sank into the tub with a long sigh, closing her eyes as the water lapped seductively around her shoulders. Nice.

It took a bit more effort than she'd hoped to clear her mind. Seth's face kept popping into it. She pushed him firmly to the back of her thoughts, promising that persistent image she'd deal with him later. This time was just for her. For a few rare, precious minutes, she intended to be thoroughly, lazily, hedonistically selfish. Reality and responsibility would catch up with her all too quickly.

The water had grown cold by the time she reluctantly rose and reached for a towel. Her eyelids still heavy, she patted the thick terry fabric over her wet, fragrant body. The warm water had left her skin soft and sensitized. Her nipples tightened as she passed the towel over them. A faint quiver ran through her when she dried the tender insides of her thighs.

She told herself she was only chilled.

The full-length mirror on the back of the bathroom door was filled with her reflection. She glanced at it, looked away, then found her gaze slowly turning back to the mirror. The hand in which she held her towel dropped to her side.

Her face was flushed from steam, and damp little ringlets of hair had escaped the pins to cling to her neck. Her fair skin glistened slightly in the light, probably as a result of the moisturizers in the bath powders. She noted the flaws, of course, as any woman would. The faint tracing of stretch marks from two pregnancies. The tiny scar low on her right side from the emergency appendectomy she'd had when she was twenty. Her tummy wasn't quite as flat as she would have liked.

But she was still slim and in reasonably good shape; her breasts, though on the small side, still firm and high. The stretch marks could have been worse—and besides, she could never be ashamed of those reminders that her body had borne two beautiful, healthy children. She wasn't a teenager anymore, but she looked pretty good for a woman of thirty-one, she decided. Would a singularly fit and attractive twenty-eight-year-old man think so?

Realizing what directions her thoughts had taken, she gulped and reached quickly for her nightgown. What was she doing? Was she possibly considering taking Seth Fletcher as a lover?

Had she completely lost her senses?

She crawled into bed and pulled the covers to her chin. Her eyelids stubbornly remained open, her gaze focused unseeingly on the darkened ceiling.

By the time the first pale light of dawn crept through the lacy curtains at her windows, she'd had too little sleep and far too much time to think. She'd finally come to a resigned acceptance that she was strongly physically attracted to Seth Fletcher. She wanted him.

She just didn't know if she was ready to let another man into her bed. She wasn't sure that she even could without letting him into her heart, as well.

Rachel saw quite a bit of Seth during the next two weeks. He ate dinner with her and the children several evenings. Sometimes Rachel prepared the meals, and others Seth insisted on bringing takeout for everyone or treating them at a kid-friendly restaurant.

On the nights when they didn't see each other, he called, usually waiting until after the children were in bed so that he and Rachel could talk without interruption. They talked about many things during those long, comfortable calls. Rachel's work. Seth's slowly but steadily building practice. The children's progress at school. Current events. Politics. Religion. Whatever occurred to them. Rachel began to look forward to those calls with an enthusiasm that worried her when she stopped to think about it, which she didn't do very often.

The one thing they *didn't* talk about was their relationship. Seth made no secret that he was courting her, though

Rachel wasn't sure even that term was appropriate. He wanted her, yes. But was he actually thinking long-term here? Surely not. And yet—would a man who was only pursuing a physical affair seem quite so content to sit around her den playing video games with her kids?

She was growing very confused.

The only real contention between them during those weeks was over Rachel's work. The first time she told Seth she couldn't have dinner with him because she planned one of her take-out dinners for three at her office, he seemed taken aback. He offered to join them, but Rachel refused, telling him she didn't think she could get any work done if he was there to distract her. He offered to baby-sit, but she turned him down for that, too. He didn't say anything more about it.

The second time it happened, the following week, Seth wasn't quite so reticent with his opinions. "What could you possibly have to do that can't wait until tomorrow?" he asked.

"Taxes," she answered succinctly. "I'm supposed to deliver a stack of paperwork to my accountant's office tomorrow, and it isn't finished yet. I had hoped to finish this afternoon, but several other things came up that had to be handled first."

"Sounds to me like you need to hire more help."

"That would be nice," she answered tiredly. "But I can't afford it."

A sound from the reception area caught her attention. Paige and Aaron were eating egg rolls and chicken-fried rice from take-out containers and watching the small portable television Rachel usually kept in the storage closet. Rachel sat behind her desk in her office, her door open so she could keep an eye on the children. She snapped her fingers at them when a developing quarrel threatened to become noisy. They subsided into mutters in response to that familiar maternal signal. Rachel knew they were bored and tired of the offices; she was, herself, for that matter.

"Rachel, I admire your dedication to your business," Seth said, though his voice didn't sound particularly admiring when he called her attention back to the phone call. "But you work too hard. You really should take more time for yourself."

"More time for you, you mean?" she asked, weariness and worry making her peevish.

He paused a moment, then said quietly, "No. I mean more time for yourself. And your children. I'd like to think being with me is something you do for pleasure, but mostly I'm worried about your health. You need rest."

His gently reproachful tone made her wince. She started to apologize but bit the words back. The children were arguing again—she thought it had something to do with what program they were going to watch next—and the tax forms weren't filling themselves in while she talked on the telephone. Her head was beginning to throb in earnest, and she hadn't eaten since breakfast. "I've really got to go, Seth. I have to finish this tonight."

"All right. I'll talk to you tomorrow then."

She murmured a good-night and hung up the phone. "Paige, Aaron," she said firmly. "Stop that bickering or I'm turning the television off."

"But she—"

"He won't—"

She interrupted them before they could continue to place blame. "I mean it," she warned. "I don't want to hear another word about it from either of you."

Two gusty, supremely martyred sighs came from the other room, but at least the quarreling stopped. Before long, both the children were engrossed in the program they'd finally settled on. Though racked with guilt, resentment, exhaustion and depression, Rachel turned determinedly back to her figures.

Taxes, she'd heard, waited for no one. Not even single mothers.

The next day, Friday, passed with blessedly few problems at work. Rachel could see that she was actually going to get away close to her usual time. At five-thirty, she cleaned off her desk and dug into her purse for her car keys, satisfied that everything had been done that needed her attention that day. She would spend the evening with her children, maybe she'd take them to see that new Disney film they'd been hinting about since it had opened last week. Maybe Seth would like to go with them, she thought, biting her lip as she regretfully remembered the way she'd snapped at him on the phone the day before.

She looked up in startled question when she heard the outer door to the reception area open. Her drivers had finished their routes and gone home early that afternoon, and today had been Martha's day off. She wasn't expecting anyone else at this hour. She usually kept that door locked when she was here alone. She chided herself now for forgetting to lock it this afternoon.

"May I help you?" she called out, trying to see who'd entered. She stayed behind her desk, one hand close to the telephone—just in case.

She realized that there was good reason for her caution when Frank Holder suddenly filled her office doorway. One glance at his glazed, bloodshot eyes and disheveled appearance told her that he'd been drinking. He leaned one meaty shoulder against the doorframe, probably to prop himself up.

She rested her hand casually on the telephone receiver. "What are you doing here, Frank?"

"I'm here to get my job back," he replied, and his voice, though gruff, was surprisingly clear. Maybe he wasn't quite as drunk as she'd first thought. She wasn't sure whether to be relieved or more worried.

"Frank, you aren't getting your job back. I've already hired someone else to replace you," she said, using the firm, don't-argue-with-me voice she had perfected with her children. "I'd like you to leave now."

"Oh, I'm sure you would," he said with a sneer. "But I don't think I will leave. Not just yet, anyway."

She sighed, carefully hiding her wariness of him behind a facade of impatient confidence. "Please don't make it necessary for me to call the police. You'll only be in further trouble if Chief Jackson finds out that you've ignored his warnings to you."

"You ain't calling anyone," Frank assured her with a cocky certainty that made her even more uneasy.

Keeping a cautious eye on him, she slowly lifted the receiver to her ear. Her stomach clenched when she heard nothing from the instrument but dead silence. She scowled. "What have you done to my phones?"

His smile was chilling. "This is between you and me, Rachel. Jackson ain't got no business interfering."

Rachel slammed the receiver into its cradle, her temper igniting at his infuriating behavior. "Get out of my office, Frank," she ordered him. "Now."

He took a step toward her, instead. "You ain't my boss anymore, remember?" he mocked her, and then moved another step forward. "You can't tell me what to do now."

Rachel visually measured the distance between herself and the door. Her desk was in front of her, and Holder firmly stationed on the other side. She clutched her car keys in one fist, ready to run in the opposite direction if he should come around one end of the desk after her. Firmness hadn't worked with him; she tried logic, instead. "Why are you doing this, Frank? You can't possibly hope to accomplish anything by threatening me like this."

He raised both eyebrows in an expression probably meant to be exaggerated innocence, but which came across, instead, as an ugly leer. "Have I threatened you?"

"You've done something to my telephone. You're trespassing on my property. If this isn't a threat, what is it?"

"I'm here to teach you a lesson," he said. "You give a woman a taste of power, and she gets carried away with it. Thinks she's as tough as a man. We're going to see how tough you really are, Rachel."

"Don't do this, Frank."

He laughed shortly. "Now you try begging," he said, though she hadn't considered her words a plea. "Well, it's too late. You pushed the wrong man when you pushed me. Maybe none of the rest of 'em have the guts to put you in your place, but I have. I ain't got nothing to lose, anyway."

"That's not true," she countered quickly, shifting her weight when he moved a couple of inches to his right.

"Sure it is. You've cost me my job and my woman. You gave me all those smiles and nicey-nice 'good mornings' when I came to work for you, then you cut me cold when I tried to be nice to you in return. Your problem is you been too long without a man, and I mean a real man, not a fuzzy-faced boy like that lawyer you've been playing with."

Rachel's eyes widened. How did Holder know she'd been seeing Seth? Had he been watching her that closely? She thought of the rusty truck that had caused her such concern before she'd forgotten it in the confusion of her growing feelings for Seth. She knew now who'd been driving that truck, as she'd suspected all along, darn it. Why hadn't she mentioned it to someone? Why had she allowed herself to be so careless?

She'd given up on trying to reason with him. Instead, she gripped her keys more tightly, wedging them between her clenched fingers as she'd been taught to do in a self-defense course she and Celia had taken at the local recreation center. *Go for the eyes,* they'd told her. She hoped it wouldn't come to that, but she was ready, if it became necessary. She had no intention of allowing Holder to hurt her. Not without one hell of a fight, anyway.

Holder took another step to his right, moving him fully out of the path of the door, and Rachel abruptly decided it was time to get out of there. She was younger, in better shape, and sober. She figured that gave her the advantage when it came to making a dash for it.

She shot around the desk and sprinted toward the door.

Holder moved with a speed that shouldn't have been possible for a man of his size and condition. He caught her by the shoulder just as she reached the door, spinning her around and slamming her against the wall with a force that knocked the breath out of her.

"That wasn't so smart, was it, boss lady?" he mocked her, his face close to hers, his breath sour enough to make her eyes water. "Now what are you going to do, huh? You going to start giving orders again? You going to fire me again? You going to yell for that police chief buddy of yours?"

Rachel shoved against him. "Get away from me!"

His fingers dug cruelly into her shoulders. He laughed. "Yeah, still giving orders," he taunted. "You really don't learn very fast, do you, Rachel?"

He lowered his face toward hers. He was going to kiss her, she realized, recoiling at the very idea. She turned her head away from him.

He caught her chin with one hand and forced her to face him again. And then he moved closer, his dark, blurry eyes gleaming with an intent that made her stomach churn.

She took a deep breath, raised her fist and slashed at his face with the keys protruding from between her knuckles. The sharp edges of the keys raked his unshaven skin, leaving ugly red welts in their path. Holder cursed and jumped back, raising a hand to his abraded cheek.

Rachel took advantage of the opportunity to run.

He caught up with her again just before she reached the outer door. He grabbed the hem of her suit jacket and jerked backward, nearly pulling her off her feet. His curses were low and vicious, his intentions worded in specific, obscene language. Rachel fought him with all her strength, aware now that this was what he'd planned all along. He was here to rape her, if not worse. And she would not make it easy for him.

She kicked, bit, scratched. Holder backhanded her with one huge fist, and the pain was enough to make her gag. No one had ever hit her before, she thought dazedly, staggering to remain on her feet. And it had hurt even worse than she'd imagined it would.

She was groping blindly for support, terrified of what would happen if she should fall, when her hand fell on the lamp that sat on a small table between the two vinyl chairs in the reception area. She swung the lamp automatically, ripping the cord from the wall socket and smashing the heavy glass base against the side of Holder's head.

He stumbled, going down on one knee.

Rachel jerked the door open and threw herself over the threshold, drawing a deep breath of the cool outside air. She hoped an ear-piercing scream would be heard by someone nearby, since she wasn't sure she could make it to her car before Holder caught up with her again.

The scream was cut off with a choked cry when she collided with something warm and solid.

"Seth!" she whispered, clutching at his shirt and gasping for breath. "Oh, thank God."

"Rachel?" He steadied her, his eyes anxiously searching her flushed and bruised face. She knew exactly how she must look. Her hair had tumbled loose around her shoulders, her blouse was disarrayed, her jacket ripped. She'd lost a shoe.

Holder appeared in the doorway, bellowing her name. Rachel noted in satisfaction that he didn't look any better than she did from their encounter. His cheek was still raw and reddened from her keys, and a nasty-looking lump was now forming at his temple, where she'd hit him with the lamp. Blood oozed in a thin line from the left side of his mouth; she thought in satisfaction that at least one of her wild swings must have connected.

Seth had gone rigid against her. With firm hands, he moved to set her aside, his gaze intent on the man staring back at him from the office doorway. "Get in your car, Rachel," he said, and she'd never heard his voice sound so hard or so coldly furious.

"Seth, no." She caught at his shirt again, knowing exactly what he'd do if she let go. "Let's just call the police."

Seth looked down at her, and touched her bruised cheek with one tender fingertip. "He hit you," he growled. "I'm going to beat him to a pulp."

"You can try," Holder blustered, but he suddenly looked much less confident. Much less brave. Fighting with a woman half his size had been one thing. Facing this angry, muscular young man was quite a different prospect. He inched toward the battered, rusty pickup he'd parked behind Rachel's car.

Seth shifted toward him, making Holder move more quickly, his steps weaving now from a combination of alcohol and the blow he'd taken to the temple.

Rachel clung determinedly to Seth's shirt. "You are not going to fight him," she said, keeping herself stationed between Seth and Holder. "We're calling the police. Leon will take care of this."

Seth moved her out of the way as easily as if she'd been a chair, or some other lightweight, inanimate object. "You go call the police," he instructed her. "I'll make sure Holder is here to help us welcome them when they arrive."

"I can't call them," she said, suddenly remembering. "He's done something to the telephones."

"Use the phone in my car," Seth replied, reaching out to catch Holder's sleeve just as the older man put his hand on the driver's door handle of the pickup. "You aren't going anywhere, Holder."

Holder snarled and tried to throw off Seth's hand, but Seth subdued him by the simple method of catching Holder's ankles with one well-placed foot and sweeping his feet out from under him. Holder landed on his backside with a graceless thud.

"You really don't want to get up," Seth advised him conversationally, poised with fists at the ready, looking as though he would gladly welcome any excuse to beat the older man senseless. "I'd only have to knock you down again."

Holder responded with a string of expletives that made Rachel gasp even as she hurried to Seth's car.

Seth didn't bat an eye. He only crossed his arms at his waist and remained where he was, looming over Holder in quiet menace.

Holder subsided into silence, nursing his wounds with one dirty hand and giving both Rachel and Seth threatening looks that would have been more ominous had he not been sitting in the dirt, bleeding and defeated.

Rachel placed two calls, one to the police, the other to Celia. Shaken by Rachel's explanation, Celia agreed to pick up the children at the day-care center and take them home.

"You're sure you're all right?" she asked for the third time, her concern evident in her voice.

"I'm fine," Rachel assured her. "Just a bit bruised."

"Why don't I keep the children overnight?" Celia suggested. "That will give you a chance to get yourself together."

"I can't ask you to do that," Rachel protested automatically.

"I didn't have any other plans," Celia persisted. "I'll tell the kids it's a surprise slumber party. They won't have any reason to worry about you."

"Well—"

"Please, Rachel. Let me do this."

Rachel sighed and agreed. To be honest, she was relieved that she didn't have to face the children until she'd put the trauma of the attack behind her, and had a chance to come up with a reasonable explanation for the bruises she would wear for several days. "Thank you, Celia."

"You're welcome. And tell Seth to give you a little extra TLC for me, will you?"

Rachel hastily brought the call to an end.

The police arrived quickly. Seth looked rather disappointed that Holder had given him no excuse for violence.

Leon was right behind his uniformed officers, having been informed of Rachel's call. He watched as Holder was loaded into the police cruiser and Rachel gave a preliminary statement, then lingered behind when the cruiser bore Holder away.

"You're sure you're okay?" he asked, studying Rachel's battered face with intent ebony eyes. "Maybe you should have that checked before you go home."

"She will," Seth assured him before Rachel could say anything. "I'll make sure of that."

Rachel frowned at Seth. "I don't need to have it checked," she insisted. "It's only a bruise."

"You'll have it checked," he replied, his patience clearly at an end, "if I have to drag you into the emergency room." His eyes dared her to argue with him.

She came very close to letting him know that she had had enough of pushy males for one day. The only thing that held her back was knowing how badly she would hurt him by comparing him to Frank Holder. Holder's arrogance had been motivated by a vicious craving to dominate and humiliate her. Seth, on the other hand, was genuinely concerned about her, and still frustrated because he hadn't been able to physically vent his hostility toward Holder.

As though he'd read her thoughts, Seth's expression suddenly gentled. He gave her a smile and touched her hand in apology. "Sorry, guess I'm still just itching for a fight. But I really do wish you'd have a doctor look at you, Rachel. Just to reassure those of us who care about you," he added.

There really was no good argument to that particular excuse. She sighed and nodded.

Leon unsuccessfully fought a smile. "Looks like I'm leaving you in good hands," he said.

Rachel hoped her cheeks didn't look quite as pink as they felt.

Leon turned his attention to Seth. "Good thing you arrived when you did."

Seth shrugged ruefully. "Rachel was handling herself quite well without me."

Rachel appreciated the stroke to her ego, but she wasn't nearly as confident about her ability to get away unscathed had Seth not arrived when he had. "I've never been so glad to see anyone in my life," she assured him fervently.

Seth looked at her thoughtfully, as though trying to decide whether to take the words personally or to assume she would have been just as glad to see anyone at that moment.

The police chief cleared his throat. "Guess I'd better be going. I want to have another little talk with Holder."

Rachel smiled at him. "Thank you for coming, Leon."

He leaned over to lightly kiss her cheek. "You just take care of yourself, lady," he murmured gruffly. "Dolores will probably call tomorrow to check on you."

"Tell her I'm fine. But I'd love to hear from her, anyway."

Leon nodded, then offered his hand to Seth. "You take care of her," he said.

"I intend to," Seth replied. Something in the somber looks they exchanged made Rachel suspect they were talking about more than the evening ahead.

Seth waited only until Leon had driven away before turning to Rachel. "Let's go see about that cheek," he said, sliding an arm around her shoulders. "We'll leave your car here and pick it up later, okay?"

She let out a long, shaky breath and allowed herself to relax against him. "Okay," she agreed.

The way her hands were suddenly shaking in delayed reaction, she wouldn't have wanted to try to drive, anyway.

Chapter Eleven

Seth never wanted to feel again what he'd felt when Rachel had tumbled into his arms outside her office, her beautiful face swollen and bruised, her dark eyes wide with fear. He was absolutely certain she'd taken a good ten years off his life in that moment.

He'd never wanted to hurt anyone as badly as he'd wanted to hurt Frank Holder for daring to lay a hand on Rachel. For the first time in his life, Seth had been filled with a violent, totally primitive rage. He'd wanted blood, and he'd wanted it to flow at his hands. He'd restrained himself only because he could tell Rachel would have been further upset if he'd given in to his bloodthirsty urges.

But, he thought, pacing the confined space of the Emergency waiting room of the tiny Percy Memorial Hospital, if Holder ever came near Rachel again...

"Seth? Where's Rachel? Is she okay? What the hell happened?" Cody Carson burst into the waiting room in a frenzy of questions, his usually laughing blue eyes filled with panic.

Seth held up both hands in a calming gesture. "Rachel's fine," he assured his friend. "The doctor is checking her out just to make sure, but she was more shaken than hurt."

"I was told that Frank Holder attacked her at her office this afternoon. They're saying he tried to—to rape her."

"It's true that he attacked her, but he didn't rape her." Seth had to fight down a renewed surge of that deadly anger. It took him a moment to get his voice back under control. "He hit her a couple of times, but she held her own. You should have seen him," he added with a sudden, unexpected little smile. "She clawed his face and smashed a lamp against the side of his head, and got in a few pretty good punches. He'll have as many bruises as she does."

Cody didn't smile in return. "He's going to have more when I get through with him."

Seth shook his head. "The police have him in custody. He won't bother Rachel again."

"Damn straight he won't. If he comes near her again, I'll kill him. I'll make sure he knows that before he makes bail."

Seth had never seen Cody look more seriously determined. He was rather surprised by the intensity of his friend's reaction. "Cody, don't go throwing threats around," he said, feeling compelled to warn. "Rachel won't appreciate it if you get yourself into trouble on her behalf."

"I won't get in trouble," Cody replied, gradually looking calmer. "But he won't bother her again, either. Besides," he added just a bit more lightly, "once Adam finds out what happened, Holder may decide he'll be safer living in some other state. Alaska, maybe."

"You think Adam will get involved with this?" Seth asked curiously.

"You can bet your boots he will, if he hears about it. Which he will. Adam seems to find out about everything that goes on in the family, even though he doesn't get involved that often. He's very protective when his family is involved, particularly the women. I wouldn't be surprised if Holder gets a visit from some hairy-knuckled guy named Vinnie."

Seth's eyes widened. "You mean your cousin would hire someone to, uh . . ."

Cody smiled and shook his head. "Just kidding. Sort of."

Which didn't sound particularly reassuring. Seth was beginning to wonder about Rachel's cousin Adam.

Rachel joined them then, distracting both Seth and Cody from thoughts of anyone else. Seth studied her closely while Cody gathered her into his arms for a quick, fervent hug. The right side of her face was puffy and discolored. She'd have quite a shiner by tomorrow morning, he predicted. She looked tired and pale and still a bit shaky, but other than that, he could tell she was going to be okay. He let out a sigh of relief.

"What are you doing here?" Rachel asked Cody when he gave her a chance to speak.

"Mike Smith called me at the bar to tell me what happened. He said you'd been taken to the hospital."

"I wasn't *taken* to the hospital, Seth drove me here," Rachel corrected. "And how did Mike Smith know about it, anyway?"

"Sherm Bostic called him. Sherm's dating that new police dispatcher—the tall blonde."

Rachel shook her head. "The Percy grapevine," she muttered. "Heaven only knows how badly the story's been exaggerated by now."

Cody's smile was a bit shaky. "It was bad enough when I heard it."

She touched her brother's face, obviously sensing the fright he'd had. "I'm fine, Cody. Really. But thank you for coming."

"You need anything? Want me to drive you home or buy you some dinner or... or something?" he offered, at a loss for further helpful suggestions.

"I'm taking her home," Seth said quickly. "And I'll see that she gets something to eat. You probably need to get back to your club." It wasn't that Seth didn't want Cody to hang around, but he was going to be the one to take care of Rachel tonight. He wanted very badly to believe that she needed him tonight, if only a little.

"Where are the kids?" Cody asked, glancing curiously from Seth to Rachel.

Rachel answered him. "Celia has them. They're going to spend the night with her."

"I'll pick them up in the morning and take them to an early movie," Cody said, and it wasn't an offer, but a statement of intent. "You get some rest."

"Cody, you—"

"I want to do this, Rachel."

Seth realized, as Rachel must have, that Cody wanted to feel as though he was doing something to help her. Seth knew exactly how Cody must feel. Rachel was so darned independent, so fully self-sufficient, that there were times when it was hard to believe she ever needed anyone else. And yet those who loved her wanted very badly to feel needed by her. At least, that was the way Seth felt.

Rachel nodded. "All right. The children have been wanting to see the new Disney movie. There's a one-o'clock showing tomorrow afternoon. You can bring them home afterward, if you're sure that's what you want to do."

Cody grinned.

"It'll be fun. I'll feed them candy and popcorn and sodas and nachos and bring them home happily sick to their stomachs."

"Thanks so much," Rachel told him wryly.

He kissed the end of her nose. "Anytime. Go home and rest now. Take care of her," he added for Seth's benefit.

Seth reflected that Cody's voice held the same veiled note of warning that Chief Jackson's had when he'd spoken the same words. Were they warning him not to hurt her further? They needn't worry. Seth had no intention of ever hurting Rachel. In fact, after today he found himself battling a strong urge to wrap her in cotton and stash her away where no one could ever threaten her again—a possessive, overprotective impulse he was quite sure she wouldn't appreciate at all.

Promising he'd help her collect her car the next day, Seth drove Rachel straight home from the hospital. He ushered her inside as carefully as if she were something fragile and breakable, she noted in mild exasperation, too tired for any stronger reaction to his overly solicitous manner.

"Are you hungry? I'll make dinner," he offered the moment they stepped inside.

"I'm really not very hungry right now," she said, wincing a bit as she slipped out of her ripped jacket.

He was at her side immediately. "What's wrong? Is something hurting you?"

"I'm just a little sore," she explained. She was deliberately understating, of course. She ached all over.

She saw the now-familiar temper flare in Seth's eyes, and knew that it was aimed at Holder, not her. He kept the emotion out of his voice when he spoke. "Would you like to take a warm bath or something? I could make a light dinner in case you're hungry later."

He was being so thoughtful and sweet that she didn't want to offend him by telling him she didn't need to be waited on hand and foot tonight. Actually, a warm bath sounded like a very good idea. For one thing, it would give her a much-needed chance to be alone for a few minutes. She could use that opportunity to quietly fall apart in private.

She didn't bother with the scented bath powders this time. She collapsed into the tub like a handful of spaghetti melting into boiling water. And though the bathwater was as hot as she could tolerate, she started to shake the moment she allowed herself to relax into it. She wasn't cold. She was remembering the look in Frank Holder's eyes when he'd thrown her against that wall and loomed over her.

She had never been that frightened for her own safety in her entire life. There had been moments during her desperate fight when she'd thought she couldn't win. But somehow she'd kept fighting. And maybe, she told herself with a faint touch of renewed spirit, maybe she would have gotten away even if Seth had not shown up when he did.

She still didn't know why Seth had arrived at her office at that moment. She hadn't been expecting him. But whatever the reason, and false confidence notwithstanding, she'd been elated at seeing him. The moment his arms had closed around her, she'd known that she was safe.

She focused on that remembered feeling of safety as she fought off the last remnants of fear. Gradually her shivers stopped and her tense muscles unclenched. The warm water soaked into her skin, and she filled her lungs with deep, cleansing breaths of warm, damp air. By the time she finally opened the drain and pushed herself to her feet, she was feeling about as strong as those wet spaghetti noodles she'd pictured earlier.

She'd forgotten to bring her robe into the bathroom with her. Shaking her head at the befuddled state she'd been in, she wrapped a towel around her and walked through the connecting door into her bedroom.

Seth was standing beside her bed, holding a steaming cup.

She stopped with a gasp, startled at finding him in the room she'd expected to be empty.

"I'm sorry," he said quickly, and set the cup on the nightstand, beside Ray's photograph. "I thought you might like some tea to—"

His words cut off abruptly. His gaze was riveted to her bare arms. She knew what he was seeing. The bathroom mirror had already shown her the rapidly purpling, hand-shaped bruises.

"It's not as bad as it looks," she said, instinctively trying to soothe the distress she saw in his expression. "I've always bruised easily."

He didn't answer, but took two quick steps forward and reached for the towel. By the time she realized his intention, it was too late. The towel was gone.

"Seth!" she gasped, automatically making an effort to cover herself with her hands.

But he was studying the dark, ugly splotch spreading across her rib cage, and the even darker one at her hip. She'd gotten those marks when she'd fallen against her desk, she remembered. And, despite her words to the contrary, they were every bit as sore as they probably looked.

"I should have beaten his head in," Seth said in a curiously uninflected voice, his gaze never leaving the evidence of her struggle with Holder.

"No, you shouldn't have." Rachel snatched her blue chenille robe off the end of her bed and wrapped it clumsily, hastily around her. Oddly enough, beneath her embarrassment at having Seth see her nude, there was an underlying chagrin that he'd reacted only to the bruises.

"I wish he'd tried just once to hit me," Seth mused, absently rubbing his right fist into his left palm.

"Bullies like Holder rarely attack someone who could easily beat their heads in," Rachel observed, using Seth's own graphic description of what he would have done to Holder if given the chance. "It took more character for you to resist violence than to have given in to it," she added, then winced at her rather sanctimonious tone. She had a tendency to fall back on clichés in awkward situations—and this was, most definitely, an awkward situation!

"Rachel?"

She was concentrating on knotting her belt tightly at her waist. She didn't look up from the task. "Yes?"

"Have I told you yet that you're the most beautiful woman I've ever known?"

That brought her head up. His tone had been quite casual, but the way he was looking at her wasn't casual at all. And this time, she was aware that he wasn't seeing the bruises.

"Seth—"

He raised a hand to her face, his warm palm gently cradling her abused cheek. "You really are beautiful."

She wished he'd stop saying that. It left her without anything to say in return... especially tonight, when she harbored no illusions about how she must look. "I—"

His fingers moved in her hair and the heavy, dark mass fell around her shoulders, the pins deftly removed. Seth seemed to be very good at things like that—too good, actually. "You—"

His mouth brushed hers. Lightly. Barely hard enough to feel. And yet she felt the contact all the way to her bare toes.

She'd forgotten what she was going to say. She stared up at him, speechless. He smiled and kissed her again. And this time he stayed long enough for her to respond.

Somehow her arms found their way around his neck, her fingers into his thick, sandy hair. For the second time that day, she found herself pressed against a man's body, but this time she knew she was in no physical danger. Her heart, however, was a different matter.

In some ways, she was far more vulnerable to Seth than she had been with the vicious Frank Holder.

He kissed her again. And again. His arms were strong around her, but he kept them locked around her waist, just holding her while he made love to her mouth. He made no move to carry the embraces further. Rachel knew he wouldn't resist if she backed away from him. Maybe it was that knowledge that kept her right where she was.

It was so quiet in the house. So still. She could hear her own pulse pounding in her ears. She thought she could even hear Seth's heart beating rapidly against her chest. She closed her eyes and parted her lips, an invitation he accepted eagerly.

Her arms tightened around his neck. In automatic response, he held her more firmly, his arms lifting her against his chest. She stood on tiptoe, straining against him, savoring every point of contact between them. Still flushed and damp from her bath, wrapped in her fuzzy robe, she felt soft and feminine in contrast to his strong, muscular body. Despite her deeply ingrained belief in their mental and social equality, she found those physical differences deliciously exciting.

As she'd discovered only hours earlier, a man's strength could be terrifying when turned against her. She realized now how wonderful it could be when the man was as tender, as considerate and as caring as Seth was being with her. She'd needed this, she thought dazedly, to help her push aside those lingering fears for good. And she suddenly needed to tell him so.

"Thank you," she whispered, her lips close to his ear, her cheek pressed to his.

"For what?" His voice was endearingly unsteady.

"For coming to my rescue this afternoon. For being here with me now."

His hands moved against her back in slow, easy strokes that soothed even as they aroused. "You're welcome," he murmured. "Though I wasn't expecting to come to anyone's rescue when I showed up at your office. I was there to apologize to you for being so impatient with you yesterday when you had to work late. I was being selfish, and I wanted to tell you I was sorry."

"Apology accepted," she mumbled, lost in the faint, masculine scent of spicy after-shave.

"As for being with you now—don't you know there's nowhere else on earth I'd rather be?"

She drew back just enough to look at him. His beautiful green eyes were utterly sincere.

He wanted her. She wanted him. At that moment, it suddenly seemed so clear, so simple. "Seth," she whispered, and brought his mouth back to hers.

He stiffened for just a moment, as though uncertain of her meaning. And then he gathered her hungrily against him and wholeheartedly accepted everything she was offering.

The belt she'd knotted so tightly loosened at his touch. Her robe slipped from her shoulders and slithered unnoticed to lie at their feet. Seth kissed the bruises on her forearms, and then knelt to press gentle, fleeting kisses to the marks on her ribs and hip. His mouth moved across her tummy and up her torso, his hands sliding slowly up and around her thighs.

Rachel gripped his shoulders through the fabric of his pale blue shirt, steadying herself when her knees threatened to buckle. The uncomfortable image of stretch marks and other physical flaws raced through her mind, but then Seth's mouth moved against her breasts and all thought fled.

She was breathing in sharp, ragged pants by the time he finally threw off his own clothing and lowered her to the bed, his own breathing labored. He fumbled for a moment with his slacks, then tossed them aside, and Rachel knew that he was still protecting her, this time from the consequences of her own choice. A moment later, he came to her, covering her restless, yearning body with his own.

Incapable of coherent speech, she gasped when he finally, carefully entered her. He moved slowly at first, giving her time to adjust, painstakingly considerate of her bruises. But Rachel soon urged him on with eager, impatient hands. She didn't want to be pampered, coddled like some fragile doll. She wanted him to make love to her without holding anything back.

She was with him completely as they raced toward fulfillment. She tumbled into the madness first, shuddering with spasms of sensation so intense she cried out. She was dimly aware that Seth wasn't far behind her. She gripped him tightly when his perspiration-sheened body grew rigid, his head thrown back, his eyes closed. And when he finally collapsed against her with a deep groan of satisfaction, she cradled him against her breasts, her lips against his damp hair, her legs wrapped snugly with his.

They lay that way for a very long time, each drawing strength from the other, seeking—and finding—unspoken reassurance that the extraordinary experience had been fully shared.

Lace-draped French doors led from Rachel's bedroom to a tiny balcony that overlooked her backyard. Wrapped in her chenille robe, she stood on that balcony sometime after midnight and let her eyes drift from the misty half-moon that seemed to hang so low above her to the heavily shadowed silhouette of the swing set she and Seth had assembled for her children. Though the October days were still warm enough, the nights were growing longer and cooler. There was just enough nip in the fresh, clear air to make her draw the collar of her bathrobe more snugly around her throat.

Seth had been soundly asleep when she'd slipped out of the bed. She'd been very careful not to disturb him. She was trying to deal with her feelings about what had passed between them earlier. She was still feeling rather stunned by the intensity of the experience.

She was aware of a faint, nagging sense of guilt. She knew Ray wouldn't have wanted her to live like a nun for the rest of her life. He had always wanted her to be happy, and would have been the first to encourage her to go on with her life. But still she felt a bit disloyal, especially when she silently, rather sadly acknowledged that what she'd experienced with Seth had been different, more shattering than anything she'd ever known before. Even with Ray.

Two bare, tanned arms circled her from behind, and she was drawn back against a warm, hard body. "What are you doing out here?" Seth asked in a deep voice, his cheek resting against her hair.

"Just enjoying the peacefulness," she said, keeping her own voice low. "No sirens wailing or dogs barking, for a change. It's nice."

"Your kids should have a dog," Seth said unexpectedly. "Aaron would probably like one."

"Dogs are too much trouble. They dig holes and poop in the yard, and always need to be bathed and dipped and fed and taken to the vet. I'm not at all sure they're worth it."

Seth chuckled, his chest vibrating against her back. "They're no more trouble than a couple of kids. And they don't talk back."

"True. But kids are eventually supposed to reach a point where they're self-sufficient. Dogs don't."

"Always an argument for everything," he said with an exaggerated sigh.

She smiled and rested her hands over his crossed wrists. "I try."

He held her in silence for a moment. She could sense that he was wearing nothing but his jeans. "You must be getting chilled," she said, snuggling more deeply into his arms.

"No. Are you?"

"Not yet."

"It'll be winter soon," he said, looking up at the clear, starry sky.

"Yes." She sighed, and hers wasn't feigned.

"You don't like winter?"

"I used to. Now I dread it."

"Why?"

She took a deep breath and recited, "Dead batteries. Frozen and broken fuel lines, air lines, brake lines, hydraulic hoses. Icy roads and parking lots. Drivers taking reckless chances with their safety and their equipment to run their routes in spite of the weather. Customers complaining even when we can't safely get to their containers. Frozen Dumpster lids. Frozen truck lids. And there's always the danger that vagrants are sleeping in the Dumpsters for warmth, though we haven't actually encountered that problem yet. And then there's—"

"Okay, I get the picture," Seth interrupted her hastily. "What about the good things about winter?"

She made a rueful face. "Sometimes it's easier to prepare for the bad things than to anticipate the good ones," she said, and she wondered if Seth was aware that she was no longer talking entirely about her business.

He had always seemed to be very perceptive where she was concerned. He turned her to face him, his face grave in the moonlight. "Just because bad things have happened to you in the past doesn't mean you should give up hoping for the best."

"I'm . . . not used to taking risks, Seth," she told him, choosing her words very carefully. "I've always needed to know where I was going, and exactly how I intended to get there. I'm a planner, a list maker. I'm at my best when it comes to taking care of other people's needs. When it comes to my own . . ." She let the words trail into a little shrug.

He heard her out, but he was smiling, his hand cradling her still-sore face. "Have you ever considered letting someone help you with your own needs?"

"I'm not accustomed to depending on other people. I've always taken care of myself," she informed him. Even with Ray, she had never been dependent, she mused. In fact, there were people who'd said that Ray was sometimes a bit too dependent on *her* competence, not that she'd ever allowed those people to bother her. She'd always been content with what she'd had with Ray.

The problem was, she wasn't so sure she would be content with such a quiet, carefully planned and orchestrated relationship with Seth.

"I know you take care of yourself, all too well," Seth assured her dryly. "But has it ever occurred to you that someone who cares about you, someone who loves you, would want to take care of you at times? Would want very much to feel needed by you?"

Even that cautious mention of the word "love" made Rachel's breath catch. She had to swallow before she could whisper, "I'm not sure I want to need anyone, Seth. If I should start needing someone, and then that person went away, what would I do then?"

He kissed her right temple, and his lips moved softly against her skin. "I can't imagine that someone who loves you would ever leave you for any reason short of death."

She sighed. "That's reason enough to be afraid, as I've learned from experience."

"I can't—no one can promise you that he won't die, Rachel." Seth was careful to keep the conversation hypothetically phrased, so she wouldn't feel it necessary to commit herself to anything just yet. "It's something you have to know will happen to everyone eventually. The philosophers say we should live every day as though it is our last. Savor every moment, treasure every smile, seize every opportunity for happiness and fulfillment. It took me a long time to start living that way, and now I have no regrets."

"That sounds like a very irresponsible way to live. Live for today and let tomorrow take care of itself."

Seth shrugged. "It's possible to accept responsibility without becoming a slave to it, Rachel. Planning and list making and organizing are all necessary at times, but not when they overshadow all the fun and adventure in life."

Which brought them back to where they'd started. Rachel was cautious, Seth impulsive. He considered her a slave to responsibility; she worried that his emotions would change as rapidly as his moods. She had to worry about how their actions would affect her children; Seth embraced her children with the same enthusiasm with which he'd pursued her, even though he and Rachel hadn't come to any agreement about where their relationship was headed. He wanted to be needed; she was desperately afraid to need.

Did those differences leave them any common ground other than the physical attraction she had never been able to deny?

Seth brushed a breeze-tossed strand of hair away from her eyes. "Such a serious expression," he said, placing a kiss on her forehead. "It's getting late, and cooler. Come inside, sweetheart, before you get chilled."

He was taking care of her again, even though she was perfectly capable of deciding whether she was too cool. Yet, again, she found that she couldn't resent his consideration for her welfare. Just for tonight, it was rather nice to be pampered. Maybe a bit too nice.

Pushing her worries to the back of her mind, she stepped through the French doors into the bedroom. Into Seth's waiting arms.

Chapter Twelve

Seth woke in bed alone again the next morning. He glanced automatically toward the balcony where he'd found Rachel during the night, but the French doors were closed. He assumed she was downstairs, probably in the kitchen. Neither of them had eaten dinner the night before. He didn't know if Rachel was hungry yet, but he was starving.

He yawned, stretched and swung his legs over the side of the bed. All in all, it had been one hell of a night, he thought ruefully. From the most exquisite lovemaking he'd ever experienced to one of the strangest middle-of-the-night conversations he'd ever become involved in; he should know by now that there was no guessing what Rachel would do, despite her claims to predictability and reliability.

As he stood, he glanced at the nightstand beside the bed. The cup of tea he'd brought her last night was still there, still untouched, long grown cold. A clock radio told him

it was just after eight o'clock. A framed photograph lay on
its face on the nightstand. It had been standing last night,
he remembered with a sudden frown. Rachel must have set
it down.

He lifted the frame and studied the smiling face of the
man in the photograph. Ray Evans. He'd had a pleasant
smile. Had probably been one hell of a nice guy, Seth
thought with a scowl.

Why had Rachel turned the photo facedown this morning? Had she been feeling a bit guilty as she'd climbed
nude from the bed she'd once shared with Ray? The same
bed in which Seth had spent such an exhilarating night? He
was fully aware that he was the first man to have slept in
that bed since her husband had died.

Seth swallowed as the eyes in the photograph seemed to
study his face. "I'm not going to hurt her," he sheepishly
heard himself mutter aloud. "I don't want to replace you
for Rachel or your children. I only want to make my own
place in their future."

He hoped Ray would have approved.

He set the photo back into its original, upright position
and stepped into his jeans. Then, carrying the full teacup
with him, he went off in search of Rachel, telling himself
that it was ridiculous to imagine that worried eyes were
watching him leave the bedroom.

As he'd expected, he found Rachel in the kitchen. She
was wearing an oversize black turtleneck sweater and
jeans. She had pinned her hair up again. If she'd been trying to look a bit distant this morning, she'd succeeded.

A pot of coffee brewed on the counter. Rachel was
busily stirring something in a large mixing bowl. Was she
planning to feed him and send him on his way? If so, she
could forget it. Cody wasn't bringing the kids home until
midafternoon, and Seth intended to stay for a while.

"Good morning," he said, and dumped the cold tea into
the sink. "You never got around to drinking your tea last

night," he added unnecessarily. Maybe just to remind her of exactly what had distracted her from her tea.

"Good morning. You must be hungry. I hope you like waffles." Rachel spoke brightly, her bland smile making it clear that she wasn't ready to discuss last night.

"I love waffles," he assured her. "What can I do to help?"

"Nothing. They're almost ready. Pour yourself some coffee and have a seat at the table."

She was talking to him as if he were one of her kids. Seth thought about remaining on his feet out of pure obstinacy, but decided if he did that, he'd be *acting* like one of her kids. He filled a coffee mug for himself, and another for her.

The kitchen table was already set for two. The morning paper rested beside one of the plates. Seth pushed it aside, uninterested in anything that wasn't taking place in Rachel's kitchen. Deciding to let her make the next overture, he sipped his coffee and watched her while she cooked the waffles.

The silence in the room must have bothered her. She cleared her throat and asked, "Did you sleep well?"

"For the most part. Did you?"

"Yes, thank you."

She was lying. Seth could tell by looking at her heavy-lidded eyes that she hadn't slept particularly well at all. Had she lain awake worrying about the major step forward they'd taken in their relationship? About his expectations for the future? Had she thought about her late husband? Even worse, had she felt any regrets?

Rachel slid a well-filled plate in front of Seth and set another at the other place. Seth waited until her hands were free, then caught her wrist and tugged. She blinked in surprise when she found herself suddenly sitting on his knee. He kissed her before she had a chance to comment. He was pleased when her mouth automatically softened beneath his, when her lips moved to return the kiss.

"Good morning," he said, smiling when he finally lifted his head.

Rachel's answering smile was a bit tremulous. "I thought we'd already said that."

"This way is much nicer," he assured her, brushing another kiss across her lips. And then he lifted a hand to touch the colorful bruise on the right side of her face. "Does it hurt?"

"It's sore," she answered honestly. "But not too badly."

"And the other bruises?"

"The same."

He stroked his thumb slowly across her lower lip, his gaze focused on her unpainted mouth. "Any other discomfort this morning? From, er, I mean, I know it's been a long time for you..."

Her cheeks pinkened beneath the bruises. "No, I'm—I'm fine." She sounded embarrassed by the question.

"No regrets?" He kept his voice light, his gaze on her mouth. He didn't want her to see quite how important her answer was to him.

Her lips trembled a moment, but her voice was steady. "No. No regrets."

He looked up, meeting her eyes, searching for equivocations. He found none. He let out a small breath of relief. "I'm glad," he told her simply.

She held his gaze for another moment, then glanced away. "Your waffles are getting cold."

He didn't try to hold her when she slipped off his knee. He was satisfied with what he'd accomplished while she'd been there.

"Do you want syrup, honey, powdered sugar or strawberries to top your waffles?" she asked, opening the refrigerator door.

He chuckled at the extent of the choices. "I'd call this a full-service place."

She laughed softly and threw him a teasing glance over her shoulder. "You just remember that when it's time to leave a tip."

"You can count on it," he promised her gruffly. God, he loved it when she laughed with him. Her whole face brightened with her smiles.

There was no longer any doubt in his mind that he loved her. Or that she had the power to break his heart.

"The strawberries sound good," he said, refusing to dwell on any negative thoughts during this rare time alone with Rachel.

He made a special effort to keep her smiling during breakfast, and was quite proud of his results. As long as he kept her thoughts off the recent developments between the two of them, Rachel was easy enough to amuse. She loved talking about her children, and she soon had him chuckling with funny stories about things one or the other had said or done.

Seth didn't mind hearing about her children. Far from it, he thought indulgently; he was crazy about her kids. He had already accepted their place in his future. He'd even begun to wonder if Rachel might be interested in having another one or two. It might be nice.

Not that he'd mind if she didn't want more children. Paige and Aaron were great kids, and he'd be proud to claim them, once he convinced their mother that the four of them belonged together.

He didn't even attempt to share those particular thoughts with Rachel. He was well aware that her smile would vanish in an instant if he started talking about the possibility of making babies with her. She still couldn't even bring herself to talk about last night without panic.

The telephone started ringing almost immediately after they'd finished their breakfast. Seth hadn't realized Rachel knew quite so many people in town, though he supposed he should have. She'd lived there almost all her life, after all, and was an established member of the business community. The Percy grapevine had been very active that morning. Everyone wanted to know if it was true that Rachel had been attacked by a former employee at her place of business.

"You have to admit some of the stories have been interesting," Rachel said wearily, after about the twentieth call. "The last rumor had it that I shot and killed Holder as he was advancing on me with a bowie knife. I don't know what made anyone think I actually keep a gun at my office."

"Rachel, you're worn-out," Seth scolded gently, studying the smudges beneath her eyes. "Why don't you put the answering machine on and get some rest?"

She shook her head. "I'm afraid one of my friends will be worried if I don't answer. I'm perfectly capable of answering the phone, Seth."

"Then you take a nap and I'll handle the calls."

She rolled her eyes at that. "And wouldn't *that* start the rumors flying!"

"I don't care."

"I do."

He sighed.

The doorbell chimed just as the telephone rang yet again. Rachel looked torn.

"I'll get the door, you answer the phone," Seth said, nudging her toward the den extension.

She bit her lip but reached for the phone when it rang again. Seth opened the door without checking to see who was on the other side.

Celia Carson smiled when she saw him. "I rather expected to find you here," she commented. "Did you stay the night?"

He didn't quite know how to answer. What would Rachel want him to say?

Celia laughed. "Never mind. I think you've already given me an answer. And I have to tell you I'm delighted."

"Your sister's going to kill me," he muttered resignedly, standing aside to let Celia in.

"Don't worry about it. She talks a tough game, but she's really a marshmallow," Celia assured him rather obscurely. "Oh, there you are," she added when Rachel appeared. "What—"

She suddenly gasped. "Oh, Rachel. Your poor face," she wailed, clutching her sister's arm. "Oh, I could kill that man!"

Seth shook his head. Rachel's siblings apparently harbored surprisingly violent impulses behind those laughing blue eyes. "You're going to have to get in line behind your brother," he told her. "And probably some guy named Vinnie."

Celia and Rachel both looked at him blankly. "Vinnie?" Rachel repeated.

"Cody says Adam will probably hire a Vinnie to take care of Holder for you," Seth explained.

Rachel groaned. "I do *not* want Adam told about this," she said fiercely. "If he finds out—"

Celia cleared her throat and tried to look innocent.

Rachel glared at her younger sister. "You've already told him, haven't you?"

"I called him this morning, right after I talked to Mom and Dad and Gran. I didn't want them to hear about it from a stranger or in the newspaper or something," Celia answered hastily. "Mom would have been hysterical if I hadn't called to assure her that you're all right. And you know how Adam gets."

"Yes, I know how he gets. That's why I didn't want him to know," Rachel said crossly. "He'll probably try to have

Holder executed or something. And I wouldn't be surprised if he tries to have me hospitalized for my bruises."

Celia giggled. "Maybe he'll offer to 'do your face' for you. You know, a little nip here, a little tuck there..." She bit back the rest when Rachel only glared at her again.

"I take it Adam's a bit overprotective of his family," Seth commented, remembering what Cody had said the night before.

"You can say that again," Celia said fervently. "And he fully expects everyone to do what he says when he starts giving orders. It's the way he was raised, I guess. His father died when he was very young, and his mother is a—"

"Celia," Rachel warned quickly.

"I was only going to say that his mother is practically a helpless invalid," Celia retorted. And then she made a face. "Or at least, she pretends that she is. Really, she's just lazy and overdemanding and I can't imagine why Adam continues to put up with her, myself, but—"

"Celia, would you like a cup of coffee or something?" Rachel interjected determinedly, making Seth smile at her exasperated expression.

Celia nodded. "Yeah, a soda sounds good. I'll get it. You sit down and rest. You probably didn't get much sleep last night," she added over her shoulder.

Rachel immediately turned on Seth. "What did she mean by *that?*" she demanded.

"I haven't the faintest idea," he soothed her. "To be honest, I'm never quite sure what Celia means."

Looking only slightly mollified, Rachel nodded. "A common enough problem," she agreed. "You didn't tell her that you—that we...er..."

"I didn't tell her anything," Seth replied. He didn't add that Celia had formed her own, quite accurate conclusions. He was sure Rachel would find that out soon enough.

"The kids were really good last night, Rach. And they were looking forward to seeing the movie with Cody. He said he'd have them home at around three," Celia said as she rejoined them with a diet soda can clasped loosely in one hand.

Celia was wearing a green knit sweater that came almost to her knees, along with a pair of black stirrup pants and several long strands of colored beads. Her near-black hair fell in a shaggy mane to her shoulders, not quite hiding the huge earrings that dangled against her neck, and her blue eyes were dramatically enhanced with makeup. Seth thought again of how different Rachel and her sister were, and yet the bond between them was obviously a strong one.

"Did the children ask why they were spending the night with you? What did you tell them?" Rachel asked Celia.

"I told them you'd had a little trouble at the office," Celia reassured her. "I didn't give them any details, and that seemed to be enough to satisfy them. You can tell them whatever you want them to know when Cody brings them home."

"I'll have to tell them the truth, of course. Or at least part of it. The way the rumors are flying around town, they'll probably hear it from their friends at school if not from me."

"They'd want to know what happened to your face, anyway," Seth noted.

Rachel sighed. "I know. I'll think of some way to tell them about it without frightening them."

"They can handle it, Rach," Celia insisted. "They're very mature for their ages. They were really cute at the mall last night."

"The mall?" Rachel repeated.

"Yeah. I took them shopping. Well, they had to have something to sleep in." Celia defended herself quickly before Rachel could chide her. "And you couldn't expect them to wear the same clothes two days in a row."

"I hope you didn't overdo it," Rachel said fretfully.

"Just pajamas and one casual outfit each," Celia informed. "And new toothbrushes, of course. It was really fun. You know how I love shopping for your kids."

"You just love to shop," Rachel retorted, though she was smiling now.

Celia had to agree. She looked at Seth with a smile. "You should've seen Aaron choosing his new clothes. As much thought as he put into it, you'd have thought he would be modeling them for the cover of *GQ*."

"A little clotheshorse, eh?" Seth grinned. He liked sharp-looking clothes, himself. Nice to know he and the kid had a few things in common besides a mutual respect for video games.

"Yeah. And he hates the color yellow with a passion. Even a yellow thread makes him shudder."

Seth laughed. Rachel smiled in response to Celia's teasing about her son's pronounced tastes. Seth was glad she was smiling again. Now if only Celia didn't say anything to—

"Yes, I really enjoyed having the kids stay over," Celia commented cheerfully. "Tell me, Rachel, did you do anything special last night? I would hate to think you wasted a whole night's worth of free baby-sitting."

Rachel's face flamed. Her smile disintegrated.

His own cheeks warm, Seth could willingly have spanked Celia Carson. Maybe that was something that should have been done more often in her childhood, he mused half-seriously.

Celia was laughing at their expressions. She patted Rachel's arm. "I'm sorry. I couldn't resist teasing you. Especially after all the lectures I've had about Damien Alexander during the past few months," she added archly.

Seth's eyebrow rose. Damien Alexander? Could Celia possibly be talking about the racy hotelier who so often made the scandal sheets with his high-rolling life-style?

"That is an entirely different situation," Rachel insisted. "You and Damien are—and Seth and I aren't—"

Both Celia and Seth waited with interest for Rachel to untangle the sentence.

Seth and I aren't...what? he wanted to ask. Lovers? Oh, yes, we are. Serious? One of us most definitely is. What were you going to say, Rachel?

But whatever it was, Rachel bit the words back, shook her head and lifted her chin. "There's the phone again," she said when the instrument gave another demanding buzz. "I'll get it. Seth, there's no need for you to hang around now if you have other things to do this morning. Celia can give me a hand around here."

"I'll get the phone," Celia said quickly, maybe in response to Seth's suddenly narrowed eyes. "You two go ahead and, um, talk."

"Was that intended as a dismissal?" Seth asked the moment Celia left the room to take the call in the kitchen.

Rachel crossed her arms at her waist and rubbed her forearms through her thick sweater. "Of course not," she said, though she didn't quite meet his eyes. "I just didn't want you to feel obligated to hang around when I know there must be things you need to do."

"I haven't felt obligated to hang around," Seth repeated clearly. "I've been here because I wanted to be with you. And because I thought you were enjoying our time together, as well."

She moistened her lips but still didn't look at him. "Seth, I—"

He waited.

She drew a deep breath. What was she going to say that seemed to take such courage?

"Seth," she began again. "I think we should slow down."

Slow down? "I beg your pardon?" he asked politely.

She twisted her hands more tightly into the sleeves of her sweater. "We...um...moved too quickly last night. It wasn't anyone's fault, really, just a combination of a lot of things, but I'm not ready...it isn't time... *I* don't have time for a, er, an affair...or anything—"

He'd lost all sympathy for her awkward embarrassment, as well as any patience he might have managed earlier. He took a step forward and caught her forearms in his own hands, pulling her toward him with a little jerk. His face was very close to hers when he said, "Make time."

"But—"

"This isn't an affair, Rachel. This is a courtship. And you might as well accept that it isn't going to progress exactly according to your careful time schedule. There are two of us involved here, in case you haven't noticed."

"But—"

"I've been pretty damned patient until now. I haven't pushed you—well, not as much as I wanted to—and I've tried to understand your fears and reservations. But last night changed things, Rachel. Last night we made a commitment, whether you want to admit it or not. And unless you can look me in the eye right now and tell me you aren't the least interested in ever making love with me again, I'm holding you to that commitment."

"But, Seth, I—"

He was on a roll, his emotions too raw, too urgent to permit argument. "I won't expect you to flaunt our relationship in front of your family, your children or your friends. I respect your reputation and your responsibilities. But we *have* a relationship, and it's about time you started admitting it. You can begin by admitting it to yourself."

"Seth, you—"

He smothered whatever she would have said beneath a firm I-think-I've-made-myself-clear kiss. And then he released her as abruptly as he'd taken hold of her.

"I'll leave now and let you think about what I've said," he announced, deliberately cool. "If you're ready to get on with this thing without all these hot-and-cold games, you know where to find me."

She planted her fists on her hips, spread her feet and took a deep breath, obviously ready to tear into him with all the temper now sparking in her shadowed dark eyes. Seth didn't give her a chance. Ignoring her sputtering, he headed for the front door, jerked it open and moved to step through it. He paused on the threshold to look back over his shoulder.

Taking one last, calculated risk, he said, "And by the way, Rachel. I love you."

He didn't take another complete breath until he was in his car and headed toward his own home. He spent most of that short trip castigating himself for being an impulsive fool and probably ruining everything.

Damn, but this love business was enough to make a man beat his head against a wall!

Her mouth open, Rachel stared blankly at her front door, which had just closed so sharply behind Seth. Her fists fell limply to her sides. Had he just said—?

Suddenly aware that she wasn't alone, she looked toward the doorway to the kitchen and found Celia standing there looking as bemused as Rachel felt. Celia, too, was staring at the front door. How much of that bizarre exchange had she overheard?

Celia slowly turned her wide eyes in Rachel's direction. Her face was alight with her amusement when she shook her head. "Wow," she said. "Now *that* was a declaration of intent if I've ever heard one."

Rachel started to say something, but had to stop to clear her throat. "Could we maybe talk about something else for a while?" she asked weakly.

Celia laughed and linked her arm through Rachel's. "My poor, shell-shocked big sister. You really have had a trying couple of days, haven't you? Let's see what we can do about that face of yours before the kids come home."

Chapter Thirteen

"Why are we coming to Seth's office, Mama?" Aaron asked, looking with interest through the side window of their car on the following Thursday afternoon.

Rachel wasn't exactly sure how to answer. It had been five days since she'd seen Seth. During that time, he hadn't called, hadn't dropped by. As he'd promised—or warned—he was leaving the next move to her.

And by the way, Rachel. I love you.

She gulped, and tightened her hands around the steering wheel as she guided her car into the parking lot of his law office. Maybe he wouldn't be in, she thought. Maybe it would be better if she waited a day or two for this.

But his black sports car was parked in front of the building, next to a tiny economy car. She glanced at her watch, noting that it was almost five-thirty. Was Seth's secretary still here, or did the little car belong to a client?

Would Rachel be interrupting something important if she went in now?

She should have called. The only reason she hadn't was because she hadn't known she was coming until she'd found herself driving toward his office instead of her home after picking the children up at their day-care center.

"Mama?" Aaron said as Rachel parked the car and then just sat behind the wheel, staring at the building. "Aren't we going in? I want to see the fish."

"I've missed Seth," Paige said from the back seat. "We haven't seen him in a long time. Do you think he could have dinner with us tonight, Mama?"

Rachel moistened her lips. "Maybe we'd better just go on home. Seth may be busy."

Two disappointed protests greeted that suggestion. Just as Rachel was about to start the car again, the door to Seth's office opened and a young, very pregnant woman walked outside, toward the other car.

Rachel decided the woman must be Seth's secretary, Maddie. She remembered now that he'd told her she was pregnant.

Maddie noticed Rachel's car and approached the driver's window, which Rachel lowered, feeling rather embarrassed that she'd been caught staring at Seth's office. "I'm Mr. Fletcher's secretary," she said, leaning slightly toward the window with a curious smile. "May I help you with something?"

"Actually, the children and I dropped by to see Seth, if he isn't busy," Rachel explained. "If he is, we won't bother him."

Maddie shook her curly head, her smile deepening. "You must be Rachel Evans."

Rachel wasn't even sure she wanted to know how Maddie had guessed that. "Yes, I am," she admitted.

"Just go on in. Seth was cleaning his desk a minute ago, and the mess it was in, it's going to take him a while. He'll probably welcome the distraction."

"Thank you," Rachel told her, feeling well trapped now. Why oh, why, had she given in to impulse by coming here? She should have known better. Every time she gave in to her impulses, rather than making specific plans, something went awry. Impulsive behavior just seemed better suited to others, like Celia. And Cody. And Seth, darn it.

Aaron already had his hand on his door handle. Rachel doubted that Seth would have been flattered by Aaron's eagerness, since it could be attributed as much to a fascination with the aquarium as a fondness for Seth.

Maddie drove away just as Rachel and her children reached the outer door to Seth's office. Once again, Rachel was aware of a sudden, cowardly urge to run before Seth spotted them, but she reminded herself that her children would probably think she'd lost her mind if she did that. She'd actually started to wonder about that, herself.

Aaron headed straight for the aquarium when they entered Seth's reception area. Rachel asked Paige to join him. "Just give me a minute to speak to Seth alone," she added in a low voice.

Paige looked curious, but obediently moved to stand beside her brother in front of the colorfully decorated tank.

Rachel tapped lightly on Seth's closed door. His voice bade her to enter. She opened the door.

"What's wrong, Maddie?" Seth asked without looking up from the pile of paperwork he was sorting on his wildly littered desk. "Forget something?"

"Maddie just left," Rachel said.

Seth's head came up with an almost comical snap. "Rachel!"

"Is this a bad time?" she asked anxiously, poised to run. "I can—"

"No, come in," he said quickly, shoving papers recklessly aside and rounding the end of his desk. "What are you doing here? Is something wrong?"

"No, nothing's wrong." Glancing over her shoulder to make sure the children were still occupied with the aquarium, Rachel pushed the door almost closed to give her and Seth the illusion of privacy. She left a one-inch opening so she could hear the children, but she didn't feel free to talk if they could see her.

Seth stopped a few inches in front of her, his green eyes studying her face intently. "Your face looks much better."

She resisted an impulse to touch her still slightly bruised cheek. "Thanks. It feels better."

"I hear Holder's going to do some time. Did you know that he'd been given a suspended sentence for beating his girlfriend a couple of years ago? That will be added to the penalty for what he did to you."

"Leon told me about it," Rachel agreed. "I didn't even know Frank had a record. He lied on his job application, and I'm afraid when I hired him I was still pretty new at managing the business. I didn't think to run an extensive reference check."

"You do so now, I hope."

"Yes, as much as possible."

"Good. It never hurts to take extra precautions."

Rachel smiled. "That sounds more like something I would have said than you."

He chuckled. "Yeah. I guess you're starting to corrupt me. I'm even trying to get my office organized," he added with a rueful nod toward his desk. "Not that I'm making much headway at it."

"Is there anything I can do to help?" she asked.

He shook his head. "Thanks, but I'll manage somehow."

"Well." She twisted her hands in front of her, very much aware that he hadn't even kissed her yet. And that she wanted very much for him to do so. Soon.

Oh, my, he looked wonderful, she thought with a silent sigh, surreptitiously eyeing him from beneath her lashes. He was wearing a beautifully knit sweater in shades of plum and green, paired with dusky gray slacks. His hair was trimmed, but still fell onto his forehead in that manner she found so endearing. His emerald eyes were bright, questioning, much too perceptive as they remained steadily on her face.

She suddenly felt the silence like an awkward presence standing between them. "The children are in the other room," she said, though he probably already knew. "Aaron wanted to watch the fish."

"He can feed them before you leave. I haven't done so yet today."

"He'll like that. Um... Paige wanted me to ask if you'd like to have dinner with us."

The corners of his mouth twitched, but he didn't smile. Rachel had the impression he was making an effort not to. "Did she?"

Rachel nodded. If he was daring to stand there and laugh at her—

"And what do you want, Rachel?" Seth asked quietly, never taking his gaze away from her face.

You, she thought immediately, shockingly. "I think it would be nice if you join us for dinner," she murmured instead, trying not to think of those nights she'd lain awake remembering their lovemaking. Aching for more.

Seth shook his head. "That isn't what I asked. I asked what you want, Rachel."

She frowned at him. "I want you to join us for dinner," she muttered grudgingly.

"Why?"

"Don't push your luck, Fletcher."

He couldn't hold back the smile this time. He grinned. "Why, Rachel?"

She exhaled loudly. "Because I've missed you, damn it."

"That's all I wanted to hear—for now," he assured her, and took her into his arms.

The kiss was all the more powerful for being so long delayed. Rachel wrapped her arms around his neck and kissed him back with a hunger that had been building for almost a week. She'd tried to ignore it. Tried to deny it. Tried to convince herself that she didn't need him, or the problems he would inevitably cause her. But she'd finally conceded defeat. She'd missed Seth desperately during this past week. His kisses. His smiles. Him.

"Mama?" Aaron pushed open the door, then tilted his head quizzically. "Why are you kissing Seth?"

Rachel blushed to the roots of her hair. Seth laughed and hugged her before letting her go. "Because kissing is nice," he answered lightly.

From the face Aaron made, Seth could just as well have said that eating worms was nice. "Yuck," the child pronounced clearly. "I wouldn't kiss a girl. Except my mama, of course," he added.

"I wouldn't kiss any other girl, either," Seth said.

Rachel thought about hitting him, just to shake some of that smugness out of his expression. Only her frequent lectures to the children about not hitting other people held her back.

"You'd kiss me, wouldn't you, Seth?" Paige asked flirtatiously, appearing in the doorway behind her brother in time to hear the exchange.

Seth swooped on Paige with a smacking kiss on the cheek. "You bet I would, sweetheart. And thank you for asking me to dinner," he added, touching the tip-tilted end of her nose with an affectionate finger. "I accept."

"Really? Cool!"

She might as well admit it, Rachel thought resignedly. Her kids were nuts about the guy.

She knew just how they felt.

Seth was ecstatic. Rachel had come to him! And just when he'd finally decided he was going to have to go after her.

He felt like punching the air and cheering. He settled for grinning like an idiot.

It didn't take him long to finish clearing his desk. He simply opened the only empty drawer and swept an arm across the surface, dumping everything into a cluttered pile in the drawer. He surveyed the now-clean desk in satisfaction; Rachel looked at him with the horror of someone for whom filing was a religion. She didn't comment, though it must have been difficult for her to resist.

"I'm ready to go now," Seth announced. "You guys choose a restaurant and I'll follow in my car. Tonight's my treat," he added, noting that the kids seemed to wholly approve of the plan.

"We could go to my house," Rachel suggested. "I could cook for us."

The children frowned, and Seth shook his head. "I feel like taking you all out tonight. I want to show you off."

Rachel automatically smoothed the hem of her rose-colored sweater over her matching wool slacks and then glanced toward the children. Seth knew she was checking the damage they'd done to their appearances since she'd sent them off to school. He could have told her that the kids looked fine, as she did, but he guessed moms were supposed to do that sort of thing before taking their off-spring out in public.

He was really going to like this family thing, he decided.

He had one hand at Rachel's waist and another on Aaron's shoulder as he ushered his family-for-the-evening through the reception area and toward the outside door. They had almost reached it when it suddenly opened.

It seemed to be his day for unexpected visitors, Seth thought as he stared at the man who stepped through the doorway. Too bad this one wasn't as pleasant a surprise as the last one had been. "Dad," he said without a great deal of enthusiasm. "What are you doing here?"

The gray-haired man with Seth's green eyes glanced first at Rachel and the children, and his attention lingered for a noticeable moment on Seth's hand at Rachel's waist. Intimidated by the man's stern manner, the children shifted closer, Paige to her mother, Aaron peeking out from behind Seth's leg. Arthur Fletcher's brow lifted a quarter of an inch as he turned his gaze to his son. "Seth," he said by way of greeting. "Were you leaving?"

Seth knew his father was pointing out that it wasn't six o'clock yet. Short of an emergency, Arthur Fletcher had never left his own office before six in his entire professional life. Just as he'd rarely missed a Saturday morning in the office—or Christmas Eve, or birthdays, or baseball game days, or school play days...

"Yes, as a matter of fact, I *am* leaving," Seth replied coolly, shoving the unpleasant memories aside. "Why are you here?"

Rachel stirred at Seth's side, looking rather startled by his cool manner toward his father. She didn't know, of course, quite how bitterly Seth and his father had parted six months ago. But Seth hadn't forgotten one cutting, hurtful word.

Arthur didn't look at all surprised by his son's chilly welcome. Seth knew it was because his father hadn't forgotten their parting, either. "I have to be in a courtroom in Harrison tomorrow morning," he explained. "Since I have to pass through here on the way, I thought I'd stop by and see your office."

He glanced around Seth's minimally furnished reception area, his attention lingering for a moment on the aquarium. Seth couldn't help picturing the plush mauve-and-silver reception area of the prestigious Fletcher Law Firm in downtown Little Rock.

Whatever Arthur's opinion of Seth's place of business, he kept it to himself. He turned to Rachel. "We're being rude, Seth," he said.

Seth nodded. "Rachel Evans, this is my father, Arthur Fletcher."

Rachel offered a hand, as composed and dignified as if greeting one of her customers. "Mr. Fletcher," she said. "It's very nice to meet you. These are my children, Paige and Aaron."

Arthur shook her hand and studied her assessingly. "You're a friend of Seth's?"

"A very good friend," Seth answered for her.

"I see."

Rachel shot Seth a look that subtly reproved him for his behavior, and then smiled at his father. "We were just going out for an early dinner, Mr. Fletcher. Would you like to join us?"

Seth somehow managed not to protest aloud. Aaron clung more tightly to his leg.

Arthur looked from Rachel, to Seth, then back again. "Yes, I believe I will join you. Thank you for asking."

Seth shouldn't have been surprised. His father had always seemed to delight in making Seth feel awkward and uncomfortable. Arthur would waste no opportunity during dinner to do so in front of Rachel.

"Rachel, you take the kids in your car," he instructed. "My father and I will follow you."

"There's no need—"

"This is the way I want to handle it, Dad," Seth contradicted curtly. "Rachel?"

She nodded and quickly ushered the children outside.

Arthur cast one last, quick glance around Seth's office. "Nice little place."

Seth didn't miss the frown Rachel directed over her shoulder when she overheard the condescending comment. Maybe now she knew exactly what she'd gotten them into by inviting Seth's father to dine with them, Seth thought.

"All right, Dad. Why are you really here?" Seth demanded the moment he and his father were in his car, Seth behind the wheel.

"I told you why I'm here," Arthur repeated patiently. "You are my son, Seth. Is it so surprising that I want to see where you work and live?"

"Six months ago, I got the impression that you didn't care whether you ever saw me again," Seth said coldly.

"You know that's not true."

Seth's reply was flat, expressionless. "No. I don't know it."

Arthur stared through the windshield ahead of him. "Then you're very much mistaken."

Seth turned right, following Rachel's car, not even particularly curious about where she was leading them. "How is Mother?"

"She's fine. Busy, of course."

"Of course," Seth repeated dryly. Being busy was a way of life for his family. Anything less was unacceptable behavior for a Fletcher.

"She told me that you haven't called her in a while."

"She's difficult to reach." *In more ways than one.*

"Yes." Arthur changed the subject. "Your practice is doing well?"

"Well enough." It could be better, of course, and he hoped it would be, eventually, but Seth saw no need to go into that. One of the things his father had predicted six months ago was that Seth would soon find himself in bankruptcy, should he try to go out on his own.

"This is a very small town, with several existing law firms. You couldn't possibly be making what you were earning with the family firm."

"Dad, just don't start, okay?"

"Fine," Arthur snapped, obviously annoyed. He crossed his arms and looked out the side window. After a moment, he asked, "Where are we going?"

"I don't know. I told Rachel to choose. You might as well be prepared that it won't be anything fancy. She'll pick someplace that's suitable for children."

Arthur nodded. "I assumed as much when I accepted her invitation."

"Why *did* you accept?" Seth couldn't resist asking. "I've never known you to be interested in dining with kids. God knows, you rarely did with us."

He was looking at his father when he spoke, so didn't miss the muscle that jerked in Arthur's jaw at the dig. Arthur let it go. "I wanted to get to know her," he said, instead. "I could tell from the way you acted with her that she is important to you."

Seth was surprised that his father knew him well enough to have interpreted his feelings for Rachel. Or were his feelings for her so obvious that even a stranger could read them? "I intend to marry her, as soon as she'll have me," he heard himself saying without pausing to think about it.

Arthur turned his head to look at Seth, apparently testing the sincerity of the words. "You're serious."

"Very."

"Have you asked her?"

"Not yet. We haven't been dating long. But I will ask her, when the time is right."

"She's divorced?"

"Widowed. Three years ago."

"And now she's looking for a father for her children?"

Seth didn't like that question. "No," he said shortly. "She's quite capable of raising her children alone. If she marries me, it will be because she loves me, not because I'm a convenient substitute for her late husband."

"Do you realize how difficult it will be, raising and supporting two stepchildren?"

"Of course. Not that I'll be supporting them entirely. Rachel runs her own business. And they're good kids. I'm looking forward to making them part of my family."

"Part of *our* family, you mean," Arthur reminded him.

Seth shrugged. "If you and Mother want to get to know them, that's fine. When—" He forced himself to stop and phrase the sentence more realistically. "If Rachel marries me, you will technically become their grandparents. If you choose to be a part of our lives, I would expect you to treat them exactly as you would any biological grandchildren you might have in the future."

"You sound as though you don't particularly care whether your mother and I are part of your future," Arthur complained.

Seth's fingers tightened spasmodically around the steering wheel. "I faced that possibility six months ago, when you ordered me out of your house."

"I was angry. And disappointed. You knew I would be when you announced that you were leaving the firm."

"Yes. But I'd still hoped that you might make an effort to understand why I had to do so."

Arthur remained silent as Seth followed Rachel's car into the parking lot of a family-style steak house. The place wasn't crowded yet, so they were able to park side by side, close to the door. Aaron jumped out of his car and immediately took Seth's hand again. Seth smiled down at the boy, thinking again that he would be very proud to claim Aaron as his son, regardless of whether Arthur ever accepted the boy as a grandchild.

Families were formed through love, he mused. Not bloodlines. It had just taken him a while to come to that realization.

Now all he had to do was convince Rachel.

Arthur's presence put certain constraints on the dinner. The children were on company behavior—quiet and shy. Rachel seemed a bit uncomfortable, which Seth supposed he could understand. After all, she must be aware that Arthur was sizing her up as a potential mate for his son.

Seth thought regretfully of how much fun they could be having had his father not shown up. But maybe it was time to get this out of the way so that he and Rachel could go on with their courtship, he decided finally.

"Seth told me you're a businesswoman," Arthur said to Rachel. "What sort of business are you in?"

"I own and operate a commercial sanitation trucking company," Rachel said. Seth heard the note of defensiveness that had crept into her voice.

Arthur frowned. "A trash-hauling company?"

"Yes," she answered without elaboration.

"Rachel employs three full-time and one part-time driver," Seth explained, feeling the need to assist her. "Her company is holding its own against several nationally owned companies that also operate in this area."

If Arthur made one derogatory remark about Rachel's business, Seth thought, he would never speak to him again.

But Arthur surprised him yet again. "I've just been retained to represent a small waste-hauling company in Little Rock. McElroy Trucking. Are you familiar with the company?"

"I've heard of it," Rachel agreed. "He's involved with a fight over local franchise taxes, isn't he?"

"Yes. And he has a legitimate complaint. I intend to win for him," Arthur said with utter confidence. He then proceeded to involve Rachel in a rather extensive conversation about the future of trash disposal and the recycling industry, proving that he'd researched his client's business extensively, as always.

Seth relaxed a bit as he turned to entertain the children by asking them about their day at school. He should have known, he thought, that his father wouldn't have said anything derogatory about the business. The Fletchers were workaholics, not snobs. To them, any successful business was a respectable one, particularly if long hours and clever management skills were required. The more money there was to be made in a business, the more it impressed them. Which was the reason Arthur had so much trouble understanding why Seth would have walked away from a highly lucrative firm to start his own comparatively small-stakes practice.

As though he'd read his son's thoughts, Arthur soon managed to turn the conversation along those very lines. "Did Seth tell you that our family law firm has been in existence since the turn of the century?" he asked Rachel.

She nodded. "Yes, he did. You must be proud of the firm's long-standing reputation."

Arthur liked that answer. He graced her with a small smile. "Yes, very much. I only wish Seth felt the same way."

Seth shot his father a warning look. "Don't."

Arthur ignored him as he so often did. "Seth had quite a future with the family firm," he continued. "A huge corner office on the twentieth floor of a downtown office building overlooking the Arkansas River. An experienced legal secretary. Wealthy clients already lined up for him. It was quite a shock for us when he announced that he was leaving us after less than a year."

"I'm sure it was," Rachel murmured. "But we're pleased to have him in Percy. He's quite an asset to our business community."

Seth smiled at her.

Arthur's smile faded.

"I have to go to the bathroom," Aaron whispered loudly.

Seth pushed back his chair. "I'll take you," he offered, then glanced over his shoulder at his father when Aaron hopped willingly out of his chair. "Behave yourself."

Arthur only frowned in response to the thinly veiled warning.

As they left the restaurant, Seth took Rachel's arm. "I have to take him back for his car. I'd like to come by your place afterward, if that's all right."

"What about your father?" she whispered. "Shouldn't you spend more time with him?"

"I think my father and I have spent all the time together that either of us cares to for tonight," Seth replied. "Besides, he's already told me that he wants to drive straight to Harrison tonight. He has to be in court early in the morning."

"All right. I'll make some coffee."

He brushed his lips across her cheek. "Good. See you in a little while, then."

She nodded and ushered her children to their car after bidding good-night to Arthur.

"She seems like a nice woman," Arthur proclaimed when he and Seth were headed back toward Seth's office.

High praise, coming from his father, Seth reflected wryly and with an odd touch of pride. "Yes, she is."

"You could do worse."

Seth rolled his eyes. "She could do better."

"Probably."

Seth wondered if his father was actually trying to make a joke. It was hard to tell at times. "I love her, Dad."

"Well—" Arthur cleared his throat, typically uncomfortable at the mention of such a strong emotion. "I wish you luck, then."

"Thank you."

"I'm sure your mother would like to meet her. And the children, of course. They're quite well behaved."

"We'll wait for an invitation."

"It isn't necessary, but I'll have her call."

Seth nodded, though he wasn't sure how Rachel would feel about officially meeting the rest of his family, especially until something more definite had been settled about their own relationship.

"Seth, I wish you would reconsider coming back to the firm. Especially if you intend to marry and take responsibility for those children, and possibly more children to come. You would have so much more to give them—"

"There's more to life than money, Dad," Seth countered. "Small-town life is good for the kids. They go to a good school, live in a nice home, have friends and family here. And I make enough to take care of them, even offer a few luxuries along the way. As my practice expands, I'll earn more. They won't go hungry."

"But—"

"Give it up, Dad. I was miserable there. And nothing I did quite pleased you, anyway. It's better this way."

Arthur surrendered with a disgruntled mutter. He'd always hated to lose an argument. His son was one of the few people who consistently thwarted him.

They parted with a handshake and a tentative awareness that the feud was at an end, despite Arthur's disappointment with the outcome. They would never be close, Seth thought with a touch of the old regret. But maybe they could work something out.

They were, after all, family.

"Well, what did you think of him?" Seth asked Rachel half an hour later, as the two of them sat in her kitchen, sipping coffee while the children watched television in the den.

"He's...intimidating," Rachel admitted, using the very same word Seth had used to describe his father. "I'm sure he's a very good attorney."

"Yes, he is that," Seth conceded. "He's not such a great father, but he is one hell of a good attorney."

"There's a lot of pain between you," Rachel observed quietly. "A lot of disappointment—on both sides. I'm sorry."

"So am I," Seth admitted. "I spent most of my life trying to live up to his expectations. I studied law because that was what he wanted, but my grades were never quite up to his standards. I even failed the bar exam the first time I took it, probably because I partied a bit too much the night before. You wouldn't have wanted to be there when he found that out," he added with a barely suppressed shudder at the memory.

"But you passed it the next time."

"Yeah. And then I went straight to work in the ol' family firm. I hated it. I made myself miserable and everyone else crazy. I just couldn't live that way. I have to be the one in control of my own actions. I can't be my father's puppet."

Rachel frowned into her coffee cup as though there were something fascinating floating around in the steaming beverage. "While you were away from the table with Aaron, your father suggested that I try to convince you to rejoin the firm. He, um, implied that it would be to my own ultimate benefit for you to do so. I suppose he thought I have some sort of stake in your financial future."

"You do have a stake in my future," he said simply. "What did you say to him?"

"I didn't say anything. I changed the subject. After all, it's not as if we—as though you and I are—"

"I told him that I'm in love with you," Seth said, cutting in.

Rachel's eyes widened and her cheeks darkened. "You—you did?"

"Yes. He'd already guessed, anyway."

She moistened her lips. "What did he say?"

"He approves. He probably thought I'd have a better chance with you if I go back to the big-money job."

"That's—that's ridiculous," Rachel stated, still looking embarrassed. "My emotions aren't affected by dollar signs."

Seth was painfully aware that she'd still never responded to his declarations of his feelings for her. He knew she wasn't a mercenary person, and that she was being completely honest when she said she didn't care about his income. But was she still having doubts about his reliability? His sense of responsibility? Had his father's visit only made her worry more that he wasn't the steady, dependable sort of man she admired?

Overachieving workaholic that she had become since her husband's death, Rachel probably understood Arthur Fletcher even better than Seth ever had.

"Rachel, I—"

"Mama, can we watch a video? I want to see *Aladdin* again," Aaron said from the doorway.

Rachel glanced automatically at her watch and shook her head. "It's too late to start a movie now, Aaron."

"But we don't have to go to school tomorrow," he argued.

"No?" Seth asked. "How come?"

"Teachers' meeting," Aaron replied, leaning against the back of Seth's chair. "We can sleep late tomorrow. Mrs. Campbell's going to come stay with us."

"Who's Mrs. Campbell?"

"She's a neighbor who helps out with the housekeeping a couple of times a month," Rachel explained. "And, occasionally, she baby-sits for me."

Seth ruffled Aaron's brown hair. "Got a day off, huh?"

Aaron nodded happily. "Three whole days before we go back to school."

"You really should do something special. Why don't the four of us go for a picnic tomorrow afternoon? How about it, Rachel?" he asked when Aaron's face lit up. "Want to play hooky with the kids tomorrow?"

"But I have to work," Rachel protested immediately. "And so do you."

Seth shrugged. "I can take the afternoon off. I don't have any appointments tomorrow."

"Well, I can't. I'm sorry, Aaron," she added when Aaron automatically wailed a protest. "I have too much to do to take off without planning. We'll do it another time." She sent a reproachful look at Seth as she spoke, silently chiding him for raising her son's hopes.

Seth frowned. "Surely you can take an occasional afternoon off."

"Of course, when I have a chance to make the proper arrangements. But not on the spur of the moment like this."

Maybe it had something to do with his father's visit. Maybe it had to do with those old, painful memories of all the afternoons his overly busy parents hadn't been there to take him on picnics, or watch him play ball, or take him to the zoo. Maybe he just needed to know that he was as important to Rachel as her business. Seth set his jaw stubbornly and said, "Fine. But do you have any objections if I take the kids out for the afternoon?"

"Well, I—"

"Please, Mama. Let us go with Seth. It'll be fun," Aaron pleaded.

Rachel narrowed her eyes for a moment in irritation at Seth for putting her in an awkward situation, but then she sighed and nodded. "All right. If you're sure you want to. I'll make the arrangements with Mrs. Campbell."

"All right! I'm going to go tell Paige." Aaron happily bolted from the room.

Seth held up both hands before Rachel could say anything. "You don't have to say it. I shouldn't have mentioned it in front of him without speaking to you first. I'm sorry."

"It really would have been better if you'd talked to me first," Rachel agreed.

"I know," he repeated. "It won't happen again. It was just a spur-of-the-moment thing."

Slightly mollified, she nodded. "Just don't make a habit of it," she warned. "I have schedules for the children,

Seth. It makes everything much easier for all of us if I try to stick to them.''

Seth bit his tongue to keep from commenting about her schedules. He was aware that it would take time for him to make a place for himself in this family that had been getting along quite well without him for the past few years.

"You're sure you can't take some time off tomorrow?" he asked again.

He thought there was a trace of wistfulness in her eyes when she shook her head, a touch of regret in her voice when she spoke. "I'm sorry. I can't."

"But you really don't mind if I take the kids out?"

"Not if you're careful." She smiled then, just a bit shyly. "My children are very fond of you. I guess you've noticed that."

"I'm very fond of them, too," Seth admitted, returning the smile. "And I'll be careful."

Their gazes held for a moment. Seth fought an almost overpowering urge to reach across the table and pull her into his arms. *Take it slowly*, he reminded himself. *One step at a time.*

He was still repeating that to himself when he forced himself to leave her with nothing more than a brief, discreet kiss at the door.

Chapter Fourteen

As had been happening to her more and more lately, Rachel found it very difficult to concentrate on work Friday afternoon. She kept looking out her office window, noting the rich blue of the autumn sky, catching a glimpse of blazing colors from the hardwood trees at the back of her business property, imagining how sharp and fresh the pleasantly cool air must feel outside. Say, on a picnic.

For at least the tenth time, she turned her attention sternly back to the bid forms on her desk. This bid was for a big job, a nearby town of twenty thousand people that was putting its residential trash collection up for private bids after providing city-owned service for several years. Like many small towns, Pineland had discovered that the rising costs of providing such service were becoming too much to handle, and had realized that private companies could handle the business with less trouble and expense for city officials and lower charges to the residents.

Evans Industries had always exclusively handled commercial accounts until now. Taking on this residential route would mean the purchase of a new rear-loader truck, more investment in recycling equipment, higher insurance, at least two more full-time employees. Rachel knew it would also involve more telephone time; residential customers tended to complain more than business customers, she'd heard. And yet there was a nice profit to be made, once the investment money had been recouped. If she was going to expand her business, this was a sensible way to begin.

A letter at the corner of her desk caught her eye. She'd opened it only that morning and had set it aside, telling herself she wasn't interested. The logo at the top of the professional letterhead held her gaze now. The letter had come from one of the largest internationally operated waste-hauling companies. It was a polite, tentative attempt to find out if Rachel was interested in selling Evans Industries. She knew the competition she gave this huge company was strictly small potatoes, yet steady enough to have caught the competition's attention. This wasn't the first time she'd been approached with an offer like this. She'd always turned them down before, never even taking the time to consider the possibility of selling her company. So why did she find herself staring for so long at this particular letter, unable to put it completely out of her mind?

She forced herself to look away from that recognizable logo. Her gaze fell, instead, on the twelve-year-old photograph of Ray and Herman Evans, standing proudly in front of their first truck. They had worked so hard to establish this business, to make it successful. Ray had dreamed of eventually competing with "the big guys," becoming as well-known and profitable as BFI or Waste Management, Inc., two of the nationally operated companies. After his death, Rachel had just struggled to hold

on to the business he'd already built up, adding a few accounts along the way to compensate for the ones she lost
through routine business changeovers. The Pineland route,
should she take it on, would be her first attempt at expan-
sion.

And now she wasn't entirely sure that was what she
wanted to do.

She touched the face of her late husband in the photograph.

"I know you would have gone after this, Ray," she said
softly. "But this was your dream, not mine."

The problem was, she'd long since lost sight of whatever dreams she might once have harbored.

She'd majored in business at the local junior college,
with the intention of becoming an office manager or an
executive secretary. Rachel had never dreamed of living in
a large city, becoming a high-powered career woman, or
taking a job that required extensive travel or relocations.
She loved Percy, enjoyed small-town life, thrived on the
security and the fulfillment that came from having a shared
history with her friends and neighbors. She liked knowing
that her children were playmates with the offspring of her
own childhood playmates, that she was doing business
with people who'd known her from infancy. She wouldn't
mind traveling a bit someday, just to experience other
places, other sights, but she hoped she would always have
a home here to return to. Friends to welcome her home.

Her dreams had been very traditional, she realized. A
comfortable income, a happy marriage, children, a nice
home. She needed a bit more challenge in her life than the
sitcom moms of the fifties... but not much, she admitted
with a wry smile. As far as Rachel was concerned, these
days there was a great deal of challenge to be found in
raising safe, happy children to be productive, confident
adults.

It took both money and personal attention to achieve that goal. Like most working mothers, especially single mothers, Rachel sometimes had a great deal of difficulty providing both. But deep inside herself, she honestly believed she was managing very well. And that made her feel good. Gave her a sense of fulfillment.

And yet, somehow, it still wasn't enough. She adored her children, was proud of the nice home they shared, cherished the closeness she had with her family, and yet there was still something missing. A hole that had been ripped through her life with the untimely death of her husband.

She'd known what it was like to be happily married. To feel part of a couple, to know that she was never really alone. To wake in the night and know that someone slept beside her, someone she loved and who loved her in return. Someone to share her joy and her pain, her accomplishments and her failures, her dreams and her fears. Someone who would be there with her even when the children went off to seek their own lives, their own mates. Someone to belong to her, and to whom she belonged.

A partner. A lover. A husband.

She set down her pencil. Her hands were trembling and she stared at them nervously. No, it wasn't an attack of nerves. It was terror.

Seth was going to ask her to marry him. She was absolutely sure that he was. He'd already told her he loved her. He'd made it quite clear that he was interested in much more than an affair. He'd even called it a courtship, and, to Rachel, a successful courtship led to marriage.

Seth seemed so confident, so certain of his feelings. Yet how could he be? They'd known each other such a short time. Rachel and Ray had dated for three years before they'd married, for over two years before the subject had even been mentioned. Yet she and Seth had known each other only a matter of weeks. It was so crazy! So impulsive. So very Seth.

He'd promised he wouldn't rush her, but she knew better than to trust that promise. Oh, he meant it, she believed that. But Seth was an impatient man. He wouldn't be content for long with platonic dates, with the occasional stolen night together. He would want more. And, she suspected, she would, too.

But what if it didn't work? What if he discovered that she wasn't really what he'd wanted, after all? What if he eventually found her as structured and organized and compulsive as the family he'd run away from? What if he discovered, to his regret, that he missed the freedom he'd found when he'd separated himself from his family? What if the love he claimed to feel for her now was really no more than a passing infatuation?

It would destroy her, she realized bleakly. In some ways, she would find that more utterly devastating than the loss of her husband. To allow herself to love someone who didn't truly love her in return would surely break her heart.

And what about the children? Wouldn't they be shattered if they grew to love Seth, to depend on him, to need him, only to lose him as they'd lost the father they could barely remember now? They had already taken to him more quickly than they'd ever taken to anyone outside of the immediate family. They longed for a father, and they'd already decided that Seth would do nicely in that role. But Rachel just couldn't be sure.

He was sweet and fun and thoughtful and kind and amusing and ... well, Seth had many wonderful qualities that Rachel could list for hours. But did he really understand what it meant to be a father? All the work, the trouble, the heartache, the expense, the worry, the sacrifice, the inconvenience, the frustration? There was great joy, as well, in raising children, but any parent could attest that it sometimes took an effort to keep that in mind. And, if there were other children—and there was a deep, secret part of Rachel that longed for another child—would Seth show favoritism? Could he possibly love another man's children as deeply, as purely as his own child? Rachel could never settle for less for Paige and Aaron.

The telephone at her elbow buzzed and Rachel nearly leapt out of her chair. She stared in appalled disbelief at her watch. Three o'clock? Where had the afternoon gone? She'd accomplished absolutely nothing! She might as well have gone on that picnic, after all, she thought with a wistful regret. She picked up the phone, forcing all her convoluted emotions out of her voice when she said crisply, "Evans Industries. May I help you?"

Seth couldn't have picked a better afternoon for a picnic. The weather was ideal. Pleasantly cool, yet warm enough that lightweight sweaters and jeans were quite adequate clothing. Cloudless blue sky. A light, fragrant breeze.

Had Rachel been with them, it would have been a perfect afternoon.

He'd followed Cody's directions to "the ultimate picnic spot," a grassy glade beside a small creek that meandered through miles of primitive woodlands. He'd parked his car at the side of a gravel road, and he and the kids had carried the picnic supplies to this spot, roughly a fifteen-minute walk from the road.

The kids were having a great time. They'd eaten a bucket of chicken, with coleslaw and potato salad on the side, followed by those little chocolate pudding cups the chicken place sold for dessert. They'd downed chilled canned sodas, and were now charged with sugar-and-caffeine fueled energy, running and squealing and laughing as they pursued the Frisbee Seth had brought with them.

Seth had long since collapsed onto the spread blanket in exhaustion. He stared in amazement at the still-hyper children, wondering why no one had figured out a way to harness that source of energy for commercial use. These two were enough to make a reasonably well-conditioned man of only twenty-eight start feeling a bit old.

"Aaron," he said, watching as the boy approached the swiftly running, shallow creek just as it disappeared into the woods beyond the glade. "Don't get in the water. Your mom would strangle both of us if you got your clothes and shoes all wet and muddy."

"Okay, Seth," Aaron said absently, his attention focused on something in the clear water. Probably minnows, Seth thought in amusement. Bugs, maybe. He clearly remembered his own boyhood fascination with such things.

Paige plopped onto the blanket at Seth's side and wiped the back of her hand across her flushed face. "Whew!" she said. "I'm pooped!"

Seth laughed. So the energy wasn't inexhaustible. He was rather relieved to hear it. "You are, huh?"

Paige nodded, then looked a bit guilty. "Oops. Granny Fran doesn't like me to use that word. She says it sounds distasteful."

"What? Pooped?"

Paige nodded again.

Seth grinned. He could just hear Granny Fran saying that. "Then maybe you'd better not say it anymore," he suggested. "Granny Fran's a pretty classy lady."

Paige smiled. "You like my Granny Fran, Seth?"

"Yes. Very much."

"Good." Paige scooted an inch closer to him and rested her little head trustingly against his forearm.

Seth looked down at her dark, pigtailed head nestled so contentedly against him and felt a hard lump form in his throat. Oh, yeah, he thought. He was going to like this fatherhood thing. A lot.

"Are you going to marry my mother, Seth?"

The unexpected question made him choke. He coughed a couple of times, cleared his throat, then said carefully, "Your mother and I haven't really talked about that yet, Paige."

"Oh. Why not?"

"Well, we haven't really known each other very long."

She looked up at him in apparent surprise. "You've known her since September!"

"This is only October," he declared. "It's only been about seven weeks since your mom brought you to my office that first time."

"That's a long time, isn't it?"

He supposed seven weeks *was* a long time, to an eight-year-old. "Not really very long," he said.

"How long do you have to know her before you can get married?"

Seth was beginning to get a bit flustered. "Um, well, there isn't a set time limit or anything. I mean, it doesn't really matter how long you know someone if you love them and want to get married. But—"

"Do you love my mother?" Paige asked the questions so simply that she couldn't possibly be aware of how difficult they were to answer.

But, then again, this one wasn't all that difficult, Seth realized abruptly. This was an answer he could give her without the slightest hesitation. "Yes, Paige. I love your mother."

"So you *are* going to marry her?"

"I would like to," he said, still choosing his words with care. "But it has to be something your mother wants, too."

"Oh. Well, I'll talk to her for you," Paige offered airily. "She probably wants to. Why wouldn't she?"

If only it could be that simple, Seth thought with a wistful smile. "Um, Paige? How do *you* feel about it? I mean, do you want me to marry your mother?"

Paige gave him a shy, sweet smile that made him decide right then that he was going to have to keep a very sharp eye on her when she got a few years older. He shuddered at the very thought of her turning a smile like that on a helpless, hormone-happy teenage boy. Maybe this fatherhood thing wasn't going to be quite such a snap, after all.

"Yes," she said warmly. "I hope you do marry her. That would make you my daddy, wouldn't it?"

"Technically, it would make me your stepfather," Seth said, feeling compelled to point out that fact. "Your father was a very special man, Paige. I want you always to remember that, and that he loved you very much. But, if your mother and I get married, I would be very proud to have you for my daughter. To have you call me Dad, if you want to. I would love you and your brother just like you were my very own children. Can you understand that?"

Paige nodded. "I won't forget my real daddy, Seth. Mama gave me his picture and told me to try to always remember him, though it's hard sometimes to remember what he was like. But I wish you could be our new daddy. We've talked about it, Aaron and me," she added. "We want a father, like our friends have. And we want it to be you."

It was almost enough to make a grown man bawl, Seth thought shakily. *Rachel Carson Evans, you're going to marry me if I have to...to...* His mouth twisted. *If I have to beg.*

He slipped an arm around Paige's narrow shoulders, gave her a hug and planted a kiss on the top of her dark head. "Thank you, Paige. I hope everything works out just the way you want it to. But don't push your mom, okay? We have to give her all the time she needs to make up her own mind. Marriage is a very important decision. She has to be very sure it's what she wants."

"She'll marry you," Paige said with a confidence that Seth envied. "She always gets a funny look on her face when you're around. Me and Aaron—I mean, Aaron and I think it's because she's in love with you. People always look funny when they're in love, don't they, Seth? At least, they do on TV."

Seth laughed. "Maybe it's just indigestion," he teased.

Paige rolled her eyes and sighed. "Oh, Seth. You're so silly."

"I am, huh?" Seth promptly tickled her tummy, causing her to dissolve into delighted giggles.

Relieved that the delicate discussion had been resolved, at least temporarily, Seth pushed his hair back from his forehead and glanced at his watch. It was almost four. Probably time for him to get the kids back home. He reached for an empty chicken container. "Want to help me pick everything up, Paige? We don't want to leave any trash behind."

"We don't want to be litterbugs," Paige agreed solemnly, stuffing used paper plates and napkins into the empty chicken bucket. "We have to keep our earth clean."

Figuring that she was quoting a slogan she'd learned at school, Seth responded with approval. He glanced over his shoulder as he started to fold the blanket. "Aaron, bring the Frisbee, and let's get going, okay?"

The spot where the boy had stood staring into the creek was empty. Seth frowned and sat back on his heels. "Aaron?" he called, raising his voice a little.

Still no answer. He pushed himself to his feet, planted his hands on his hips and took a quick survey of the glade, catching no glimpse of Aaron's green-and-navy striped sweater. "Aaron!"

Paige sighed gustily and shook her head. "Sometimes you can yell right in his ear and he doesn't hear you if he's thinking about something else," she said. "That boy can be more trouble!" she chided with the superiority of two extra years of maturity.

"You finish gathering these things up, and I'll go get him, okay? And don't you wander off," he added hastily. "Stay right here."

He began where he'd last seen Aaron, standing by the creek at the very edge of the woods. "Aaron?"

There was a path, of sorts, along the bank of the creek. Seth followed it several yards into the woods, calling the boy's name in a louder and more anxious voice. He finally stopped, realizing that he was completely out of sight of the glade now. He couldn't leave Paige alone.

"Aaron!"

The silence that followed his shout was a vaguely ominous one.

Rachel leapt out of the passenger side of Celia's little car almost before Celia had brought it to a complete stop beside the other cars and pickup trucks parked along the side of the gravel road several miles outside the Percy city limits. An ambulance was also parked nearby. Rachel couldn't even look at it without shuddering.

Three men stood at the end of the well-trodden path that led into the woods toward the glade Rachel remembered from past picnics with her family. It had been years since she'd been here, but she clearly remembered that the woods went on for miles beyond the little creek that ran through the area. And that those woods were full of old caves and crumbly ravines that had caused painful falls for many an unwary hiker. Cody had fallen once as a teenager, and had to be carried out by his friends. He'd spent weeks on crutches afterward. And then had headed back for the woods the day after the cast had been removed from his ankle.

"Cody knows these woods better than anyone," Celia reminded Rachel as though she'd read her thoughts. "He'll find Aaron."

"Mama!" Paige broke away from the cluster of men at the edge of the path. Rachel hadn't even seen her standing with them.

"Paige." Rachel caught her daughter in her arms. "Are you all right?"

"I'm fine," Paige replied, looking rather surprised by the question. "Aaron's the one who's missing."

Missing. The very word made Rachel's throat clench even more tightly than it had been since Celia had shown up unexpectedly at her office to tell her that Cody had called and reported that Aaron had disappeared into these woods during his picnic with Seth. She had added that Cody and Seth and a dozen volunteers and police officers were looking for the boy. Rachel had immediately insisted on coming to personally monitor the progress of the search.

"I shouldn't have let him come," Rachel muttered, more to herself than to anyone else. "I should have told Seth no."

Paige stiffened. "Aaron's the one who ran off, Mama," she insisted. "Seth was watching us just like he was s'posed to. He told Aaron not to go to the creek, but Aaron did it, anyway."

"The creek!" Rachel repeated with a gasp.

One of the men nearby overheard. "The creek's only a couple of feet deep at its deepest point," he assured her. "I wouldn't worry about that. The boy's probably just wandered off the path and got turned around. Happens all the time with inexperienced hunters. They'll find him, don't you worry."

But Rachel was worried, of course. She was worried sick. She kept picturing those ravines, thick underbrush, wild animals—who knew what dangers lurked out there for a child who was barely six years old? And it was getting dark. Poor Aaron must be terrified.

"Seth called Uncle Cody from his car phone," Paige said, hanging on to her mother's hand. "Uncle Cody came with some other guys, and then the amb'lance came. Everybody's out in the woods now, yelling for Aaron. Is Aaron going to get in trouble, Mama?"

"No, Paige, Aaron isn't in trouble," Rachel said. "I just hope he's okay." *Please, God, let him be all right.*

One of the men stepped forward, and Rachel greeted him with a tight smile. "Hello, Jim. You've been helping with the search?"

He nodded and patted her arm awkwardly. "Yeah. Jake called me," he explained.

Rachel nodded at the mention of Cody's partner. She suspected that Cody had headed for the woods as soon as Seth called, leaving instructions for Jake to call for more help. "Thank you for coming, Jim. Have you heard anything?"

Jim shook his head. "Not yet. Aaron's been missing about an hour and a half, close as we can tell. But don't you worry, Rachel. Pete Cunningham's kid was lost for ten hours out there once, and he turned up just fine."

Ten hours. Rachel felt her stomach turn. One of the other men nudged Jim and muttered something that made Jim swallow and say, "I'm sure they'll find Aaron sooner than that. He's just a little kid. How far could he get in an hour?"

The man who'd interrupted before rolled his eyes and pulled Jim away. "Let's go help 'em look," he said gruffly. "Ms. Evans can stay with her little girl now."

Celia slipped an arm around Rachel's waist. "They'll find him, Rach. He'll be fine."

"I hope you're right," Rachel whispered, holding her daughter close to her side. "Oh, I hope you're right."

It was a very long half hour later that a shout came from the path. Celia and Paige had been sitting on the trunk of Celia's car, talking in low voices, while Rachel paced, unable to sit or stand still. It was almost completely dark now, the only light coming from the headlights of the vehicles parked around them and the flashlights the search parties carried. Rachel whirled in response to the rapidly approaching sounds of men's voices and heavy footsteps. She gasped and darted forward when two uniformed paramedics stepped onto the road, carrying a stretcher between them. A tiny body lay on the stretcher, and Cody and Seth walked closely on either side of it.

"Aaron!" Rachel put out a shaking hand to touch her son's tousled head, reassuring herself that he was breathing and all in one piece.

He wore a neck brace and his right arm was splinted, his face was scratched and filthy and tear streaked, and his clothes were torn and dirty. He looked up at Rachel with huge, apologetic eyes. "I'm sorry, Mama. I was chasing a rabbit and it kept running and I got lost. And then I got scared and I ran some more and I fell into a big hole. I hurt my arm. And then I heard Seth shouting my name, and I yelled and he and Uncle Cody found me."

"We think his arm is broken," Cody explained, putting a hand on Rachel's shoulder. "But other than that, he seems fine."

"You can ride in the ambulance with him if you want, ma'am," one of the paramedics offered. "We'd like to get under way now."

Rachel nodded, her hand still resting on Aaron's head, her gaze still focused on his weary little face. "All right. Celia, you'll bring Paige?"

"Of course," Celia replied, her hands on her niece's shoulders.

"Rachel." Seth came around the side of the stretcher, reaching out to Rachel with one dirty, badly scratched hand. He was almost as disheveled as Aaron, she noted when she glanced his way. His face looked pale in the artificial light from several sets of car headlamps. "I'm sorry," he said. "I know you must have been frantic."

"I don't blame you, Seth," she said distractedly. "I knew you weren't experienced with children. I shouldn't have let them come without me."

His hand fell to his side. If possible, his face went even whiter. Cody murmured something Rachel didn't catch and didn't take time to ask him to repeat.

The paramedics carefully loaded Aaron into the ambulance, and Rachel climbed in behind him, her attention fully claimed by her frightened, wounded child. A moment later, they were under way.

Chapter Fifteen

By the time Aaron's broken arm was set and he was taken home, fed and tucked into bed, Rachel was exhausted. Celia and Cody were still hanging around, Celia staying close to Paige while Rachel was busy with Aaron. Rachel wasn't quite sure why Cody hadn't left yet. She would have thought he'd head for his club, but he said only that Jake could handle everything alone for an evening. He waited until Aaron was in bed and Celia was tucking Paige in before he cornered Rachel in the kitchen.

"I think we need to talk," he said as she poured herself a cup of coffee. He was sitting at her table, a half-eaten sandwich on a plate in front of him, a full cup of coffee steaming at his side. His face was unusually grave, his eyes intent and serious. "It's about Seth."

Rachel had just been thinking about Seth, as a matter of fact. She'd seen him briefly in the hospital emergency room waiting area, but she'd been preoccupied with Aaron and hadn't had a chance to talk to him. Later, she'd been told that Seth had waited only until he'd known for sure that Aaron would be all right and then had left. She'd assumed that he'd gone home to clean up and change, and had more than half expected him to show up at her door this evening. Or at least to call. He'd done neither.

"What about Seth?" she asked Cody, taking a chair across the table from him.

"You really hurt him this afternoon," Cody said with the frankness of a sibling. "I was surprised at you, Rachel. The poor guy didn't deserve it."

Her eyes widened in shock. "What are you talking about?" she demanded. "I hardly had time to speak to Seth this afternoon! And I assured him that I didn't blame him for what happened to Aaron."

Cody snorted. "Yeah, right. You basically told him it was all your fault for trusting him with your kids in the first place. Real nice, Rachel."

"That's not what I said."

"Didn't you?"

I knew you weren't experienced with children. I shouldn't have let them come without me. She could almost hear her own words repeating inside her head.

"Oh, Cody, I didn't mean it the way you make it sound. Surely you know that. Surely Seth knows."

"How could he know? It was exactly what you said, Rachel. He was already blaming himself for letting Aaron get out of his sight. Aaron admitted that Seth told him not to wander off, but Aaron ran off, anyway, chasing that rabbit. Paige told us that she was the one who'd distracted Seth with a lot of questions, and you know how easily she can do that," he reminded her.

"Anyway," he continued relentlessly, "Seth called me for help barely fifteen minutes after he noticed Aaron was missing, because he knew I was more familiar with the woods than he was. And because he wanted to make sure someone was watching out for Paige while he kept looking for Aaron. By the time I got there, the guy was half-frantic, but determined to find Aaron. Rachel, he did exactly what he should have done under the circumstances. It could just as easily have happened if the kids had been with me. Or with you."

"Oh, Cody, I know that. Anyone who's ever watched children knows how quickly they can get away. I only meant that Seth probably didn't realize that because he's had so little experience with them. I honestly didn't mean to make him feel that I didn't trust him with my children."

"It's what you said," Cody repeated stubbornly.

Rachel groaned and buried her face in her hands. Remembering her words. Remembering Seth's expression. Maybe she *had* meant the words more than she'd realized. Maybe all her emotional worries during the afternoon, combined with her stark fear for Aaron's safety, had made her lash out at Seth in reaction, without even realizing it.

She must have hurt him very badly.

"I'll call him," she said, lifting her head and glancing toward the telephone. "I'll explain."

"Look, Seth's been my friend for a long time," Cody said. "He and I lost touch for a few years, but there was a time when I knew him probably better than anyone. I know he's spent most of his life trying to prove himself to the people he cares about, and usually feeling like he failed them. Nothing he ever did was right, as far as his family was concerned. It finally just got easier for him to quit trying."

Rachel winced. "Are you saying I'm like Seth's family? That I'm too demanding, that I expect too much from people?" she asked in a whisper.

Cody reached across the table to take her hand. "I love you, Rachel. You're a very giving, very capable person. You expect a great deal from others, but you demand even more from yourself. All I'm saying is, it's okay to make mistakes sometimes. It's okay to be human. You have to give yourself permission not to be perfect, not to be Superwoman. And you have to give Seth credit for trying, even when he makes mistakes."

Rachel's cheeks burned. She wouldn't have taken this from anyone else, she realized. She would have heatedly denied every word of it. But Cody was one person who harbored no illusions about himself, or others. He accepted people as they were, flaws and all, and enjoyed them, anyway. And he'd never been anything less than completely honest with her.

"Do you think Seth can forgive me for what I said? For what my words implied?" she whispered.

Cody smiled and squeezed her hand. "The guy's so crazy about you he'd forgive you anything," he assured her. "I never thought I'd see my ol' buddy fall so hard and so fast, though I certainly can't fault him for his taste. He's a great guy, Rachel, and you're a very special woman. You belong together."

She tried to return his smile but found that she couldn't. "I'm scared."

"I know. Hell, I would be, too," he said. "Why do you think I've worked so hard at *not* falling in love with anyone? It looks like a very painful process, as far as I'm concerned. But it's too late for Seth, I guess. And it's too late for you, too, isn't it, sis?"

Rachel stared at him, then nodded. Very slowly. With a sudden, shocking, undeniable conviction that Cody was right. It really *was* too late for her. She was in love with Seth Fletcher. Probably had been for weeks, despite her fierce resistance.

When had it happened? When she'd come home to find him struggling to put together a swing set for her son? When he had rushed to assist her the night Holder had called with his ugly threats? The night they'd made love? Or maybe the first time he'd looked up from his house of cards and flashed that bright, sexy smile at her?

All these weeks, she thought dazedly, she'd been fighting so hard to resist him. Asking herself if she really wanted to get involved with him, if she really wanted him to become a part of her life. And all the time, it had already been too late.

"I have to talk to him," she said, thinking of him alone now, still shaken from his fear for Aaron, utterly convinced that he'd let her down when she'd trusted him with her children. God, she'd been cruel with her thoughtless words. Even though she hadn't really meant to be, it had been inexcusable of her. "I have to explain...."

"Do you really want to try to do that over the phone?" Cody asked quietly.

"No," Rachel said instantly, shaking her head.

"Then what are you waiting for? It's getting late. The guy's probably into a heavy depression by now. Go put him out of his misery."

Rachel moistened her lips. "Now?" She wasn't at all sure she was up to that tonight. It had been such a difficult, traumatic day....

But it had been just as hard for Seth. And he was alone now. Not surrounded, as she was, by people who loved despite flaws.

"Can you think of a better time?" Cody asked, still wearing that sympathetic, understanding smile.

Rachel shook her head. "No. But the children..."

"Celia and I will watch out for the kids. And in case you're interested, I don't have any plans till morning, so there's no need for you to rush back home."

She flushed and smiled at the same time. Impulsively she stood and threw her arms around her brother's neck. "I love you," she said, and kissed his cheek.

"I know. Now get lost."

It occurred to Rachel as she parked in front of Seth's neat little brick rented house on the other side of town that she'd never even been inside it before. They'd driven past it once, after taking the children out for dinner. Seth had said that it was the first conveniently located place he'd found to live when he'd moved to Percy, and that he had planned to build a new place eventually.

His car was parked in the driveway, and there was a light on in the front window. She took a deep breath and rang the doorbell, then nervously wiped her hands on the knit slacks she'd changed into after taking Aaron home from the hospital. She didn't know quite what she was going to say. It wasn't at all like her to take chances like this. To go into something this important without careful forethought and planning.

The door opened, and her pulse went into double time.

Seth had showered and changed since she'd seen him last. His hair was still damp, that thick forelock tumbled boyishly over his eyes. He wore a gray sweatshirt and black sweatpants and a pair of white socks. No shoes. There was a deep, angry-looking scratch on his right cheek, and another on his chin. His eyes were shadowed, looking weary and dispirited.

Rachel thought he looked wonderful. "May I come in?" she prodded when he only looked at her without saying anything.

"Oh, yeah. Sure." He moved aside to let her pass, then closed the door behind him. "Is Aaron all right?" he asked.

"Aaron's fine. He was sound asleep when I left. Cody and Celia are baby-sitting."

"Is he in any pain? Does his arm hurt very badly?"

Rachel shook her head, touched by the obviously sincere concern in Seth's expression. "He's fine," she repeated. "Once the fright wore off, he began to enjoy all the attention."

She stepped closer to him and reached up to lightly touch the swollen abrasion on his cheek. The clean, soapy scent of freshly showered male tickled her nostrils. "Did you put anything on this?" she asked him.

Seth stood very still beneath her touch, his eyes impossible to read. "No. It's okay. Just a scratch."

"It's rather deep. Do you have any antiseptic? You don't want to let it get infected."

He shook his head, dislodging her fingers. "It's okay."

She let her hand fall. "You look tired," she said. "Have you eaten?"

"Rachel. Why are you here?"

She took a deep breath. "I came to thank you. And to apologize."

He frowned. "What do you mean?"

"I want to thank you for taking such good care of Aaron this afternoon. Had you not acted so quickly in getting help, he could have been lost for hours in the dark. He'd have been terrified. And I want to apologize for not thanking you sooner. My only excuse is that I was so distracted with worrying about my son that I couldn't seem to think of anything else."

Seth stared at her for a moment, his expression heartbreaking, then turned his head. "I let him get lost," he said gruffly. "You were right, Rachel. I don't know anything about taking care of kids. I should have waited until you could go with us before trying something like that."

She shook her head. "I should have been with you this afternoon, but not because you aren't fully capable of taking care of the children, Seth. I should have been there because I belonged there. Because my children deserve to know that they are more important to me than a few hours of paperwork. And so are you."

"Rachel, I—"

"You didn't lose Aaron, Seth. He lost himself. He could have just as likely chased that rabbit into the woods had I been there with you, and he would have been just as lost. Children are capable of disappearing very quickly, as many perfectly responsible parents have learned to their dismay. I plan to have a long, stern talk with him about what he did as soon as he recovers a bit, to let him know that when he's told not to wander off, I expect him to follow orders. Maybe you should be with me when we have that talk," she added. "After all, it was your instructions that he disobeyed. We don't want him to make a habit of that."

Seth looked at her questioningly. "You make that sound as though I'll be around to give further instructions in the future."

She nodded bravely. "I certainly hope you will be," she murmured.

He touched her face with the fingertips of one hand, and she felt the tremor in them. Was he so very unsure of himself? she wondered. So very unsure of her?

"I still feel like I let you down this afternoon," he said, as though in answer to her unspoken question.

"No," she whispered. "You didn't let me down, Seth. You never have. But I've let you down, over and over. I was afraid to care for you, afraid to let you into my life and into my heart. I was so afraid of being hurt again, of being left alone again if something went wrong."

"I've never wanted to hurt you, Rachel." Seth cupped her face between his hands. "Don't you know that by now?"

"I trust you, Seth," she said, looking up at him without hesitation. "With my children, and with my heart. I love you."

"Oh, God." He closed his eyes and rested his forehead against hers.

"I know it would serve me right if you've changed your mind about loving me," she continued doggedly, staring at the pulsing hollow of his throat. "I've been a coward and a shrew. I work too hard and I worry too much and I don't laugh or tease enough. I expect too much from people. I'm a compulsive list maker and obsessive about details and schedules and I—"

"I love you," he said, raising her face to his. He touched his lips to hers, lightly, tenderly. "I love you," he said again, then kissed her harder.

She caught her breath and clung to him, relief making her light-headed. Only now did she see how much she'd risked throwing away with her fears and doubts. "Seth," she whispered, holding him tightly, inhaling that wonderful, clean-male scent, savoring the strength of his arms around her. Knowing without doubt that he loved her.

She gasped when he suddenly swung her into his arms, then laughed when he began to move across the room with quick, determined steps. "I take it you're about to give me a tour of your house?"

His grin was wicked and utterly male. "No. Only the bedroom."

She kissed his scratched jaw. "Good."

An hour later, Rachel still couldn't have described Seth's bedroom. He hadn't bothered to turn on a light when he'd carried her in. They'd undressed by touch, made love with only the dim illumination spilling in through the open bedroom door. And then they'd made love again.

As far as Rachel knew at that moment, this was the most beautiful bedroom in the whole world.

She kissed his cheek, his jaw, soothing the raw scratches he'd suffered during his search for her son. And then she kissed his lips, lingering to explore every centimeter of his mouth before moving on to nuzzle his throat. Her fingers slid slowly, luxuriatingly down his body, tactilely approving every firm, warm inch of him.

Seth groaned softly and tangled his fingers in her wildly disheveled hair. "Oh, man, Rachel. You're going to cripple me."

"You want me to stop?" she asked, delicately touching the tip of her tongue to his left nipple.

"No," he said on a choked laugh. "Oh, no. Don't stop."

She kissed his chest, then snuggled her cheek against his flat stomach. She smiled against his skin. What a beautiful, beautiful man he was. She was no longer surprised by her responses to him, no longer questioned the unfamiliar passion he elicited from her. She'd been extraordinarily blessed to find love for a second time. She intended to treasure this very special gift. This very special man.

"I love you," he said, smiling down at her.

"I love you," she repeated.

"Will you marry me?"

He asked so casually, so confidently. Had it not been for the unsteadiness in his fingers as they rested against her face, the wild pounding of his heart beneath her cheek, she might not have known how much her answer meant to him.

"Yes," she said, her voice clear, firm, certain. "I'll marry you."

Drawing her into his arms, he rolled onto his side, looming over her as he kissed her deeply, with a renewed enthusiasm. "Thank you," he said when he finally gave her a chance to breathe again. "I won't ever let you down, Rachel. You or the kids. I promise you that."

"I know you won't." She reached up to rest her hand against his uninjured cheek. "Don't you know how much I admire you, Seth? For having the courage to be yourself, to go after what you want and what you need."

"I probably won't ever get rich running a one-man law office in Percy," he warned her, only half-teasingly. "I expect to make a comfortable living, but nothing like the big bucks my father's always pulled in through his operation."

"I don't care about that. I never have. I love living here. I wouldn't ever want you to go back to your father's firm where you'd have to work all the time and be miserable."

"And I won't interfere with your work, either," he assured her. "I shouldn't have pushed you to take off this afternoon. You do what you have to do, Rachel. I'll understand."

"I've had an offer from a very large organization that wants to buy my business," she said, watching his face as she spoke. "It's a good offer, a very nice profit."

"But I thought you were thinking of expanding the business."

She shrugged, the movement brushing her bare shoulder against his arm. "Taking on more business will only mean more hours I'd have to spend away from you and the children," she said. "I don't know if I want that."

"It's your decision," Seth said firmly. "I'll back you up in whatever you decide. We'll get by just fine, whatever you want to do. But please don't feel that you have to sell the business to please me. I really don't resent you working. I just need to know that I'm as important to you as the job," he explained, with a trace of his former uncertainty.

"I'll never give you reason to doubt that again," Rachel promised. "We'll talk about the business later. We'll decide together what course to take. After all, it affects both our futures now."

Resting on one elbow, Seth twirled a strand of her hair around his fingertip. "Would it be very difficult for you—selling Ray's business, I mean?" he asked quietly.

"Ray started that business to take care of his family," she answered. "It has done that very well for the past few years. If I sell it, the money will go a long way toward providing for the children's future. That was all he ever wanted—for them to be secure, and happy. He and I had always planned for me to quit working and spend more time with them while they were small. I've always regretted that I haven't been able to do that."

"You can do that now," Seth observed. "And if you ever want another child...well, I'd like that," he said. "Not that I'd ever favor another child over Paige and Aaron," he added quickly. "They're great kids, Rachel. I already love them."

"I know. I saw your love for them on your face this afternoon when you brought Aaron out of those woods," she whispered, her eyes stinging with happy tears.

Seth took a deep breath. "I know you loved Ray," he said, not quite meeting her eyes. "I know you were happy with him."

"Yes, I was."

Sensing his vulnerability, Rachel selected her next words with great care. "I was only twenty-one when I married Ray. Our relationship was very warm, very comfortable, based on mutual interests and shared goals. We were happy, and we shared a very special love. But I've changed in the past ten years, Seth. I've learned that there can be more to life, more to love, than I ever even dreamed when I was twenty-one. More intensity, more passion, more laughter. I want it all now. And I've found it all—with you. I love you in some ways more than I've ever loved before. I want to be your wife, your lover, your partner, the mother of your children. I want you, Seth Fletcher. Only you."

He smiled, and his eyes were alight with pleasure at her words. "I love you, Rachel. I've never loved anyone before, and I'll never love anyone again the way I love you. I want to spend the rest of my life with you."

It was an exchange of vows as binding, as sacred, as the formal ceremony that would soon follow. From this moment, Rachel thought in wonder, her life was joined with Seth's.

"Be patient with me," she whispered, "while I learn to dream again."

His smile deepened. He caught her close, holding her tightly against his pounding heart, their flesh melded as tightly as their futures. "Trust me, Rachel," he said, his voice gruff with emotion. "I have dreams enough to share."

He kissed her lingeringly, then drew back with a laugh of pure joy. After a moment, Rachel's tremulous laughter joined with his.

Epilogue

Lila Twining was sitting on Frances's living room sofa, sipping tea, when Frances rejoined her after answering a telephone call. Lila looked up with a smile, then raised her eyebrows as she studied her friend's face. "From the way you're smiling, that call must have been good news," she commented.

Frances laughed and walked over to her old upright piano, on which rested several framed photographs. Her late husband, her children, her grandchildren, her great-grandchildren. She felt very proud as she studied those much-loved faces, her gaze lingering for a moment on a recent photograph of Rachel and the children.

"Yes, it was very good news," she agreed. "Rachel just called to tell me that she's getting married again."

"To that nice young man you told me about? Seth?"

Frances nodded happily. "Yes. I can't wait for you to meet him the next time they're here, Lila. You'll like him."

"From what you told me, I'm sure I will. This is wonderful news, Frannie. Rachel and the children have needed another man in their lives."

Frances chuckled and turned away from the photographs. "Not a very modern thing to say, my friend."

"Ah, but I'm not a very modern woman," seventy-something-year-old Lila acknowledged without regret.

"That's true. And I happen to agree," Frances admitted. "Rachel and the children did need someone. And I'm sure Seth will do quite nicely."

Lila set her teacup down on a needlework coaster and smoothed her wool skirt over her bony knees. "Well, that takes care of one of your grandchildren, Frannie. Now you have only three more to marry off."

Frances laughed softly. "You make it sound as though I had something to do with Rachel's engagement. I didn't, you know. I only nudged her along a bit when I had the opportunity."

"Then you can just as easily nudge the others," Lila said with a firm nod of her silvery head. "Especially Adam. Thirty-eight is more than old enough for him to be starting his own family."

"Yes. And I'd love to see Cody settled down, as well," Frances said.

"At least Celia has plenty of time. She's still young."

Frances turned her eyes back to that grouping of photographs, studying the beautiful dark-haired, blue-eyed face of her youngest granddaughter. She sighed. "Yes. Celia has time. But..." A note of worry had crept into her voice.

"Celia's heading for trouble, isn't she?" Lila asked sympathetically, knowing her friend's concerns.

"I hope not," Frances replied. "But I can't help worrying. She's so restless, so hungry for adventure. If only she could find the right person to share those adventures with."

Lila patted Frances's hand. "She'll find someone, Frannie. Just as Rachel did."

Frances smiled again. "Yes, just as Rachel did," she agreed, and mentally added a photograph of that nice young Seth Fletcher to her cherished family grouping.

A Note from the Author

Family relationships have always intrigued me, maybe because of my own large and diverse extended family. I've examined family connections often in my writing—from my first Special Edition, *Healing Sympathy,* in which the orphaned heroine assembled her own "family" of equally lonely misfits (which eventually included the emotionally battered hero), to the more recent "Family Found" series, which involved a group of six siblings separated as small children and finding each other as adults. Close families, stepfamilies, dysfunctional families, foster families—they all fascinate me, and all provide unlimited inspiration for my work.

A Man for Mom is the first book of a new series, "The Family Way," and Rachel Carson Evans is a very Special Woman to me—a widowed mother of two who has become so overwhelmed by her responsibilities to her children and her late husband's business that she has almost forgotten she has needs of her own. Rachel is strongly influenced by another Special Woman—her grandmother, Frances, known to the family as "Granny Fran." It is Frances who encourages Rachel to enjoy life to the fullest. Enter fun-loving young attorney, Seth Fletcher...and a new family is formed.

In the next three books of "The Family Way" series, Frances's other grandchildren will find new families of their own, usually when they least expect to do so, and in ways they couldn't have predicted! I'm having a wonderful time helping Granny Fran play matchmaker. I can't wait to see what she has in store for Celia, Cody and Adam! I would love for you to join me in finding out.

* * * * *

*If you liked A MAN FOR MOM, you'll love
BEGINNINGS, a story by Gina Ferris Wilkins
featured in the 1995 Silhouette Books collection
THREE MOTHERS AND A CRADLE,
available in bookstores now.*

Silhouette®

SPECIAL EDITION™

COMING NEXT MONTH

#961 RILEY'S SLEEPING BEAUTY—Sherryl Woods
That Special Woman!
Abby Dennison's last adventure before settling down had landed
her in trouble that was seemingly inescapable. Only Riley Walker
could call her back from a terrible fate—but would his love be
enough to save her?

#962 A FATHER'S WISH—Christine Flynn
Man, Woman and Child
When she had Alexander Burke's baby, Kelly Shaw gave it
up for adoption, thinking he didn't want her or the child. Now
she was back in his life, and old flames had begun to ignite
once again....

#963 BROODING ANGEL—Marie Ferrarella
Blue blood had met blue collar when Mary Elizabeth Clancy and
"Mitch" Mitchell loved and lost years ago. Now a tragic twist of
fate had brought them together, and only Mitch's determination
could prevent them from losing each other again.

#964 CHILD OF HER HEART—Arlene James
Gail Terry had finally found the daughter she'd thought lost to
her. She never expected to fall for the child's guardian, rancher
Rand Hartesite, whose sexy charm—and dad potential—were
hard to resist.

#965 THE GIRL NEXT DOOR—Trisha Alexander
Simon Christopher was Jenny Randall's best pal—but her secret
feelings for him had long ago gone beyond friendship. Now
opportunity knocked at Jenny's door—along with Simon, who
suddenly realized that just being friends could never be enough!

#966 A FAMILY FOR RONNIE—Julie Caille
Forced to share guardianship of her nephew with old flame
Luke Garrick didn't make things easier for Alicia Brant.
Especially when both wanted sole custody—and both still
desperately felt the love they'd once had....

Take 4 bestselling love stories FREE

Plus get a FREE surprise gift!

Special Limited-time Offer

Mail to Silhouette Reader Service™

3010 Walden Avenue
P.O. Box 1867
Buffalo, N.Y. 14269-1867

YES! Please send me 4 free Silhouette Special Edition® novels and my free surprise gift. Then send me 6 brand-new novels every month, which I will receive months before they appear in bookstores. Bill me at the low price of $2.89 each plus 25¢ delivery and applicable sales tax, if any.* That's the complete price and a savings of over 10% off the cover prices—quite a bargain! I understand that accepting the books and gift places me under no obligation ever to buy any books. I can always return a shipment and cancel at any time. Even if I never buy another book from Silhouette, the 4 free books and the surprise gift are mine to keep forever.

235 BPA ANRQ

Name	(PLEASE PRINT)	
Address	Apt. No.	
City	State	Zip

This offer is limited to one order per household and not valid to present Silhouette Special Edition® subscribers. *Terms and prices are subject to change without notice. Sales tax applicable in N.Y.

USPED-295   ©1990 Harlequin Enterprises Limited

Silhouette celebrates motherhood in May with...

Debbie Macomber
Jill Marie Landis
Gina Ferris Wilkins

in

Three
Mothers
& a Cradle

Join three award-winning authors in this
beautiful collection you'll treasure forever.
The same antique, hand-crafted cradle
connects these three heartwarming romances,
which celebrate the joys and excitement of
motherhood. Makes the perfect gift for yourself
or a loved one!

A special celebration of love,

Only from

Silhouette®
™

—where passion lives.

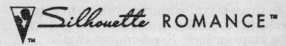

HE'S MORE THAN A MAN, HE'S ONE OF OUR

Fabulous Fathers

FATHER IN THE MAKING
Marie Ferrarella

Blaine O'Conner had never learned how to be a full-time father—until he found himself in charge of his ten-year-old son. Lucky for him, pretty Bridgette Rafanelli was willing to give him a few badly needed lessons in child rearing. Now Blaine was hoping to teach Bridgette a thing or two about love!

Look for *Father in the Making* in May, from Silhouette Romance.

Fall in love with our Fabulous Fathers!

Silhouette

ROMANCE™

FF595

SILHOUETTE®

Desire®

1995

Don't let the winter months get you down because the heat is about to get turned way up...with the sexiest hunks of 1995!

January: *A NUISANCE*
               by Lass Small

February: *COWBOYS DON'T CRY*
               by Anne McAllister

March: *THAT BURKE MAN*
               the 75th Man of the Month
               by Diana Palmer

April: *MR. EASY*
               by Cait London

May: *MYSTERIOUS MOUNTAIN MAN*
               by Annette Broadrick

June: *SINGLE DAD*
               by Jennifer Greene

**MAN OF THE MONTH...
ONLY FROM
SIILHOUETTE DESIRE**

MOM95JJ-R

DREAM WEDDING
by Pamela Macaluso

Don't miss JUST MARRIED, a fun-filled series by Pamela Macaluso about three men with wealth, power and looks to die for. These bad boys had everything—except the love of a good woman.

***

"What a nerd!" Those taunting words played over and over in Alex Dalton's mind. Now that he was a rich, successful businessman—with looks to boot—he was going to make Genie Hill regret being so cruel to him in high school. All he had to do was seduce her…and then dump her. But could he do it without falling head over heels for her—again?

Find out in DREAM WEDDING, book two of the JUST MARRIED series, coming to you in May…only in

JM1

Announcing
the New Pages & Privileges™ Program
from Harlequin® and Silhouette®

Get All This FREE
With Just One Proof-of-Purchase!

- **FREE Travel Service** with the guaranteed lowest available airfares plus 5% cash back on every ticket

- **FREE Hotel Discounts** of up to 60% off at leading hotels in the U.S., Canada and Europe

- **FREE Petite Parfumerie** collection (a $50 Retail value)

- **FREE $25 Travel Voucher** to use on any ticket on any airline booked through our Travel Service

- **FREE Insider Tips Letter** full of fascinating information and hot sneak previews of upcoming books

- **FREE Mystery Gift** (if you enroll before May 31/95)

And there are more great gifts and benefits to come!
Enroll today and become Privileged!
(see insert for details)

PROOF-OF-PURCHASE

Offer expires October 31, 1996   SSE-PP1